DEATH SAILS

in the
SUNSET

Roger Keevil

DEATH SAILS IN THE SUNSET

by Roger Keevil

mail@rogerkeevil.co.uk

www.rogerkeevil.co.uk

Printed by CreateSpace, an Amazon.com company
Available on Kindle and other devices

To C, W, and C, my constant travelling companions on so many cruises!

Chapter 1

"Good lord! Andy Constable! I don't believe it!" The white-uniformed ship's officer's face was split by an incredulous grin as, hand extended in greeting, he advanced across the towering atrium of the brand new cruise liner *Empress of the Oceans*. "What the bloody hell are you doing here?"

Detective Inspector Andy Constable's own features lit up in recognition. "Derek? You are kidding me!" He shook the other's hand warmly. "Well, of all the people I expected to see today, you're probably furthest down on the list. Although I've got to say, it's a treat to see a friendly face after the day we've had."

"We?"

"Sorry." Constable turned to the younger man standing immediately behind him in the boarding queue. "Derek, this is my sergeant, David Copper. Copper, this is Derek Crane. We were at police training college together."

"*My* sergeant?" queried Crane. He exchanged brief handshakes with Copper. "You've gone up in the world, Andy. Chief Superintendent now, is it?"

"Just D.I., I'm afraid," smiled Constable.

"So what are you doing here mob-handed?" asked Crane. He suddenly looked apprehensive. "Look, come over here a second. We're holding up the queue." He drew the two detectives aside. "This isn't official, is it?"

Constable laughed. "Nothing of the kind, thank goodness. As for why we're here, long story, which I can sum up in one word - volcano."

"Oh, you're one of that lot, are you?" Crane's face cleared.

"And as for you, I might ask you the same question. How come you're all togged up like an Italian admiral instead of the sober blue serge of Her Majesty's constabulary?"

"There's another long story, which I will bore you with at a better time. For now, let's get you two sorted."

"Yes, well, we were standing in a nice orderly queue until now, quietly waiting for somebody to tell us what to do."

"Oh, I think we can do better than that. Come with me - what's the point of having a few rings on your sleeve if you can't pull rank now and again." Crane led the way towards the head of the queue which snaked across the atrium in the direction of the Guest Relations desk.

"How do you mean?"

"The answer to *your* question," continued Crane over his shoulder, "is that I hold the lofty position of Head of Security of this floating monster. Which I reckon gets me certain privileges. Lydia!" He greeted the attractive brunette behind the desk with effusive warmth. "You are exactly the girl I need. I do believe you're allocating staterooms for our unexpected guests, are you not?"

"Yes, sir, I am," answered the receptionist with a smile, in which Constable thought he could detect a touch of wariness. This was evidently not the first time Derek Crane had attempted to exercise his considerable charm towards her.

"This gentleman," explained Crane, indicating Constable, "is a very old friend of mine, and I'm guessing that he's had a pretty grim day, which I'd like to make a lot better. So, knowing how full the ship isn't, I'm hoping that you can find him something rather better than the broom cupboard in the bilges which we are allocating to the rest of our volcano victims. What do you think? Mmmm?" He leaned forward across the desk and favoured Lydia with a winning smile and the look of a hopeful puppy.

Lydia laughed. "Derek, you are a very bad man." The hint of a French accent robbed her words of any real censure. "Let me see what I can do." She consulted her computer screen and tapped a few keys. "I have a balcony stateroom on Deck 6. I am sure your friend would like that."

"I'm sure that my friend's friend would like that very much," replied Crane. He turned to Dave Copper. "David, do you think you'd be comfortable in a balcony stateroom?"

Copper, somewhat bewildered, gave a nod in agreement. "Er ... yes ... I should think so."

Crane turned back to the receptionist. "Now, the thing is, Lydia, my friend Andy here is a senior British police officer. Very senior indeed. And isn't Deck 6 the deck where most of the suites are? So, as none of our esteemed guest list of passengers are actually paying for the cruise in the first place, and if I promise to be extremely nice to you, is there any chance ...?" He let the question hang in the air.

Lydia giggled and capitulated. "Derek, you will get me into

trouble. Let me look ..." More clicks on the computer keyboard. "All right. I have 6218, which is a suite midships, and 6220, which is the balcony stateroom next to it. How's that? Sir?"

"That's perfect." Crane leaned over the desk and deposited a peck on the slightly surprised girl's cheek. "You will go straight to heaven."

"Not if my supervisor catches me," retorted Lydia with a smile whose warmth and sparkle belied the tone of her words. "So, if you can give me your passports, gentlemen, I will make the arrangements."

"Lydia, you're an angel," said Crane, as Constable and Copper handed their passports across the desk.

"Yes, I know I am," said Lydia. "Now for goodness' sake, Derek, go away and let me do my job."

"Your wish is my command, beautiful one. We'll come back later. Come on, Andy - you look as if you could do with a drink. Let's go and find a nice quiet bar and we'll do some catching up." He headed for the curving staircase leading upwards as the two slightly bemused detectives followed, leaving the still-immobile queue behind them exchanging puzzled glances and muttering beneath their breath.

*

Nobody could say, mused Andy Constable, that it had started out as an ordinary day. The past week had not exactly lived up to expectations, if those expectations had been for a lazy week lounging in the Costa Blanca sun and generally unwinding, courtesy of a lucky win in the police station Christmas draw. But that morning, with a successfully-solved murder case under their belts, an unexpected knock at the door from the local police captain had led to an even more unexpected motorcycle outrider escort to the airport, amid profuse expressions of thanks for Constable and Copper's assistance. But from then on, the descent into chaos and confusion had been rapid.

It all started with an announcement over the public address system at Alicante airport. Safely checked in for their flight, and breathing a sigh of relief to be on the way home for a return to normality, the amplified words echoing through the departure lounge's lofty spaces had caused Constable's heart to sink.

"DerryAir regret to announce the cancellation ...."

Responding to the invitation to report to the airport's enquiries desk for further information, Constable and Copper eased their way towards the front of a crowd of over a hundred passengers, where a harassed young woman in the uniform of DerryAir's ground staff was trying to make herself heard above the growing hubbub. Her words confirmed their fears.

"I'm terribly sorry, ladies and gentlemen, but I'm afraid that it's all out of our hands. The British air traffic control authorities have closed all U.K. airspace until further notice, so there aren't any flights going anywhere at the moment."

Cries of protest arose.

"Well, how are we supposed to get home ...?"

"My kids go back to school tomorrow ..."

"Look, I've got a business to run ..."

"Isn't there some other way ...?"

The volume rose, until nothing could be heard of the woman's further attempts to soothe the increasingly restive crowd.

Dave Copper turned to Andy Constable. "I can't be doing with all this racket, guv," he muttered out of the side of his mouth, and filled his lungs with air. "Quiet!!" he bellowed at the top of his voice. A total hush fell.

"Here, who the hell do you think you are, telling us what to do?" An overweight thirty-something man sporting an impressive array of neck tattoos, his face flushed with an unbecoming mixture of annoyance and sunburn, squared up to Copper.

"I'm a British police officer. Sir." countered the sergeant, a quiet calm smile on his face. The surrounding hush became, if possible, even more intense. "So shall we all pay attention to what this nice lady is saying, and hear what she is trying to tell us? Would that be a good idea? Sir?"

The man appeared to shrink visibly and his eyes fell as the crowd, after a moment's pause, seemed to draw a collective breath, and turned as one back to face the enquiries desk, where the airline official's smile directed at Dave Copper left no doubts as to the depth of her gratitude.

"Nicely done, David," murmured Andy Constable appreciatively. "Fine example of crowd control. I can see that the next time things get a bit out of hand at the football, we shan't need to issue any shields or helmets. We'll just send you in."

"Shush, guv, I'm trying to hear."

" ... so as some of you might have seen on the news, this new ash cloud from the Icelandic volcano has now spread across most of northern Europe. All airspace north of Paris is closed, so we are not the only airline affected. In fact ...," the woman smiled ruefully, "it's total chaos. The plane that you were due to fly back on was virtually the last aircraft to get out. So please, everyone, bear with us - I know it's a very awkward situation, but we will do our best to get something sorted out for everybody."

"What about trains?" suggested a voice in the crowd.

"That's one possibility we may have to look at, sir. But for now, I'm afraid the only thing we can do is to ask you to be patient, and we'll get back to you as soon as we can. In the meantime, if you would like to come and collect them from me, we have some vouchers which you can exchange for something to eat and a drink or a coffee while you're waiting."

The crowd, its annoyance now reduced to subterranean mumbling, obediently formed a surprisingly orderly queue at the desk. As Constable and Copper, bringing up the rear, arrived to take their turn, the woman's smile turned back from the professional to the personal as Dave Copper stood before her. She saw a young man in his late twenties, with rather unkempt light brown hair, a ready smile, and an air of not wishing to take the world too seriously.

"Thank you so much for that, sir. You saved my life there," she dimpled.

"Oh, I don't think it was quite as bad as that," said Copper.

"Well, maybe not," returned the woman. "But I've known some people get really nasty when we have to cancel, so I'm glad you were there. And they say there's never a policeman around when you want one."

"Two, in fact," put in Andy Constable. "But as the senior officer of the two," he smiled, "I always let the junior ranks do the donkey work. So you should know that your knight in shining armour on this occasion is my sergeant, David."

"Well, David, it's very nice to meet you. I'm Danni. Danni Boyd. And I'm very glad that you turned up on your white charger."

"Glad to help," muttered the increasingly embarrassed Copper.

"Look, I'll tell you what I'll do," continued Danni. "Forget the drinks voucher. Here's a couple of passes for the V.I.P. Lounge. You can wait in there in comfort instead of sitting around on these horrible metal chairs, and everything's free. Please, go and have a drink on me, while I see what we can do to get this mess sorted out. We've got people on the phones all over the place. I'll come and find you and tell you what's happening when I know." She favoured Dave Copper with a final smile and a bat of her eyelashes before turning and disappearing into the inner office.

"What is this effect you have on women in Spain?" remarked Andy Constable. "Has the past week taught you nothing?" Without waiting for a reply, he turned and headed towards the stairs which led to the V.I.P. area.

*

"You know, guv," mused Dave Copper, as he worked his way down his second tumbler of 18-year-old single malt whisky, courtesy of the extremely well-stocked bar of the V.I.P. lounge, "I could probably get used to this."

"The scotch, the surroundings, or the hanging about without the faintest clue as to what's happening?" Constable's tone was acerbic.

"Come on, guv." Copper swung his feet round from the recliner chair in which he had been sprawled untidily, and looked towards his superior. "Let's lighten up a bit. After all, technically we're still on holiday. And if we're going to be stuck in a situation we can't do anything about, I can think of much worse places than here. Just remember those other poor bug... - other poor so-and-so's off our flight. They're having to make do with a cup of coffee and a limp cheese sandwich or whatever, while we're here sat in comfort. Which reminds me, I'm going to go and get another plate of those nibbles. Want some?"

"If you like."

"And a drink?" coaxed Copper. "How about a *cafe cortado* and a brandy? Just as a sort of farewell to Spain?"

"Oh, all right." Constable sighed gustily. He took a breath and, in a characteristic gesture, ran his fingers through his dark brown hair, sprinkled with enough grey to confirm his forty-odd years. He yawned and gave a stretch which took in all of his six-foot height, shook himself slightly, and seemed to come to a conclusion. "Sorry, David," he continued, as his colleague returned with the refreshments and placed them on the coffee table between them. "We're not even back at the station yet, and I seem to have slipped back into miserable old grouch mode. It's not knowing what's going on that I hate. Not being in control of my own fate."

"Hell's bells, guv, do we have to get philosophical at this hour of the day? And anyway, when were we ever in control of our own fate in our job? It kind of absolutely doesn't go with the territory. You know what it's like - you're sat there at your desk, ploughing through some mind-numbing forms which nobody will ever read, and the next minute, the phone rings, and suddenly we're off chasing the bad guys. Suits me."

"I dare say you're right."

"So what I reckon is, if hanging about at an airport is inevitable, we might as well sit back and enjoy it."

"Hmmm. Not the most P.C. remark you'll ever make, sergeant."

"Well, in that case, guv, if you're not very careful, I shall wheel out my famous power of positive thinking again and see if that gets us anywhere. After all, it got us to Spain in the first place. Maybe it'll get us home."

As if on cue, the frosted glass door of the lounge opened, and Danni put her head round it. "Oh good - you're here." She advanced on the two detectives with a beaming smile on her face.

Constable stood. "And where else would we be, other than enjoying your very kind hospitality while we wait for the volcano to belt up and let us go home?"

"Ah, well, I have some good news there. I think you'll be pleased. Now, we've got everybody's luggage downstairs, so if you'd like to come with me, you can collect it and then I'll take you over to the parking bays where the coaches are waiting."

"Hell's teeth!" riposted Constable. "You're not sending us home on a blasted coach, are you? That's going to take forever!"

Danni laughed. "Oh no, nothing like that. Sorry, I'm not explaining this very well. You're going home by sea."

"You what?"

Danni smiled at Dave Copper's bafflement. "Don't worry, David - you won't have to swim. It's all very simple. DerryAir is owned by a great big international corporation, which also owns several cruise companies. And it just so happens that one of them has just taken delivery of a new ship from the builders in Italy. She's on her way from the shipyard to the U.K. on a sort of trial cruise for invited guests - including our owner! How's that for a coincidence? And even better, the ship called in to the port of Cartagena this morning. There's plenty of room on board, so the management have arranged for all the passengers from your flight to join the ship before she sails this afternoon. It's only about an hour or so down the motorway, so we're loading up the coaches now. You're going on a cruise!" she finished triumphantly.

Constable turned to Copper, whose grin had grown increasingly radiant as Danni's explanation unfolded. "David - this power of positive thinking thing - you don't by any chance have designs on the job of Chief Constable, do you? Because if you have, I'm putting in for retirement first thing on Monday." He turned back to Danni. "This is all very good of you. I don't really quite know how to thank you."

"No thanks needed," replied Danni. "I'm only too pleased that we were able to sort things out. And it was the very least I could do after David's rescue efforts for a damsel in distress." She leaned forward and deposited an impulsive kiss on the slightly surprised sergeant's cheek. "Right then, boys." She resumed her customary professional briskness, leavened with a grin and a sideways flash of her eyes at Dave Copper. "Follow me, and we'll get you on your way."

"Boys?" murmured Constable.

"Take what you can get, guv," answered Copper out of the side of his mouth. "And stop talking about retirement. You don't get to be a miserable old sod again until we're back at the station, remember?" He cheerily picked up his hand luggage and fell in behind Danni's retreating form, leaving Constable to follow in his wake.

*

The twisting approach road through the mountains suddenly crested a rise, revealing the city of Cartagena spread below. Modern neighbourhoods studded with elegant apartments surrounded a red-roofed core, where a maze of streets with the occasional glint of glass-walled office blocks was dotted with the swell of church domes and the gleam of glazed tiles from the fantastic pepper-pots of grand municipal buildings. The battlements of a small castle keep on a crag overlooked a large

12

inlet almost encircled by the embrace of steep hills on both sides, each promontory crowned with a formidable fortress, and along the quays of the harbour, crouched in readiness, the long low grey shapes of Spain's navy floated awaiting a call to action. And, at a pier only yards from the city's waterfront ramparts, dominating everything and towering a full sixteen storeys from the waterline, rose the huge but stylish shape of the *Empress of the Oceans*. One hundred and forty-two thousand tons of dazzling white steel, her elegance accentuated by a narrow line of gleaming gold along the full thousand-foot length of her hull, and punctuated by a row of scarlet lifeboat deck-housings, the vision was crowned by a proudly flared funnel bearing the gold and turquoise logo of OceanSea Cruises.

"Holy moley!" breathed Copper from his seat next to the coach window. "Will you take a look at that?"

"As you so rightly say, holy moley," agreed Constable alongside him, trying his best to remain matter-of-fact in his reaction, and almost succeeding. "And you thought that Ewan's yacht in the harbour at San Pablo was impressive!"

"I take it all back, guv," responded Copper. A slow grin began to spread across his features. "You're never going to tell me we're going home in that?"

"*Ladies and gentlemen, may I please have your attention.*" Danni's voice came over the coach's loudspeakers from her seat at the front. "*As you can see, we are just arriving in Cartagena, and in front of you, I'm sure you've noticed the Empress of the Oceans which is going to be your home for the next few days.*"

"Happy to be proved wrong?" muttered Constable to his colleague.

"On a scale of one to ten, only about twenty-seven."

"*We shall be arriving in the port in a few minutes, and then we'll try to get you on board as quickly as we can. We've emailed ahead all your details, so if you can please just have your passports ready ...*"

Descending from the coach, the detectives could see that the vehicle's hold was being rapidly emptied of its luggage by a team of baggage-handlers from the ship.

"Don't worry about your cases." Danni materialised at Constable's shoulder. "They'll all be taken direct to your cabin."

"Hang on, we haven't got a cabin."

Danni laughed. "You will have when you get on board. I gather they've got everything under control." She held out a hand. "I hope your little cruise makes up for today's aggravations. Have a nice relaxing trip."

"We'll do our best." Constable took the proffered hand. "And thank you again for looking after us."

"My pleasure. Goodbye, David."

"Do I get another kiss?"

"Of course." Danni obliged with another peck on the cheek and a slightly shy smile. "So, if you'd like to follow everyone else up the gangway there, the crew will look after you from then on. And I have to go back to the airport and get to work sorting out arrangements for the people on tomorrow's flights."

"Best of luck with that." Constable looked up at the ship looming above him. "Come on, David - let's get aboard before they sail without us."

*

"... and so I said, 'What we really need is another body', and the guv here said, 'David, you're a bloody genius!', and he sussed the whole thing pretty much on the spot."

"Yes, well, sergeant, I think that's quite enough about your genius. And I'm sure Derek doesn't want to know the whole story of our alleged holiday."

"Don't believe a word of it, David," retorted Derek good-humouredly. "Nothing makes me happier than when the evil-doers get their comeuppance, especially when it's at the hands of my old mate here. He used to show us all up when we were at college because of his dazzling deductive skills. I'm only jealous that you two still get to do good work at the sharp end of things. I have to admit I got a bit jaded after I'd done my years in the force, and that's how come I was seduced by the power of money and the glamour of a life on the ocean wave. But the worst I seem to have come across on my previous ships is the odd case of petty pilfering from the ship's shops, or one of the grease-monkeys tries to sneak his girlfriend on board, or else a couple of the waiters decide to go berserk and have a howling scrap down in the crew's quarters over something completely incomprehensible."

"Well," said Constable, "You know the old Chinese curse. '*May you live in interesting times.*' Think yourself lucky that you've said goodbye to those three-o'clock-in-the-morning phone calls which end up with you scrambling around in a muddy ditch looking at somebody with their head bashed in."

"You're probably right," agreed Derek. "I suppose it's not such a torture to wake up every morning with a new set of palm trees outside the cabin window. Not long to wait now. Back to Southampton, then a couple of quickie two-day Channel-hops to finish bedding the crew in, and then it's off to the Caribbean on the official maiden voyage."

"So isn't that what this is?" asked Dave Copper.

"Lord, no!" replied Derek. "This is just what they call a shake-down. We always do it with every new ship we commission, and this one's fresh out of the yard. Can't you smell the new paint?"

"So what's it all in aid of, then? I mean, you've got passengers, haven't you?"

"Free-loaders," smiled Derek. "Somebody at head office had a bright idea. They thought that, instead of spending a fortune in world-wide advertising, they would let other people do the work for us. So somebody put together a list of a thousand or so of the great and the good from various different countries – TV celebrities, media people, supermodels, sports stars, business leaders, that sort of thing, plus several hundred travel agents - and they've been invited along for a free cruise, all-found, courtesy of the company. No expense spared. We've got all-sorts - Americans, Brits, Germans, Japanese - even some Russians. The idea is that they will all be so impressed by the ship and the service that they will rush home and go on TV and into the press to tell everyone who will listen how marvellous we are, and the world will then beat a path to our door with bookings."

"And is it working?"

"We'll see. So far so good. Everybody came aboard in Genoa on Saturday and Sunday, and then yesterday we were in Barcelona taking people out on trips to see the sights. And then tomorrow we're round to Cadiz, and then it's straight back to the U.K. - two days at sea, and into Southampton on Saturday. And touch wood ..." Derek tapped the arm of his chair, "it's all going fine so far. People seem to like the ship."

"I'm not surprised," remarked Constable. He looked around the bar the three were seated in, perched six decks above the floor of the atrium, where the brightly lit scenic lifts were

15

swooping up and down in a perpetual ballet over the nine-storeys. Everywhere was the gleam of Venetian glass and the glint of multi-coloured mosaics, the swirl of figured marble columns and the massive loom of striking statuary, the delicacy of painted panels and the plump opulence of luxurious leather upholstery. "She's quite a work of art."

"No surface knowingly un-decorated, by the look of it," put in Dave Copper.

"That's Italian designers for you," replied Derek. "But when they're on a cruise, people like to see their money - even if they're not spending any! Right, you two." With a brisk change of pace, he sat upright and drained his coffee cup. "Sup up. Let's get back down to Guest Relations and get you your ship cards, then we can get you to your cabins and you can unwind a bit. I've got things to do - today's excursions will be back before long, so I'd better cast a friendly eye over my team to make sure they don't let anybody unsavoury on board." He grinned. "Not that we haven't got a few of those already, but that's another story, and you didn't hear me say it. Come on - let's go back and see the lovely Lydia."

Down on the atrium floor, the snaking queue and the previous faint air of stress had been replaced by a calm serenity modulated by the leisurely tones of soft jazz music provided by the musician seated at the glass-lidded white grand piano in the middle of the central dance floor. Waiters from the curving bar wrapped around the foot of the spiral staircase were serving coffees or cocktails to couples dotted about on sofas and in cosy niches. And behind the Guest Relations desk, Lydia looked up with a well-practised smile as the ship's officer and the two detectives approached.

"Good afternoon again, gentlemen. I hope Mr. Crane has been looking after you."

"Of course I have, Lydia," said Derek. "You know I can schmooze the punters with the best of them, especially if they happen to be old friends." He turned to Andy Constable. "Right, guys, I'm going to leave you in the tender care of Lydia while I go and pretend to work. Just remember to do everything she tells you, and you won't go far wrong. Well, it works for me." He leaned across the desk and flashed a roguish wink.

"Derek ..." began Lydia in protest.

Derek held his hands up in mock surrender. "All right, all

right, I know. I'm a very bad man. Look, I've gone already. Catch you later, chaps." He disappeared through an adjacent door marked 'Crew Only'.

Lydia drew a slightly flustered breath. "So, gentlemen, if I can just give you these ..."

"You and Mr. Crane seem quite good friends," remarked Constable blandly. "I thought from what he was telling us that this was a brand new ship."

"Yes, sir, so it is, but the crew has mostly been drawn from the experienced staff of our other ships. And Derek ... Mr. Crane and I both used to work on the *Countess of the Oceans* before we were transferred to the new flagship for the first voyage. So if I can just show you ..." Lydia made a renewed effort to return to the matter in hand, but was forestalled by Dave Copper.

"So how does this all work, then? Derek was telling us that everybody on the ship is on some kind of freebie."

"That's correct, sir. All our passengers are on board as guests of the company, but apart from that, it's just like a normal cruise. Everything is all-inclusive - you can order anything you like in the bars, there is entertainment in the theatre and in the lounges, and we have a programme of excursions if you wish to join any of our trips ashore. My colleagues across at the Excursions Desk will be happy to arrange things for you." She pointed to another desk across the atrium, where a display of large illuminated photos of various tourist sites indicated some of the wares on offer. "So I just have to give you this ..." She handed over a small coloured card. "This shows you your table number in the Imperial Dining Room - that's on this deck, just through that lounge there. We have one dinner seating at 7.30 for this cruise instead of the usual two, so if you show this to the maître d' at the door he will have you shown to your table. And lastly, your ship cards. I'll just process them with your names." She produced the Britons' passports from beneath the desk.

"What are they for?" asked Copper.

"They're like your ship's passport, sir. They act as your stateroom key, and for your safe as well, and you have to show them every time you order something in the bars and when you come back on board after you've been ashore. Otherwise Security won't let you on to the ship ..." Lydia laughed. "And then I'm afraid you really would have to walk home. So please don't lose it, sir. So, it's Mr. Copper, first name ..." She leafed through the passport pages. "David. Now if you could just look towards the camera here, sir ..." She gestured to a small eye mounted on the desk. Click. "That's fine. So now we have your photo on the system, and nobody else can use your card." A few swift clicks at the keyboard, a muted whirring, and a plastic credit-type card adorned with Copper's name and a picture of the ship was handed over. "Now yours, Mr ... Constable. First name ..."

"Andy is fine," interposed Constable swiftly. "Don't worry about the full thing - I never use it. So, I look here, do I? Great. Thanks very much for all your help, Miss ..." Constable leaned forward to read the name-badge adorned with Canada's maple leaf flag. "Miss Carton."

"You're very welcome, sir. And please, call me Lydia. And do let me know if there is anything else I can do for you. Now, if you wanted to go up to your staterooms, I'm sure your luggage will have been delivered by now. You're on deck six, and if you go round to the elevators in the hall there, you'll be there in no time."

*

The scenic lift disgorged the two detectives into a hall richly adorned with gleaming brass and glass light fittings, shedding a warm glow on the frescos on the walls of the double staircase leading up and down to adjacent decks.

"It's all a bit O.T.T., all this decoration, isn't it, guv," commented Copper.

"Oh, I don't know," replied Constable. "I suppose if you're going to call your ship *Empress of the Oceans* you're going to want something a bit palatial. And anyway, I dare say the passengers appreciate a bit of luxury. As Derek said, if you're going to spend a lot of money on a cruise, you'd want to see some evidence of it."

"Except that this lot on board aren't paying a bean, according to Lydia."

"Well, lucky old them. And lucky old us, come to think of it. So I'm not going to start complaining."

"I wonder what sort of people they've got on board."

"I dare say we shall find out in due course. Anyway, why are we standing here nattering? Let's sort out where we are. You're in number ...?"

"6220, which looks as if it's ..." Copper consulted a plan on the nearby wall. "Through here." He led the way into the corridor behind the lifts, inserted his card into the slot in the appropriately-numbered door, and pushed it open with his foot. "Oh yes - I think this'll do nicely."

The cabin, in subtle tones of cream and peach, was surprisingly roomy. A double bed, on which Copper's suitcase was already waiting, occupied the central area. A door to the left revealed a compact but smart shower room with marble walls and an abundance of chrome fittings, while at the far end of the room, beyond a sofa and a coffee table on which stood a basket of fruit and an ice-bucket with a bottle of champagne, patio doors opened on to a balcony which looked straight across to Cartagena's castle ramparts.

"Very nice," approved Constable. "And this is what they're giving the other ranks. I'm almost afraid to think what Derek has rustled up for me."

"Tell you what, guv - you go next door and find out, I'll get some of my stuff unpacked, and then I'll come and find you. That way, you won't have to be embarrassed by the unwarranted luxury they've lavished upon you."

"Not only that, but I shall be spared the sound of you grinding your teeth in paroxysms of jealousy."

"Something like that, guv," Copper grinned. "Go!"

Constable's suite next door was twice the size of Copper's cabin. The bedroom area was partially curtained off with velvet drapes held back with gold tasselled ties, and a dressing room led to the en-suite bathroom containing a full-size bath with an array of controls for the numerous water-jets. The living area was furnished with sofa and armchairs, a desk, and a dining table set for two with crystal glasses, silver cutlery, and a tall vase containing an elegant arrangement of roses and willow twigs. More champagne - a finer label, the inspector noted - waited alongside.

"Bloody hell!" murmured Constable to himself. "How the other half do live!"

A tap on the door heralded the arrival of Dave Copper.

"Bloody hell, guv!"

"That's what I said," returned Constable with a smile. "Want to swap?"

"You know, I don't reckon I do. I shall be quite cosy in my little crib next door, thanks all the same. This is a bit above my pay grade. Have you had a look outside?"

"Not yet. That's next on the list." Constable slid open the patio doors and led the way out on to the double-width balcony, where teak steamer chairs and a table were laid out alongside a chest which, on inspection, revealed contents of soft cushions and red check blankets. "Every comfort provided."

Copper leaned over the rail to look at the quayside far below. "Wow, that's quite a drop. How's your head for heights, guv?"

"Not a problem," replied Constable, as with a sigh and a slight groan he settled himself into one of the chairs, stretched out his legs, and let his eyelids droop. "It's not heights I'm afraid of - it's the ground. Or in this case, the water. So please try not to go over, because I'm not jumping over afterwards to save you."

"That's a deal." Copper altered his focus. "Hallo, hallo, what's all this then?"

Constable winced. "Sergeant Copper, would you do me the inestimable kindness of not doing your impression of a village policeman in a comedy whodunnit, at least until we get back on to British soil?"

"Sorry, guv, it just slipped out by accident."

"So what *is* all this then?"

"Bunch of coaches turning up down below, guv. About half a dozen of them. Not your ordinary coaches either. They look more like the sort of executive buses your average premier division team goes off in for away matches. Very smart."

Constable joined Copper at the rail. "That will no doubt be the happy holiday-makers returning from their excursions as Derek mentioned. Like he said, no expense spared."

True enough, the coaches were disgorging a flock of brightly-clad tourists whose animated chatter could be heard seven decks above. Ship cards produced from pockets and bags, they formed a more or less orderly queue at the small pavilion where the ship's security staff, Derek Crane prominent in oversight, were processing them and waving them aboard up the gently-sloping gangway.

Constable glanced at his watch. "I don't know about you, David, but I'm in serious danger of dozing off. How would it be if we give it an hour or so? That'll give me a chance to unpack, have a shower, and put my feet up for a bit, and then you can come back here and we'll see this bottle of champagne off."

"And then dinner, I presume? Sounds like a cunning plan to me, guv."

A little over an hour later, and moments after the popping of the champagne cork had been the cue for two very relaxed detectives to sit back on Constable's balcony chairs with contented smiles on their faces, three long deafening blasts from the ship's siren echoed across the bay of Cartagena. At the same time, a modest but noticeable increase in vibration indicated that the vessel's engines were slowly but surely pushing her sideways from the pier. As the *Empress* began a stately turn in her own length to point towards the narrow mouth of the harbour, Copper raised his glass to his colleague.

"Here's to going home, guv." A pause. "I say - you know at the airport you weren't too pleased with me because I misread what the paper said about the volcano?"

"Yes ...? And ...?"

"Am I forgiven?"

Constable chuckled. "Shut up and drink your fizz!"

"Always happy to obey orders from a superior officer, sir," smiled Copper in reply. He raised his glass. "Well, bon voyage."

Chapter 2

"Pardon me, but have we met?"

The seatbelt signs on the afternoon flight from Kennedy to Heathrow had just been switched off.

"I don't think so."

"Well, I'm sure I know your face from somewhere. I never forget a face. Now let me think ..."

With a practised smile and an almost imperceptible sigh, Jacqueline Best closed her magazine and turned her attention to her companion in the adjacent seat. The woman was obviously intent on striking up a conversation.

"I suppose you might have seen me ..."

"No, don't tell me," interrupted the woman. "I'll get it in a minute."

Jacqueline fell silent, a faint smile still on her lips, one impeccably-shaped eyebrow raised in enquiry and her head slightly tilted to one side. Her glossy dark hair, cut in a bob which stopped just short of severe, fell back to reveal a discreet pearl stud in her ear. Her black suit, which to an uninitiated eye might be thought of as plain but which to any fashion correspondent would have shrieked 'couture', flattered a figure just the plump side of medium, and displayed a modest froth of white lace at the throat. Her dark eyes were piercing, distracting from the fine crows' feet at their corners. She wore make-up, with touches of lipstick and blusher, but so expertly applied as to be virtually undetectable as art. Many other women in the vicinity of fifty, concerned at the passage of time, would have sold their souls to achieve the look.

"I know!" exclaimed the woman. "You're on TV, aren't you?"

"I guess you got me," admitted Jacqueline.

"It's Pastor Best, isn't it? I've seen you on that religious channel - oh, what's your church called?"

"The Community of the Great Shepherd."

"That's the one! Oh, this is so exciting. I am so pleased to meet you. I'm Geraldine, by the way - Geraldine Coe, but everybody calls me Gerry."

"Well, good to know you, Gerry. So, are you a follower of our Community?"

"I used to be, all the time. Not so much lately, with the kids and all. I used to watch it a lot when your husband was on. Oh, what a great man he was - such an inspiring speaker. You know, when I would watch him, I could feel the Lord entering my soul, and I just wanted to help with the great work he did. I've sent in so many contributions, and it's such a joy to meet the person who's actually received them."

"People have been so generous," agreed Jacqueline. "And I'm glad to know that my husband touched your heart, like he did for so many people."

"It's sad that you lost him - last year, wasn't it?"

"That's right. He was gathered just over a year ago, but I felt it was my duty to take over as Pastor of the Community and do what I can to keep his work going." Jacqueline drew a tiny handkerchief from her sleeve and dabbed the corner of her eye. "We had such a short time together - only two years, but I know that those precious days were just a rehearsal for eternity."

"Oh, that is such a comfort," said Gerry. "What a beautiful thing to say. And I will be thinking of that next week."

"Next week?"

"Why, yes." Gerry leaned in closer and dropped her voice to a more confidential tone. "I've lost my husband too, you know, just recently."

"My dear, I'm so sorry to hear that."

"Well, I say I've lost him." Gerry let out an incongruous giggle. "I know exactly where he is." She dropped her voice further. "He's in my suitcase. In an urn. We had him cremated, and he always said that he wanted his last resting place to be in the Holy Land, so I'm going down to Jerusalem, and I'm going to scatter his ashes there. How about you?"

"I'm sorry?"

"What happened about your husband?"

"Oh." Jacqueline seemed slightly taken aback by the question. "Oh, yes, he was cremated as well. But the body is such a transitory thing, isn't it? So I let the crematorium make all the arrangements for the scattering. After all, I have everything that he left me - all the memories, and the work to carry on with."

"And is that what brings you to Europe?"

"Oh good lord, no." Jacqueline laughed. "Nothing like that. No, I've had a very generous invitation to go on a trip on board a

23

new cruise liner, so I'm flying on down to Italy to do that."

"That sounds so exciting. And who knows, you may meet all sorts of new people - new friends for your Community."

"You might be right," mused Jacqueline. "I hadn't thought of that."

"Would you like a drink before we start serving dinner, madam?" The flight steward appeared at Jacqueline's elbow.

"Champagne, please." Jacqueline took the glass and settled back in her seat, a quiet smile playing about her lips.

*

"Good morning, sir. Welcome to Italy." The hostess in the uniform of OceanSea Cruises, clip-board in hand, greeted the first of a stream of passengers emerging from the arrivals hall of Genoa's tiny airport with a warm smile. "May I have your name, please."

"Boyle."

"Just a moment ... Ah yes, here we are. Dr. Lancelot Boyle. Right, Dr. Boyle, if you would like to let my colleague here take your case ..." She indicated one of several porters in yellow jackets bearing the OceanSea logo, waiting alongside a luggage trolley. "... and if you would just bear with me for a few moments while I check our other passengers on your flight, I'll take you round to where the bus is waiting."

Lance Boyle leaned against a nearby pillar, reached into a jacket pocket, and produced from a silver case a cigarette which he placed between his lips.

"Oh sir," called the hostess urgently, "I'm afraid you can't do that. There's no smoking within the airport building."

"Don't worry about it," replied Boyle with an easy smile of reassurance. "It isn't a real cigarette - just an electronic one. Water vapour and a little shot of nicotine for those poor addicts among us who can't give up the habit. See?" He held it out for inspection. "I know, everyone says a medical man shouldn't be smoking, but this is the one vice I can't kick, so I compromise."

"That's all right then, sir. Sorry." The hostess turned back with relief to her other customers.

"No problem."

For a man in his early fifties, Dr. Lancelot Boyle looked remarkably good. A fraction over six feet tall and with broad shoulders, the unbuttoned single-breasted jacket he wore showed no sign of the middle-aged spread so common among others of his generation. Thick light-brown hair swept back from a face unlined apart from the subtlest laughter creases at the corners of the clear grey eyes, and the classically-straight nose and hint of a cleft chin would not have looked out of place on a renaissance statue. How much was due to nature and how much to art was difficult to gauge, but as one of America's most prominent cosmetic surgeons, numbering a large quantity of film stars, television celebrities, and society women among his clientele, both acknowledged and un-acknowledged, Lance Boyle was possibly his own finest advertisement. And, no stranger to self-promotion, he was always ready to accept an invitation to do an interview or make an appearance for any celebrity magazine or television programme that wanted him.

"Hello once again, ladies and gentlemen." The hostess, microphone in hand, stood at the front of the bus as it began to navigate its way out of the airport car park. "We're now on our way to the port of Genoa, where our brand new flagship, *Empress of the Oceans*, is waiting to welcome you on board. My name is Sally, and I'd just like to tell you a little about what's going to happen today. We shall be arriving in the port soon, so if you can have your passports and the invitations we sent you ready, we'll get you all on board as quickly as we can. Don't worry about your luggage - that will all be delivered direct to your staterooms. Now, we're overnight in port tonight, because we have people from all over the world arriving later today and tomorrow, so please feel free to use the ship just like a hotel until we sail tomorrow evening."

"How soon can I get a drink?" called a voice from the back of the bus.

Sally joined in the general laughter. "As soon as you like, sir. Everything is on the house. You are our guests."

"How about getting off the ship? Can we do that? I mean, is there shopping in Genoa?"

"Of course, madam. Lots of it. If you'd like to come and see me or one of my colleagues at the Excursions Desk, we'll be pleased to tell you what we can arrange."

As Lance Boyle stepped into the ship's atrium, he gazed around to get his bearings, impressed by the extravagance of the décor. And, boarding procedures completed and following the directions of a smiling white-gloved attendant, he made his way around to the scenic elevators and took the journey up to his deck. Just as he was about to step out, his eye was caught by a familiar face in the adjoining elevator as it passed his, heading downwards. "Well, well," he murmured to himself. "You just never know who you're going to meet. This could be fun."

*

"*That's* Christopher Columbus's house?" The speaker was clearly not impressed.

"Baxter darling, don't be so snooty." Anita Holm's cut-glass accent came as a total contrast to the rich New York tones of her companion. "We weren't all lucky enough to be brought up in a mansion."

"Maybe you're right," agreed Baxter. "But you'd expect something better from someone who went around the world discovering countries. I mean, this guy used to mix with kings and queens, and this is just a ... well, it's a dump!"

The judgement was a little harsh. In the context of the elegant shopping colonnades and baroque palaces of Genoa, the tiny two-storey house to which the guided tour had brought its patrons did not stand out in terms of glamour, but in terms of historical significance it was unrivalled. The birthplace of Christopher Columbus, a humble Italian sailor who rose to gain the patronage of Spanish sovereigns King Ferdinand and Queen Isabella, and went on to claim the riches of the New World for the Catholic monarchs, provided a claim to fame of which the Genoese were rightly proud, and they did not intend any visitors to their city to forget it. But as the tour guide continued his lecture to the small group who had just exchanged the comfort of their air-conditioned bus for the dusty heat of a late-morning city street, his invitation to enter the house did not raise a great deal of enthusiasm from an increasingly bored Baxter.

"Look, Anita, there's only so much history I can take. What say we lose this guy and get a coffee somewhere? It's too hot to stand around."

"Leave it to me, darling. Tact isn't exactly your strong point, is it? Giuseppe, per favore ..." Anita advanced on the guide, and after a few brief words was rewarded with a slight bow, a broad white smile, and a wave of the hand as he ushered his other guests into the building. "There you are. It's all sorted. The tour ends here anyway, and then there's an hour of free time before the coach takes us back to the ship for lunch. So, I can see some cafes over there by the opera house. You can treat me to a very large cappuccino." She turned and plunged with no apparent fear into the maelstrom of scooters negotiating the busy road junction with no regard for any traffic regulations.

Anita Holm, tall and slim and in her forties, was the archetypal English lady of the sort which is virtually guaranteed success in the world of American media. Born in London, she had studied journalism, worked for one or two undistinguished titles on the fringe of the fashion world in her twenties, but had seized the opportunity to transfer to a sister publication in New York when a colleague had let slip that she was applying for a job in the lifestyle section in the American magazine, and that she had heard that the editor particularly wanted an Englishwoman 'because everybody knows the English have got class, and that's what the readers want'. And Anita had, no doubt with Hamlet in mind, popped in between the election and her hopes, and the friend, a friend no longer, had had to sit in London and watch Anita's sudden and startling rise to prominence on the back of an interview, unexpectedly scheduled because of the illness of another journalist, in the home of one of the film world's hottest leading ladies. Startling headline-grabbing revelations tumbled into her lap, and from then on, Anita became the darling of the media. Blessed with a flawless complexion, eyes of an unusually deep blue, naturally silver-blonde hair cut in an elfin style, and the carefully-cultivated accent of a member of the lesser aristocracy, she was soon to be found on the sofa of every talk show offering her opinion on the latest trends in fashion, furnishings, dining out and theatre. Her television series as a house doctor for the aspiring middle classes seeking to achieve a chic lifestyle on a budget was one of the ratings hits of the season. And with such a growing influence among those with an appreciable degree of disposable income, it was little wonder that OceanSea Cruises had selected her as one of the leading opinion-makers who should be invited aboard their new flagship.

Coffees ordered, Anita pushed her white-framed sunglasses on to the top of her head, leaned back, and surveyed her companion. "You know, Baxter, I still can't get over the coincidence of meeting you of all people on this trip."

"I don't see why you should be surprised. The number of times we run into each other in TV studios."

Baxter D. Wall took a sip of coffee, crossed his legs, and raised a lazy eyebrow. From his two-tone blue-and-tan deck shoes and his immaculate cream designer jeans to the pale blue short-sleeved linen shirt and the now-casually-discarded baseball cap bearing the crest of one of Newport Rhode Island's smarter yacht clubs, he exuded an air of money and style. The impression was not a false one. Only son of Walter Wall, who from modest beginnings owning a single carpet store in Brooklyn had risen to become one of the most remarkable products of the American dream, Baxter was now heir to a considerable fortune and a business empire which encompassed media, publishing, and the vast chain of WalterMart discount warehouses spread throughout the United States. Walter, fully occupied with establishing his own commercial success, had never got around to marrying until his fifties, but by then his wealth had bought him the entrée into higher social circles than those normally open to an ordinary shop-keeper, and he had enjoyed a brief but profitable marriage with the only daughter of the president of a rival conglomerate who, having presented him with a healthy male child, had had the good taste to die promptly in a boating accident, shortly after her own father's death. Baxter's upbringing had therefore had all the advantages which money could buy - the best schools, entry into the Harvard Business School, eased by his father's endowment of an impressive new library, and an introduction to the top executives of any corporation which caught his eye. Walter, still with a firm grasp of the tiller in his eighties, saw no reason why his son should not work for a living. And so Baxter, in his thirties and with all the advantages good looks and money could provide, was now a trader with one of Manhattan's most prestigious share-dealing and finance houses.

"Dad knows the president of the shipping line very well," he continued. "They used to play golf together. And I needed a holiday anyway, so it was all arranged."

"And I imagine your father has probably got shares in the line too," drawled Anita. "He seems to have a finger in every other pie. So remind me again, why haven't you brought that wife of yours along?"

"Ellen has other fish to fry," replied Baxter shortly.

"Oh?" More was evidently required.

"She is spending the next two weeks at the house at Cape Cod with some of her opera friends, if you really want to know. They are talking about a new production of one of the Ring operas, and they want her to sponsor it."

"Well, why not, darling? You two aren't exactly short of a bob or two, are you? So, you not interested, then?"

"No."

"Darling, that was rather sharp. Anyone would think you'd got something on your mind. Everything all right there, is it?" enquired Anita delicately.

"Perfectly, Anita, but thank you for asking." Baxter did not seem at all disposed to be drawn into a discussion. "Now, if you will excuse me, I think I'll take a walk around the square to stretch my legs."

"Do, darling. I'll just finish my coffee. Take as long as you like. I'll be here." Anita replaced her sunglasses, picked up one of the tiny amaretto biscuits from the plate alongside her coffee, and bit into it with a speculative look in her eyes.

*

"Good evening, sir. Can I get you a cocktail before dinner?" The smiling barman greeted Ira Veal as he hitched himself on to a bar stool in the Diadem Lounge.

"Manhattan," was the gravel-voiced reply.

Undeterred by the brevity of the answer, the barman continued to smile as he briskly mixed the drink and placed it on the bar with an accompanying dish of pistachios. "Your cocktail, sir. I hope you're enjoying yourself on board."

"Haven't had much of a chance to yet." Ira took a rather grumpy swig of his drink. In contrast to the mostly elegantly-dressed women and smartly-jacketed men dotted about at the bar's tables, he presented something of a dull spectacle. Less than middle height and heavily built, his voice had an unattractive raspy quality and his jowly face, although clean-shaven, still managed to create the impression of untidy stubble, although the eyes were sharp, missing nothing. A sports jacket of an indeterminate grey-brown colour strained across his shoulders.

"No, sir? Well, please let me know if there is anything I can do to make your trip more pleasurable. My name is Ryan, and I am always going to be on duty in this bar before dinner."

Ira seemed to relax a little. "Thank you, Ryan. I'll remember that." He took a further sip. "Good Manhattan."

"So, sir, have you just come aboard today?"

"Yes. Should have been yesterday, but the idiots at StatesAir lost my luggage somewhere between Chicago and London, so I spent a day there waiting for it to catch me up. Well, at least it gave me a chance to check up on some old contacts to see what's going on in England. But not a word of apology from the airline. They're sure going to regret that."

"Really, sir? Do you think that complaints like that get taken seriously? I know from what customers have told me that it happens all the time."

"Not to me, it doesn't. And I think they're going to have to take it seriously when they see the size of the headlines I'm planning."

"Headlines, sir? What do you mean?"

"In the 'Investigator'." And in response to Ryan's blank look, "My newspaper, the 'National Investigator'. Third biggest circulation in the States, son - don't tell me you haven't heard of it! If there's a story there, we'll find it. And with a little of my front page special treatment, I guess those people at StatesAir will be grovelling pretty soon. That should mean a few free first-class flights." Ira drained his glass. "Get me another of these."

"Can I have your ship card, please sir?"

"How come? I thought all this was free."

"It is, sir. But we have to process everything through the computers for stock control. I'll just be a second." Bleep. Whirr. A receipt was produced. "There you are, sir. Your good health. And now you can relax and enjoy your holiday."

"Holiday?" spluttered Ira with a laugh. "That's a joke. I don't take holidays, sonny. Wherever I go, I'm working."

"So how come you're on board, sir?"

"Because I go where my editor sends me. And my editor has got some very useful contacts, so when he found what sort of people were going to be on this little pleasure cruise, he finagled a ticket for me to come along. With a passenger list like this, if I can't get a story, I don't deserve to be doing my job. And there's one or two people I've got my eye on already. That stopover in London might have been useful after all."

The bar had been growing steadily more crowded, and the

rising level of chatter made it difficult to hear clearly. Ryan looked around and realised that his fellow bar staff were becoming overwhelmed by the crush of passengers wanting a drink before the restaurant doors opened.

"I'd better go, sir. But I hope you have a good trip. Maybe I'll see you again tomorrow."

Ira smiled. "Maybe, son. That all depends on what tomorrow brings."

*

Marisa Mann viewed the sunlight's sparkle in the enormous solitaire diamond on her left hand with considerable pleasure. Marisa loved jewellery, and the ability to afford impressive pieces such as this latest acquisition from one of the smartest shops on Barcelona's Ramblas was still new enough to give her an extremely warm glow of satisfaction.

Marisa was one of those celebrities of whom it could honestly be said that she had risen without trace. First bursting into public awareness on the television reality show 'Big Sister', where her deliberately attention-seeking behaviour had led to scandalised newspaper headlines and a voracious public demand for more coverage in equal measure, the former Marisa Fellows' win on the show had been swiftly followed by a highly-publicised but short-lived tempestuous affair with the show's presenter, Guy Chapman. The form of marriage ceremony beneath the palm trees of a Caribbean beach in the show's aftermath had swiftly been judged invalid by a horrified local magistrate. From that point, Marisa was scarcely ever out of the headlines. A truly fabulous creation, with lavish tumbling blonde hair, large hazel eyes above strikingly sculpted cheekbones, and invitingly pouting lips, her tall slim figure, curves subtly enhanced, had a willowy grace seldom bettered on a catwalk. Her reputation as a party girl was constantly being reinforced by photographs in celebrity magazines of her alighting from a limousine outside a fashionable Hollywood nightclub, or hanging on the arm of a fading rock star at a world title fight at Madison Square Garden.

A notorious Las Vegas wedding to a film extra had lasted all of forty-eight hours before a swift and acrimonious divorce amidst accusations of violence, until within weeks Marisa was being seen in the company of Yehuda Mann, seventy-seven-year-old billionaire owner of the international chain of Vacation Inn

31

hotels. Marisa's wedding to Huda had managed to eclipse all her previous activities in terms of press coverage as well as extravagance - the bride had worn a Parisian designer gown with a thirty-five foot train, all in jet black silk encrusted with one-and-a-half million crystals, as she took her vows on a specially-created island in the lake in the grounds of a Bavarian castle, where black swans swam wearing silver collars, and where the guests toasted Marisa and Huda with vintage champagne in gold-plated silver goblets which were afterwards presented to them as souvenirs. But, as might have been expected, the happiness was not to last. Within two months, the bride was pictured sporting with a lifeguard on an Acapulco beach while the groom was heading take-over negotiations in London for a rival hotel group, and telephone calls to lawyers were soon taking place. In return for an agreement not to contest the case and a not-wholly-surprising admission of non-consummation of the marriage, Marisa found herself with a divorce settlement running into well over six figures.

"Mind if I join you?"

Marisa languidly turned her head and looked up. At the side of her chair in the elegant cafe overlooking the bustling square, eyebrows raised in enquiry, stood Philip Anders. Marisa found herself looking into warm brown eyes set in a face tanned to a healthy bronze with just a hint of olive, with a smiling mouth of impressively white even teeth, all set beneath an immaculately-combed quiff of thick dark blonde hair with a touch of natural streaking. There was the suggestion of an accent - Australian or South African perhaps, but it was too faint to be certain. The question was voiced in tones which clearly did not anticipate rejection. And Marisa could see no reason not to be seen in the company of a well-put-together young man in his late twenties.

"Not at all. Sit down." Marisa searched her memory. "Philip, isn't it?"

"That's right, but please, call me Phil. I'm flattered you remembered. We didn't really have a chance to get acquainted properly last night, what with you being at one end of the dinner table and me at the other. Maybe we can do something about that tonight?" Phil lowered himself with a casually fluid movement into the chair next to Marisa's own.

There was something quietly cat-like about Marisa's smile.

"I don't see why not. Last night I got stuck between that middle-aged woman who just wanted to talk about the work of her church and that poisonous little journalist who was pretending to be friendly, but I could tell all he wanted was a free interview."

Philip laughed. "I don't really think you can blame him for that. After all, you are a pretty hot property in the magazines at the moment. I suppose he thought it was too good a stroke of luck to pass up."

"I am nobody's stroke of luck!" Marisa's voice was sharp and emphatic.

Philip was instantly apologetic. "No, of course not. I'm sorry - that came out all wrong. I suppose I mean that when somebody like that finds himself sharing a meal with somebody like you, he's kind of going to think it's his birthday and Christmas all at once. I mean, you're you, and he's ... not exactly Prince Charming, is he?"

Marisa relented. "And I suppose you are?" Her eyes swept over Phil in appraisal. He did not seem in the least disconcerted by the inspection, and gazed back steadily. Marisa suddenly became more girlish and animated.

"Anyway, I am going to put all the blame on you for last night. When I arrived at the table it was half empty, and before I knew it that Veal man was holding out a chair for me, so I was left with no choice. And it wasn't till after that that Dr. Boyle and that other woman came in, and then you were the last of all." Marisa pouted in mock reproof. "Didn't anyone ever tell you it's rude to keep a lady waiting?"

Phil held up his hands in surrender. "Sorry - not my fault. My flight from Bangkok didn't get in to Rome until late, and there weren't any connecting flights up to Genoa until the next day, so the airline got me on one of the new high-speed trains. *Frecchiabianca*, I think they call them. Very smart, and very very fast! I just about made it to the ship before she sailed. But say what you like about the Italians, their trains certainly run on time."

Marisa was intrigued. "So what were you doing in Bangkok?"

Phil shrugged dismissively. "Oh, just a business meeting. It was only a stopover on the way from Sydney. My father has a P.R. company, so he's got all sorts of contacts all over the Far East. But

I'm sorry it all meant you got dumped on a table full of strangers. Although ..."

"What?"

"I thought I heard Dr. Boyle say he knew you."

Marisa frowned. "He may be right. Perhaps I did meet him, but that would be a long time ago. But you know what people are like - you meet them once, and they go around telling everyone you're one of their friends."

"Star-followers, eh?" Phil smiled in sympathy. "I bet you get that a lot. Hey, I hope you don't think ..."

"No, not at all." Marisa swiftly put out a hand to forestall his apparent intention of getting up to leave. "No, please, stay and have a drink. On me." She looked around and beckoned a hovering waiter.

Phil settled back. "Well ... if you insist."

*

"May I have your table number, sir?" The plump maître d', with an accent which may well have been genuinely French, greeted Constable and Copper at the door of the Imperial Dining Room. "Thank you. If you would like to follow me ..."

The two detectives had been allocated a small table just off-centre in the enormous restaurant, which spread over two decks with balconies of tables surrounding the central space, where a gigantic chandelier consisting of thousands of pieces of crystal interspersed with drops of golden and turquoise glass glittered as it swayed almost imperceptibly with the movement of the ship. At one end, a graceful double-horseshoe staircase, its glass treads seeming to float in mid-air, was wrapped around what appeared to be a monumental ice-sculpture, which on closer inspection was revealed to be a wine store whose racks glinted with a muted ruby richness from its towering racks of bottles. Waiters in gold-lapelled tailcoats and bus-boys in striped waistcoats of turquoise and blue moved purposefully between tables dazzling with the white of linen, the sharp gleam of silver and glass, and the soft brightness of flower arrangements.

"Good evening, gentlemen. Welcome to the Imperial Dining Room." The young waiter, his name-badge bearing the flag of Greece, seemed to appear from nowhere as he held Andy Constable's chair for him. "Allow me ..." With a flourish he unfolded the napkin from the place setting and placed it across

34

Constable's knees, and then briskly repeated the action for Dave Copper. "I will be serving you throughout this cruise. My name is Timon."

"Of Athens?" quipped Copper, catching sight of the badge.

Timon smiled patiently. It was obviously not the first time he had heard the remark. "No, sir, not quite, but it was a very good guess. I actually come from Piraeus."

"You'll have to get used to his sense of humour, I'm afraid, Timon," said Constable.

"That's quite all right, sir." Timon was unperturbed. "I used to get it all the time on my last ship, but I put it down to the fact that we attract a very intellectual clientele. So ..." He consulted a small clipboard. "It's Mr. Constable and Mr. Copper, I think. Is that right?"

"Andy and David will do fine."

"I don't think my maître d' would approve, sir. They like us to be rather more formal than that."

"Well then, you're just going to have to be Mr. ..." Copper picked up the name card on the table. "What the hell is that?"

"Papanicolaristides, sir," replied Timon blandly. "Don't worry, nobody else can pronounce it either. Which is why everybody in management shortens it to Tides." Copper seemed to be having difficulty avoiding choking. "Yes, I know ... and I am a waiter. Sometimes fate plays tricks with names."

"Oh, I wouldn't say that," said Constable drily. "You ever found that, David?"

"Me? No, never, guv," replied Copper in similar vein. "Why would you think that?"

"Right then, Timon - Timon it is, and we promise no jokes. Okay?"

"Thank you, sir. So, perhaps I may call you Mr. Andy and Mr. David? And now, let me give you your menus. And I will be back in a moment to take your order."

Copper browsed down the six courses listed on the menu. "I say, guv, I thought I was developing a taste for good food in Spain, but this lot takes the biscuit. There's stuff on here that I've only read about in the eating out section in the Sundays. I think I'm going to enjoy this."

"Yes, well, don't get too used to it. Don't forget that in a few days time you're back in the world of dishwater coffee and gristle pies in the station canteen."

"I'd better fill my boots while I've got the chance, then, hadn't I?"

As the two Britons gave Timon their order, their attention was drawn by a gust of laughter from the adjacent table.

"They seem to be enjoying themselves," remarked Copper. "Is that another one of your tables?"

"Yes, sir. One of six. And yes, they are a very ... jolly party." There was reserve in Timon's reply. "Well, mostly."

"Here, just a minute." Copper's eye was caught by the most animated member of the group. "That's never Marisa Fellows, is it?"

"You mean Mrs. Mann, sir? Yes, I believe it is."

"Who are you talking about?" enquired Constable.

"The one at the far end, guv. The Baywatch Blonde look-alike."

"And who exactly is she?"

"Don't tell me you haven't seen her in the papers, guv. She's all over them."

"Not the sort of papers I read, apparently. So tell me."

Copper drew a breath. "American reality TV star, mixes with all the celebs, famous for being famous - that's about it in a nutshell. Oh, and she's just picked up squillions in a divorce settlement."

"No wonder she seems a popular girl," commented Constable drily. "So, Timon, are they all with her?"

"Oh, no sir. Everyone on that table is travelling on their own. I think Mr. Wall's wife was supposed to be here - that's the gentleman at this end - but she didn't come."

"All Americans?"

"No, sir. Five of them are, but there is an English lady, and also an Australian gentleman, I think."

"And all of them having a good time and keeping you busy, no doubt?"

"That's right, sir."

"Well, apart from that chap on the far side, guv," pointed out Copper. "He's not exactly the life and soul, by the look of him. He looks as if he's chewing a wasp."

"Mr. Veal, sir. No, he does not laugh very much. And he does not say very much either. But I think he listens a lot."

"Look," said Constable, "talking about keeping you busy, Timon, if you have six tables to look after, you'd better not spend all your time talking to us."

Timon smiled. "You are right, sir. So, I will take your order through, and then I will bring you some wine. Will a bottle of house red and a bottle of white be sufficient? Or I could bring you the wine list if you would prefer to have something different."

"I think house wine will do us very nicely, Timon," grinned Copper. "Right, guv? I'm sure someone's driving this thing, and I'm very glad it's not me."

Chapter 3

For a few moments on awakening, Andy Constable could not think where he was. The glimpse of light entering through the small gap in the curtains showed a completely unfamiliar room. And the low-pitched vibration, just discernible at the edge of consciousness, was accompanied by occasional distant metallic thuds. As memory gradually returned, he rolled over and looked at his watch. Just after seven. By rights he should have been waking up in his own bed at home. As he looked around the luxuries of the suite, slowly coming into focus as his eyes adjusted to the dim light, he smiled quietly. As a second-best, this wasn't too bad. He threw back the covers, padded to the window, and drew the curtain. Below, the roof of a cruise terminal building was inching nearer as the *Empress of the Oceans* nestled steadily closer to the quayside. Beyond, a parking area where a line of coaches, already streaming through the adjacent dock gate, was beginning to form into a neat echelon. And beyond that, Cadiz.

Andy reached for the phone and dialled the number of the next-door cabin.

"Mmpph??"

"By which I take it, David, that you are not exactly up and about yet?"

"Not so's you'd notice, guv, not really. What time is it?" A pause. "Good grief! What is this, the middle-of-the-night call to say my day off has been ruined by some psychopath murderer again?"

Constable laughed. "Not exactly, sergeant. But as I've been given this extra enforced holiday, I thought it would be churlish to waste it. So I intend to get up, take a little light breakfast, and then see what the day has to offer. How about you?"

A sigh. "And you need your faithful sidekick to help you enjoy it to the full, is that it?"

"Something of the kind."

"Guv, couldn't I lay off being the sergeant until we're actually back on U.K. soil?"

"Not a chance," retorted Constable good-humouredly. "I'm thinking in terms of an eight o'clock breakfast. I'll come and hammer on your door." He replaced the receiver half-way through the grudging grunt of agreement.

The Catherine the Great buffet restaurant was perched right at the top of the stern of the ship, with panoramic full-height windows through which the sun was already streaming from a cloudless sky. Constable and Copper navigated their way through the clusters of passengers milling around the various food stations and weighing up the rival claims of the numerous styles of eggs, fresh fruit or chocolate muffins dotted among the immense array on display, and took a table by the window with a vista of the city spread beneath them. Dave Copper yawned.

"I take it there's another cunning plan, guv?"

"Not really. I thought we'd just get off the ship, and then take the day as it comes."

"Good morning, gentlemen." A familiar voice greeted the two Britons as Timon appeared alongside their table with a laden tray of used crockery.

"Oh ... hello, Timon," said Constable. "What are you doing up here? Aren't you based in the restaurant?"

"They move us around, sir. In the evenings I am in the Imperial, but at breakfast time I work up here, and then at lunchtime I will be in the Crowning Glory bar out by the pool."

"They don't give you a chance to get bored, then?" remarked Copper.

"No, sir, you would not think so. I hope you slept well?"

"After a couple of bottles of wine, no trouble," smiled Copper. "And I dare say the motion of the ocean helped to rock me to sleep as well. I went out like a light."

"And do you plan to go ashore?"

"We were just talking about that," said Constable.

"You should go to the Excursions Desk after breakfast, sir. Down in the atrium. They have trips - maybe you could go on one."

"We'll see. In the meantime, speaking of breakfast, I'm starting to feel hungry."

"Yes, you should help yourselves, sirs, and I should take all these things back to the kitchen, or I will be in trouble with my boss for talking too much. I will see you later." Timon steered an expert course through the gathering crowds and disappeared through a swing door.

Breakfast consumed, Copper leaned back with a satisfied

sigh. "You know, guv, this concept of unlimited freebies is starting to become addictive. If this is what cruising is like, I could easily develop a taste for it."

"Yes," retorted Constable, "and if you carry on putting it away at this rate, you could easily develop a considerably expanded waistline, at which point you will be of considerably less use to me if I want to send you off in pursuit of some scarpering villain. So, purely in the interests of efficiency in the workplace, get on your feet, and since we're in Cadiz, we'll go and singe the King of Spain's beard."

"You what? Aren't we likely to get ourselves nicked for that sort of thing?"

Constable emitted a sigh of despair and settled back into his seat. "This keeps happening. The history teachers at your school weren't very good, were they?"

"I should be used to this by now," muttered Copper resignedly. Being on the receiving end of one of his superior officer's lectures on some of the more esoteric events of world history had long ago become a regular feature of his working day.

"So come along, David," coaxed Constable. "Are you honestly going to tell me that the phrase 'singeing the King of Spain's beard' doesn't ring any bells?"

Copper dived deep into his memory banks. "Hang on a sec, guv." He screwed up his face. "Drake, is it? Something about the Spanish Armada?"

"And ...?"

"Got it! The Spanish were putting together a fleet to invade England ..."

"Because ...?"

"I don't know. Something to do with Mary Queen of Scots?"

"It usually was at that time. This is good. Keep going."

"And so Francis Drake sailed down here, attacked Cadiz and burnt the Spanish ships, and texted home that he'd singed the King of Spain's beard!" finished Copper triumphantly. "How's that?"

"Not bad, David," admitted Constable with a smile. "I have hopes for you yet."

"Didn't stop the Armada though, did it, guv?"

"It did not, but that is a lecture which I think we'll save for another day." The inspector rose to his feet. "In the meantime, let's take Timon's suggestion, and go and see if the Excursions Desk can tell us what this place has to offer. And since it's only eight or nine decks down, out of respect for your waistline - and mine, if I'm honest - we'll take the stairs."

As the pair arrived at the Excursions Desk, a young woman was just putting papers away and switching off computer terminals. She greeted them with a slightly breathless smile. "Goodness, gentlemen, you're only just in time! Another thirty seconds and you'd have missed me. My name's Sally. What can I do for you?"

"We just wanted to know what's on offer in Cadiz," explained Constable. "Not knowing the place."

"I'm afraid you've missed this morning's guided walking tour of the city," said Sally. "They've just left, but I could put you down for the afternoon tour if you're interested. Or we've got a couple of coach trips going off in about fifteen minutes, sir. I can probably squeeze you on to one of them, but you'll have to be quick. There are some buses going off to Seville to see the sights there - the cathedral is wonderful, I gather - or else if you're a fan of sherry, there's a trip later to Jerez to visit some of the bodegas."

"Not really me, guv," commented Dave Copper. "I'm more of a beer man myself. What do you reckon?"

"Or," continued Sally, stealing a look at her watch and failing to make the action unobtrusive, "I can give you a city map and you can decide for yourselves what you do."

Andy Constable took pity on her. "That's perfect. And you're in a rush, and you mustn't keep your other guests waiting on account of us. So give us a map, and go."

"Thank you, sir." With a smile of relief and a flurry of activity to close down the desk, Sally fled towards the stairs.

"Right then, David. Let's get back upstairs to get ourselves suited and booted, slap a bit of Factor 15 on the nose to stop it burning, and then it's off to see where this map takes us. Agreed?"

"You're the boss, guv."

Twenty minutes later, the Britons were greeted by Derek Crane as they stood in the queue waiting to have their cards processed as they left the ship.

"How's it going, guys? Everything all right?"

"Just off for a wander," replied Constable.

"Well, don't wander too far," grinned Derek. "And make sure

you're back on board by six, or we'll sail without you."

"No danger," remarked Copper. "We've not long had breakfast, and I'm already in the mood for lunch."

"Less talking, more walking," smiled Constable, as he pushed his colleague in the direction of the gangway.

*

"Well, there's something I never knew." Andy Constable was standing in the first plaza the Britons had reached after leaving the ship, a typical example of the great public spaces which Spain does so well, with a soaring monument to one of the more significant punctuations in the nation's history, set in a frame of immaculate gardens and florid baroque architecture.

"Will I regret saying 'Oh yes, and what's that, then?', guv?" asked Dave Copper in the tones of a man who felt that he had already had his prescripted history lesson for the day.

Constable ignored the implication of the remark and consulted again the notes on the back of the map he held. "Apparently, according to this, Cadiz was the capital of Spain for a while during the Napoleonic Wars."

"In fact, guv," replied Copper, in elaborately casual tones, "I think you'll find that at one point it was pretty much all of Spain."

"Sorry?"

"I expect what that goes on to say," continued Copper airily, "is that during the Peninsular War, once the French armies had taken over the whole of the rest of the country, the Spanish and the English armies who'd come to help them were bottled up here with their backs to the sea. Bit of luck it was here really, when you come to think of it. It meant the good old Royal Navy could get in and re-supply them." He smiled blandly at his astonished companion. "I suppose that would have been payback for that little episode with Sir Francis Drake."

"How in the name of all that's holy …?" Words appeared to fail Andy Constable.

"Sharpe, guv," explained Dave Copper with a grin. "I watched the series on TV, and I've read a couple of the books. It's all in there. History lessons by default. Never underestimate the educative power of populist literature, sir."

Constable erupted in good-humoured laughter. "I have to say, David, that that is one of the finest examples of 'the biter bit' that I have ever been subjected to! Good man - I'm proud of you!"

He clapped the other on the back. "Right then - as you now appear to be holding the baton, I am appointing you as our official guide for the day. Lead on."

The two detectives set out. In the old city perched on its headland, they strolled the park-lined ramparts, whipped by the same stiff breeze which had once blown galleons home across the tumbling ocean, laden with the silver of the New World. They surveyed, through fissures in the walls of an ancient fort, the array of rocks lying in predatory wait at the approaches to the harbour. They took their ease in a pavement cafe, sipping powerfully strong coffees as they overlooked a wide and almost deserted strand. And in the cathedral, a massive stone sentinel standing fortress-like virtually at the water's edge, a huge saint-studded reliquary, heavy with sanctity, gleamed with the light of a forest of candles reflected in that same plundered silver.

"What next, then, guv?" enquired Copper as the two descended the steps of the cathedral museum after viewing its opulent array of treasures. "Although I have to say, to be perfectly honest, that what I'm hoping for is lunch, beer, and a siesta. I reckon I'm about cultured out for one day."

"That sounds like a perfectly sensible suggestion, David," agreed Constable. "And I've got a feeling that most people will probably have taken advantage of OceanSea's generosity in providing free distractions, so with a bit of luck, the ship will be nice and quiet. I might even stretch out and get a few rays later on, while we still have the sun."

"Good thinking, sir. That pool on the top deck looks pretty inviting. If we head back now, I can grab a quick swim before lunch. Deal, guv?"

"Deal."

*

The warbling of the bedside telephone dragged Dave Copper from sleep, a heavier slumber than he had probably intended, courtesy of the third lunchtime beer.

"I'm guessing, guv," he croaked, "that you have appointed yourself as my personal alarm service."

"David," returned his superior, "you will sleep your days away if allowed, and you will miss all the finer things in life. And since, if you consult the sheet of the day's activities which the cabin steward so kindly left for you, the management are serving

43

what they describe as a 'Classic Elegant Tea' in the Maria Theresa Lounge in about five minutes, I think it would be churlish to decline their gracious invitation."

"I suppose I wouldn't mind a cuppa, if you're absolutely determined," grunted Copper reluctantly. "Give me two minutes."

At the door of the Maria Theresa Lounge, the Britons were greeted by a white-gloved liveried attendant, who showed them through to a table decked with crisp linen and sparkling silver. A three-tier stand bearing a selection of minute canapés and dainty cream-laden pastries was flanked by a pair of bone china cups and saucers.

"Just as well I actually put some trousers on," remarked Copper, as he noticed a passenger in shorts being politely but firmly denied entrance to the lounge amid profuse expressions of regret and explanations of the dress code. "This is all rather more than the cup of tea and a bun I was expecting."

"Good afternoon, gentlemen. Do you prefer Indian or China tea?"

"Timon!"

"Yes, sir, it is me again." Timon stood at their side, two silver teapots on the trolley he pushed.

"There appears to be no getting away from you," smiled Constable. "Do they never give you any time off?"

"Oh yes, sir, they do. Don't worry. But this afternoon I am working for my cabin mate, because he is Filipino and very religious, and he wanted to go to the cathedral in Seville, and he got permission if someone would cover for him. So here I am. Indian or China, or my colleague over there has herbal teas as well?" Timon gestured to a stewardess in a turquoise and gold cheong-sam who stood behind a table bearing an array of dishes, each labelled with a different type of infusion.

"Indian is fine."

As Timon continued to pass among the other guests in the lounge, Dave Copper looked around him.

"This is all very posh, isn't it, guv? They really seemed determined to push the boat out - sorry, didn't mean to say that."

"Obviously pitching for a better class of clientele than your average fun booze cruise," responded Constable. "I have to say, from what I've seen, that they seem to be making a pretty decent job of it."

"So do we have any thoughts as to what's on offer this evening?"

"According to the Ocean Times," said Constable, producing a folded copy of the ship's daily bulletin from his pocket and surveying it swiftly, "we sail at six-thirty, with 'Quayside Entertainment', whatever that may be, and then there's dinner at seven-thirty as usual, there's a show on in the theatre at nine-thirty, and after that I might go and lose a few quid on the roulette tables in the casino."

"I never had you down as a gambler, guv."

"There are many things you don't know about me, sergeant. No, actually, I'm not a gambler by nature, but as it's a one-off, I thought I might have a go."

"D'you know, guv, I might keep you company. I might have a go at the Blackjack."

"You play Blackjack?"

"Well, not exactly," admitted Copper with a grin. "But I have seen 'Casino Royale' - do you reckon that'll help?"

*

Sharp at six o'clock, as if summoned by the deep-throated call of the ship's siren, the last two excursion coaches swept on to the dock alongside the *Empress of the Oceans* and disgorged their chattering throng of passengers, who swiftly headed for the gangway as members of the below-decks crew busied themselves dismantling the small shore pavilion and gathering up its rope barriers. Constable glanced at his watch.

"Spot on time," he remarked to Copper, as the two stood on the top deck, leaning on the ship's rail and looking out over the rooftops of Cadiz, already starting to acquire a warmer glow as the sun began to decline and turn the terracotta tiles of the older buildings from a dazzling orange to a more mellow amber. "There goes the half-hour warning. So I'm assuming we'll be sailing on schedule at half past."

"So what's this 'quayside entertainment' you were going on about then, guv?" asked Copper.

Constable pulled a face. "I have not the remotest idea, David ..." Movement at the end of the quay caught his eye. "...but I think I can make a reasonable guess."

Round the end of the cruise terminal, where they had been hidden from view, a brass band in immaculate uniforms, buttons

45

gleaming and plumes nodding, had just struck up and were marching down the quay towards the middle of the ship, to a growing round of applause from the increasing number of passengers who were lining the rails. As Constable looked down, he could see that people on many of the stateroom balconies below him were also contributing to the swelling audience. The band reached a point opposite the entrance to the terminal, came to a smart stop and, with a flourish, unfurled a banner.

"What's that all about then, guv?"

"As far as my dreadful Spanish goes, David," said Constable, "which you will remember is not very far, it looks as if they're the Municipal Band of the Order of Santa Maria, or some such. Of course ... they have these marching bands everywhere in Spain. Each neighbourhood seems to have its own. Don't you remember all those musicians we saw trooping into San Pablo for the fiesta there?"

"Truth be told, guv, my attention was pretty much elsewhere at the time. I was rather too busy making notes for you while we tried to sort out a murderer."

"Well, anyway, there's your evening entertainment. They've obviously come to play us out of the harbour."

Perfectly on cue, the band struck up with a spirited rendering of the traditional Spanish tune 'Valencia'. They were good. The proud musical spirit of the nation echoed around the space between the ship and the building as tune after tune poured from the players' instruments. Halfway through the recital, in response to a fanfare, a team of dancers, flamenco costumes swirling, darted out from the terminal to contribute their dazzling display to the concert. Castanets clacked and trumpets tooted. In a slightly unexpected interlude, what seemed to be five shepherds in fleecy capes and pointy felt hats joined the band to give a wailing recital on instruments which appeared to be a cross between an adenoidal recorder and an undersized bagpipe. At the end of thirty minutes, the concert ended with a flourish of flounces and a triumphant crescendo of brazen exuberance. The audience, by now crammed several deep along every available stretch of railing, burst into vociferous applause, to which the ship appeared to add its own tribute of three long low cries from the voice of its siren, perched high on the funnel.

"And we're off," said Dave Copper, as a steady increase in

46

vibration, felt rather than heard, was accompanied by the gradual appearance, inch by inch, of clear water between the quayside and the ship's hull. He consulted his watch. "Half six on the dot. These OceanSea people are pretty good on their time-keeping."

"Which means," replied Andy Constable, "that we have exactly an hour until dinner."

"Or," countered Copper, "three-quarters of an hour to get down to the bar for a sundowner before we eat."

"You're in for a rude shock when we get back to the U.K., lad," remarked Constable. "All this open bar stuff is going to your head. Before we know where we are, you'll be wandering into the pub next to the station and asking for a free pint of Pina Colada."

"Fat chance of that with the landlord of the *Collar and Cuffs*, from what I know of him, guv."

"In which case, as a special treat, you shall have your sundowner. Seven-fifteen in the Diadem Bar it is."

*

Andy Constable brushed a speck of dust from his cuff and took a last glance out of the window. Cadiz was already diminishing to a distant blur astern, as the *Empress* forged her way sturdily westwards through the vigorous Atlantic chop, heading directly towards the declining sun on her way towards Cape St. Vincent. He closed the cabin door and headed down towards the bar.

"Hi, guys. You seem to be fitting into the cruise routine without too much trouble."

"Derek!" Constable put down his glass of wine, stood, and shook hands with his erstwhile colleague. "Well, as your company seems determined to offer us the full range of its hospitality, it would be ungrateful to refuse. And David here appears to be acquiring a slightly worrying taste for some of the more bizarre cocktails on offer, little umbrellas and all." He peered at Copper's glass with a suspicious eye. "What exactly is that again?"

"Corpse Reviver, guv," replied the younger man cheerfully. "I thought it wouldn't do any harm to try and get on the wavelength of some of the Friday nighters who come falling out of the bars in town, pre- and post-loaded to the eyeballs on cocktails and shots and stuff. And you never know - in our line of work, a corpse reviver might come in handy once in a while!"

"Tasteful as ever," remarked Constable. "Speaking of work,

Derek, you seem to be singularly unoccupied every time we see you."

"Don't be fooled by appearances, Andy," countered Crane. "I am, even as we speak, working extremely hard." And in response to Constable's quizzically raised eyebrow, "The pre-dinner schmooze is regarded by those at the top as an essential part of the function of a ship's officer. Look around you."

It was true. Dotted about the bar were several of Crane's white-uniformed colleagues, smiling and chatting to groups of passengers as they sat around the lounge or passed through in the direction of the dining room.

"And so," continued Crane, "if you have no objection, I will join you for a small mineral water - there are limits to what the management will allow us to get away with." The order given to a passing waiter, he leaned back in his chair with a sigh. "And they won't open the dining room doors until exactly half past, so you're in no rush. Actually, it's a treat for me to sit down for five minutes. For you lot out front, everything might seem all very calm and relaxed, but there's an awful lot of frantic paddling going on underwater."

Dave Copper opened his mouth as if to crack a joke, but in response to Constable's swiftly voiced 'Don't you dare!', thought better of it.

"Anyway, you don't have to worry about things like that for the next forty-eight hours. As far as you're concerned, you can have a nice relaxing couple of days at sea doing as little as possible before you have to rejoin the real world when we dock on Saturday morning. I'd take full advantage if I were you."

The scream which echoed down through the atrium cut through a hundred conversations like a knife. There was a second of absolute silence, before a further scream from above unleashed a hubbub of amazement and speculation. Derek Crane was on his feet in an instant.

"What the hell's that?" He looked upwards, to see a face looking over a jutting balcony high above, accompanied by a frantically waving arm.

"Somebody ... oh, somebody ... come quickly!"

Without a word, Crane raced in the direction of the lifts. Constable and Copper exchanged a mute look and, without further consultation, followed on his heels.

"Stand back, please! Security!" Crane firmly pushed aside a group of passengers standing in front of a set of opening lift doors, stepped inside with the other two Britons in close attendance, and pushed a button.

"Where are we going?" asked Constable.

"Eight," replied Crane shortly. "That was the Library and Internet Lounge. Let's see what on earth is going on."

The three emerged from the lift and hurried along the open corridor which led to the Internet Lounge on the opposite side of the atrium, to be greeted by a white-faced and trembling girl of about twenty, dressed in the universal crew uniform of turquoise jacket and white skirt.

"Oh, Mr. Crane, thank goodness it's you. Come and see."

"What's happened?"

The girl pointed wordlessly.

"Oh my god," breathed Crane. Over his shoulder, Constable and Copper could see what appeared to be a man leaning on a desk and looking intently at the computer screen in front of him. The impression was misleading - this man would never consult a computer again. The weight of the torso was supported by a half-concealed stack of books which had prevented the body slumping entirely. And protruding from between the shoulder-blades, bright against the plain white shirt of the victim, stood what looked like a green and silver twisted glass shaft.

As Constable and Copper took in the scene, Derek Crane was already speaking swiftly into his walkie-talkie. "Get me four of the security staff up to Eight immediately - I want the Internet Lounge cordoned off. This section is going to be out of bounds to all passengers - they're going to have to use the fore and aft lifts. You'd better put out an announcement on the P.A. - tell the passengers there's been an accident, but that they should carry on into dinner normally. No point in disrupting the whole ship. Oh, and get the doc up here at once. ... Why? Because there's a bloody body in the library, that's why!"

"Derek, do you want us out of your way?" Andy Constable gestured back towards the lifts.

"Lord, no. Stick around, please. You never know, it might be helpful. I'm a bit out of practice with this sort of thing, and whatever we're telling the passengers, this certainly ain't no accident. It looks far more in your line than mine." Crane turned

49

to the girl, still standing to one side with her hand to her mouth. "So, what happened ..." He glanced at the name badge. "What happened, Portia?"

"I really don't know, Mr. Crane. I just walked in and found him."

As Crane was about to continue, another white-clad officer carrying a medical bag appeared from the corridor.

"Hello, Derek," he boomed cheerfully in a ringing Irish accent. "They tell me you've got a patient for me."

"I suspect it's a bit late for you to call on your healing skills, doc," returned Crane drily. "But you'd better come and have a look." He turned to Constable. "Andy, would you mind taking Portia under your wing for a second? Just get a few basics for me if you can. Is that okay?"

"Of course," said Constable. "Shall we go and sit down over here?" He led the way into one of the library alcoves, sat the girl in one of the tub chairs, and took a seat opposite her. "So, what's your name again?"

"Portia, sir. Portia Carr."

"And what do you do on the ship?"

"I'm part of the Animation team, sir. I dance in the shows, but I also help out with some of the daytime activities, like excursions or quizzes."

"Well, look, Portia, I'm an old friend of Derek Crane's. We used to work together. So if you can just tell me what you know, I'll pass it on to him. For a start, what were you doing here?"

Portia took a breath and seemed to be concentrating her thoughts. "I just came up here to lock up the library cabinets, sir. It was on my rota for today. We open them for an hour and a half every morning and every afternoon, so I just get the key from Guest Relations, open the cabinets and put the register out for people to sign when they borrow a book, and then come back an hour and a half later and close things up."

"So just to be clear, the library opened at six o'clock, and that's the last time you were here?"

"No, I popped back after half an hour to check on things, but there was nobody about because we were just about to sail, so I went up on deck for the Sailaway Party."

"So the library isn't staffed all the time?" put in Dave Copper.

"Oh, no, sir. It's done on a trust system."

"Hmmm," said Copper. "Strikes me that there's somebody not too trustworthy round here."

"So you came in here ...?" resumed Constable.

"Yes, sir. Just before half past seven. And at first I thought there wasn't anyone here. But then I saw Mr. Veal."

"You know him?"

"Not really, sir. But I recognised him from when he was a passenger on one of the excursions I was working on, in Barcelona."

"Hang, on, guv," interrupted Copper. "Veal - isn't that the guy who's on the table next to us at dinner. The miserable one?" Copper glanced across in the direction of the dead man, where Crane and the doctor were engaged in conversation. "Not that he's got a great deal to be pleased about at the moment."

"Yes, thank you, David. So, Portia ... what then?"

"That's all, really. I saw Mr. Veal, and it took me a second or two, but then I noticed that thing sticking out of his back, and I realised he'd been stabbed, and I just screamed."

"And that's it? You didn't see or hear anyone else?"

"I didn't see anyone, no. And there was quite a lot of noise and music coming up from the bar downstairs, so I don't suppose I'd have heard anyone either." Portia took a breath and her eyes widened. "You mean ... you mean whoever did this might have been around?" Her hand went back to her mouth again.

"Look, Portia," said Constable kindly, "whoever it was, they're certainly not here now. So, I think that'll do for the present. Now, do you have a friend?"

"Yes, sir. Sally, my cabin mate."

"Well, I suggest you go and find her, sit down with her in a corner somewhere, and tell her the whole thing again. Get it out of your system - chase the demons away. I'll pass all this on, and Mr. Crane might want to have another word with you later."

With a shaky smile of thanks, Portia fled towards the lifts, past the newly-stationed security staff, and was soon heading downwards. Constable and Copper returned to where Crane and the doctor were standing over the body.

"She doesn't know much," reported Constable briefly. "Walked in, found him, screamed. So what's the score here?"

"Eamonn here can tell you better than I can." Crane

51

gestured to the doctor. "Doc, this is an old police colleague of mine, Andy Constable, and Dave Copper, who works with him. They're only here thanks to that volcano."

"Eamonn Holliday," smiled the doctor, shaking hands. "Police, eh? Well, you two could turn out to be a godsend. Violent death is a bit out of my usual range of experience. A couple of heart attacks and the odd emergency appendectomy in mid-ocean is about as exciting as my life aboard ship has been. Murder is a very different thing, and I can't see how this can be anything other than murder."

"So," said Constable, "First principles. He's definitely dead, then?"

"Oh, dead is definitely what he is," confirmed the doctor cheerfully. "You don't get stabbed in the heart and walk away from it."

"How long?"

"Minutes. He's not cooled down as far as I can tell. I'll see if I can give you any more when I've got him downstairs and taken a closer look."

"Downstairs?"

"To the Medical Centre. I've got a fully equipped miniature hospital down there. We could take out your tonsils, fill your teeth, and even deliver a baby if we had to. Not that I feel up to carrying out a full post-mortem - I think my nurses would probably have a fine case of the heeby-jeebies if I took a swing at that - but it's my first proper corpse, so you can't blame a feller for being a bit curious. So, Derek, if you can spare a couple of chaps and you've finished with the poor guy, I'll take him off your hands."

"Do you want them to fetch a stretcher?"

"I don't fancy getting him on a stretcher with that glass thing sticking out of him, whatever it is. I've got a better idea. This chair's on castors - I think it'll go a whole lot quicker if we just wheel him into the crew lift round the corner. Get him out of sight as fast as we can."

"We'll give you a hand, doc," volunteered Dave Copper. "Guv, can you ...?"

"That's grand of you," replied Holliday. "So, if you can keep him steady, it's just here to the left."

As the crew lift doors closed on the doctor - "No, that's fine, my nurse at the bottom can help me with him." - Copper allowed his face to split in a grin.

"*Doc* Holliday?" he gurgled. "Is he kidding? You'd have thought with a name like that, he'd have chosen anything but medicine!"

"Let him who is without sin ..." commented Constable wryly.

Returning to the library, the two Britons found Derek Crane in conversation with yet another ship's officer, this time with a uniform bearing the insignia of a considerably higher rank than Crane's own.

"Chaps, this is the Staff Captain. We've been weighing up the situation, and I've explained all about you. He wonders if you can help us out."

"Aren't you going to put back into Cadiz?" asked Constable. "Wouldn't that be easiest?"

"Far from it," retorted the Staff Captain. "An American-owned ship under a Panamanian flag with British officers and about twenty different nationalities in the crew trying to deal with the Spanish authorities? I don't think so. Plus we're well out of their territorial waters, so I'd be far happier to let the British police handle the matter when we get to Southampton. And as Derek informs me that you two are in fact serving British police officers ..."

" ... you just wondered if we'd help you out," echoed Constable.

"I think I can say, on behalf of OceanSea, that we would very much appreciate it. And obviously, I'd like to think we could rely on you to handle this as discreetly as possible."

Constable sighed, then smiled ruefully. "Well, since you put it so nicely, and as the company has been kind enough to treat us to its generous hospitality and take us home, I suppose it's the least we can do." He turned to his colleague. "If that's all right by you, sergeant."

"No problem, guv," responded Copper cheerily. "I was wondering what on earth I was going to do all day tomorrow anyway. I don't mind singing for my supper." He turned away, then stopped. "Just one thing though, Captain. Is it all right by you if we actually have our supper before we start? I'm starving."

Chapter 4

In the Imperial Dining Room, the atmosphere was one of fevered but subdued surmise. The announcement of an accident had obviously led to all manner of speculation, and covert glances were being cast from adjoining tables in the direction of Ira Veal's empty chair. At the table itself, a silence seemed to have fallen over the occupants, who appeared to be studiously avoiding looking at one another.

"Mr. Andy - is it true?" hissed Timon, appearing at Constable's shoulder as he finished his main course.

Constable raised a non-committal eyebrow. "Is what true?"

"About Mr. Veal. My section head heard it from one of the room service waiters. This 'accident' they announced has something to do with Mr. Veal, and they say he is dead, and that it is no accident at all."

"Fat chance of keeping the lid on things, then, guv," remarked Dave Copper.

"You cannot keep secrets on a ship like this, sir," Timon pointed out. "It is a very close community. Everybody hears everything. In fact, I myself could tell you ..."

Timon's discourse was interrupted by the arrival of Derek Crane. "Andy, David, sorry to interrupt your meal, but I've got a snippet which might interest you, and it might very well have a bearing on this business." He cast a sideways glance at the adjoining table. "Look, I can't really talk here. I hate to drag you away, but ..."

"No problem, Derek. I can't say that murder sharpens my appetite particularly. I think I've had enough for now, and if my sergeant here has many more dinners like last night's, he'll never get through his next fitness test, so it's probably a kindness to stop him before he gets to the puddings. So, after you."

Crane led the way to the atrium, gestured to the detectives to take a seat in one of the more secluded alcoves, and beckoned to Lydia Carton at her place at the Guest Relations desk.

"Sit down a second, Lydia. You remember I told you that Mr. Constable is a senior British police officer? Well, he has agreed to help me in this business of Mr. Veal, so will you please tell him what you just told me."

Lydia turned to Constable with a look of concern on her face. "I thought it was a little strange at the time, sir, and it's the first time I've known it happen like this."

"Known what exactly?"

"The table arrangements, sir."

"You'd better start at the beginning, Lydia," coaxed Crane.

Lydia took a deep breath. "There's a system on all our ships, sir. Whenever we get a new batch of passengers arriving on board, a list goes through to the maître d' with all the preferences - what language people speak, what size of table they would like to be on, whether they wish to dine with friends from another cabin, and so on - so that he can work out the table plan for the restaurant for dinner. It's normally very complicated, because we usually have a full ship and so there are two sittings, but this time it is just the one. And on this voyage, my department at head office received an email from our New York agents, specially asking that several of the passengers should be placed together on one particular table. And this table was the one that Mr. Veal is ... was on."

"And do we know where this request originated?"

"Yes, sir. I looked it up while Mr. Crane was coming to fetch you. It came from our Chairman, who was passing it on from the editor of the 'National Investigator'."

"What on earth had it got to do with him?"

"You don't know?" asked Crane. "But you do know the 'National Investigator', I assume?"

"Not personally. Only by reputation. It's some sort of American scandal rag, isn't it? 'Elvis Helped Aliens Abduct My Hamster', that sort of thing, right?"

"More or less. Celebrity revelations, scandals, cover-ups - the stuff that's meat and drink to the British red-tops, only more so. Careers finished in the blink of an eye. And here's the thing - Ira Veal was their chief reporter."

Andy Constable began to smile slowly. "And Mr. Veal had hand-picked a table of ... what, potential victims? Is that the theory?"

"It sounds plausible, guv," commented Copper. "We know what some journalists can be like."

"So who are these lucky individuals?"

"I have the list here, sir," said Lydia. "It is Mr. and Mrs. Wall -

except that Mrs. Wall did not come, for some reason - Dr. Boyle, Mrs. Mann, Mr. Anders, Miss Holm, and Mrs. ... sorry, I should say Pastor Best."

"And these are, I take it, what you described as 'the great and the good', Derek?"

"According to someone they are, obviously. So my guess is, we need to find out what it is about each of them that was of interest to Ira Veal."

Constable thought for a second. "Here's a suggestion. If you can corral them at the end of dinner - keep them together but away from other people - then we can talk to each of them and find out what relationship there was, if any."

"There's a couple of staff meeting rooms next to my office. We could put them in one, and you could use the other."

"So where will you be?"

"Would you mind if I delegate this bit to you, Andy? I've got to go and see the Captain and bring him up to speed, then I want to have a word with the doctor, and I need to get in touch with the shore authorities in the U.K."

"That's fine, Derek. You leave the heavy lifting to us. Just pop a notebook and a pen into the hands of my trusty sergeant here, and we'll slip effortlessly into the old routine. It'll be just like being at home."

"Bit different from chewing over a case in the station canteen though, guv," remarked Dave Copper. "Still, it'll make another chapter in my autobiography, if I ever get round to writing it. 'A Death On The Ocean Wave' - how's that for a title?"

"Delusions of grandeur," sighed Constable. "Let's settle down to a little routine police work, shall we?"

*

"They're all next door, Andy." Derek Crane popped his head round the door of the room in which Constable and Copper had installed themselves as a make-shift interview room. "I've put Sanjay, one of my security guys, in with them, just to keep an eye on things - I thought it might not be a bad idea to discourage them from chatting too much among themselves."

"Good thinking, Derek," responded Constable. "See, the old training paid off."

"Do you want them in any particular order?"

"Not really, no. I suppose we may as well work our way

down the list which Lydia put together, which I think you've got, David?"

"Right here, guv." A riffle of paperwork. "Which means that our first victim is Mr. Wall."

"Andy, I'll shunt him in your direction, and then if you don't mind, I'll shove off and get on with the hundred and one things which this business seems to have dumped on my plate. Any problems, have a word with Sanjay and he'll page me."

"That's fine, Derek. Leave it to us. We've done this sort of thing once or twice before." A rueful smile. "Why should today be any different?"

It was only a matter of moments before the door opened with some considerable force, and Baxter D. Wall strode aggressively into the room.

"The Security Officer says you want to talk to me. Can somebody tell me what is going on, and who the hell you are."

Andy Constable looked up from his chair and smiled calmly. "You're Mr. Wall, I take it?" And in response to a curt nod, "Please take a seat, Mr. Wall - sergeant, just push that door to, would you - and I'll happily explain the situation. My name is Constable - I'm a detective inspector in the British police force, and this is my colleague, Detective Sergeant Copper. Now, as you are I'm sure aware, there has been an ... incident involving one of the guests on your dinner table on board this ship this evening, and the Head of Ship's Security has asked us to assist him in looking into the matter."

"Yeah," grunted Baxter. "I heard. But why would he do that? What has it got to do with you?"

"Not a thing, sir." The inspector's smile grew, if anything, calmer. "But it so happens that Mr. Crane and I are old colleagues, so you might say that I'm just helping out a friend."

"But I'm an American citizen. So was Veal. And this isn't a British ship. So what are you doing asking questions?"

"Again, you're absolutely right, Mr. Wall. Except, of course, that the next legal jurisdiction we shall be entering will be the United Kingdom when we dock in Southampton, so my colleagues there will probably be asking a great deal more questions than me. All I'm asking for is a little help in trying to establish some facts so that anybody who is not involved can be delayed as little as possible."

Baxter's face took on a wary look. "I'm starting to feel that I should be talking to my lawyer."

"I'm sure if you think that's necessary, sir, we could arrange a call." Constable glanced at his watch. "By my calculation, it's still the middle of the business day in the United States. Why, do you think there may be a need to take some legal advice?"

Baxter shifted slightly uneasily. "No, of course not." He assayed a smile which was not wholly convincing. "It's what we Americans do as a matter of habit." He made a visibly conscious effort to relax. "We're not used to the politeness of you British police. So go ahead ... inspector, did you say it was? Ask me your questions."

"And I hope you won't mind if my sergeant here takes a few notes as we go along, just to make sure nothing slips my mind. So, can we just have a few details about you - full name, and so on."

"My name is Baxter D. Wall - I live in New York City."

"And what do you do, sir?" Constable took in the expensively-tailored suit, the hand-made shirt, and the general air of sleek prosperity. "That is, of course, if you do actually work."

"I do. I'm a trader with a firm in Manhattan."

"Oh yes, sir? Which one."

Baxter allowed himself a contented smile. "I doubt if you would have heard of us. The firm is very, very discreet - we have some very important clients who would not be at all pleased if their business affairs were to be made public."

"Names that would be familiar to us?"

"Oh, I think so." Baxter emitted a small chuckle. The temptation was irresistible. "What's that column they have in the 'London Times'? The 'Court Circular', is it?"

"So," Constable eased on smoothly, with just a very slightly raised eyebrow, "shall we just say a firm of high reputation, then. And how did it come about that you are aboard this particular voyage?"

"That's down to Dad, I guess." And in response to Copper's quizzical look and poised pen, "You may have heard of my father, sergeant. Walter Wall. President of WalterMart. Just about the biggest retail outfit in the U.S. Among other things."

"Oh, right, sir. Yes, of course I've heard of them. I think they own one of our big supermarket chains in the U.K., don't they, sir?"

"I really wouldn't know, sergeant. That's Dad's side of things, not mine."

"But as for you being on the ship, you say your father ...?"

"Oh, Dad knows the president of OceanSea - well, the holding company, anyway. So he fixed it for us to come on this trip."

"Us, sir?"

"My wife and myself." Baxter's reply was curt.

"But - forgive me, sir - I gather your wife isn't with you."

"No, she was ... unable to come," answered Baxter tersely. "Look, aren't we getting off the point? I'm sure my family relationships are all very fascinating, but what's this to do with what happened tonight?"

"You're right, sir," apologised Copper. "Forgive me. Of course, it's much more important to find out about your relationship with Mr. Veal."

"I can tell you that in one word, sergeant. None."

"Excuse me, Mr. Wall," resumed Constable, "but that seems a little surprising."

"Surprising or not, it's the truth, inspector. Before I came on board this ship, I'd never set eyes on the man."

"But you knew of him, of course? I mean, the 'National Investigator' doesn't exactly hide its light under a bushel in your country, from what I gather, and he was a very prominent part of their reporting line-up."

"Naturally I knew of his paper - who doesn't? But I've never read the thing, and I would have no reason to know any of their staff."

"Well, now, that's somewhat at odds with some information that we have been given, Mr. Wall. You see, I've been told that prior to this voyage, the Investigator's editor made a special effort to compile a particular list of guests who would be dining on the same table as Mr. Veal. And your name was on that list. Now why do you suppose that might be?"

"I can't tell you anything more than I've already said, inspector. I didn't know the man. What do you want me to say?" Baxter's lips shut firmly.

"Of course, I take your word for it, Mr. Wall," responded Constable. "Well, maybe somebody else has the answer to that. So then, going on from that, you would obviously have no reason to wish him dead?"

"Of course not."

"Nor any knowledge of anyone else's reason to cause him harm?"

"No."

"So, then, just one or two questions about your movements early this evening. Oh, purely in the interests of ruling out a few possibilities," added Constable hastily as Baxter's hackles visibly rose. "Can I ask where you were when we sailed?"

"I was in the fitness centre."

"Not watching the entertainment with everyone else then, sir? The band and the dancers?"

"I saw a little of it from my balcony, but to be frank, inspector, that kind of thing isn't my style. Too much noise and stamping around, so I went up to the gym. Did a workout, had a sauna and a shower, and then went back down to my suite to get ready for dinner."

"And was anybody else about?"

"Nobody, inspector. The place is usually deserted at that time - that's why I go up there then. Most of the people who use it go first thing in the morning."

"So, you saw nobody, and nobody saw you."

"Well, the guy behind the desk was there when I arrived - I saw the back of him when he was putting out some fresh towels, but I don't know if he saw me. Probably not. And he wasn't around when I left."

"And I don't suppose by any chance you saw Mr. Veal during any of that period."

Baxter gave a derisive smile. "I don't think Ira Veal was the sort of guy you'd find in a gym."

"Unless he was on the trail of a story, of course, Mr. Wall. I suppose we have to bear that in mind."

"Well, you suppose all you want, inspector, but the plain fact is, I didn't see him, he didn't see me, and that's it. If you're after some kind of alibi, I can't provide one. Sorry. And since there doesn't seem to be anything else I can tell you, if you'll excuse me, I'd rather be some place else." Baxter got to his feet.

Constable followed suit. "Not a problem, Mr. Wall. As I say, this is all quite unofficial, and any help you can give us is purely voluntary. Although much appreciated, of course. So I hope that, if anything occurs, you won't mind if I ask you if we can have another chat?"

"Find me if you need me, inspector." Baxter grimaced. "After all, I'm not exactly going to get off the ship, am I?" He turned and was gone.

"Nice helpful gentleman," remarked Copper. "We didn't exactly get a lot out of him, did we? Do you buy all that guff about him not knowing Mr. Veal at all?"

"Not for one second. I don't think I'd go so far as to suggest that they were drinking buddies, but I get a sniff of something not quite right."

Copper guffawed. "He wasn't too forthcoming about his wife, was he? What do you reckon to a bit of hanky-panky there? Or ... maybe it's more a case of Mr. Veal knowing something *about* Mr. Wall, guv, rather than knowing him personally."

"Not quite the most brilliant deduction you'll ever make, Copper, considering that our victim was an investigative reporter. The clue is rather in the question, wouldn't you say?"

"And there's no-one to back up Mr. Wall's account of his movements, which never helps."

"You say that, sergeant, but we haven't got an account of Veal's movements either as yet, so let's not jump ahead of ourselves."

"Maybe Derek Crane can rustle that up for us, guv. Do you want me to get in touch and ask him?"

"No, leave that for the moment. Let's carry on working our way through the people on that dinner table. Who's next on the list?"

"Chap called Lancelot Boyle. Lancelot? Strewth!"

"Right then. Why don't you pop next door and get him in here?"

*

"Please take a seat - it's *Doctor* Boyle, isn't it?"

"Lance is fine." Boyle sat in the chair facing the inspector, his casual tone and pose nevertheless betraying signs of tension.

"I think, if you don't mind," replied Constable, "that we'll keep it a little more formal, Dr. Boyle. After all, we are investigating a sudden death."

"Yeah, I'm not really clear on that. The Security Chief cooped us all up next door and said that somebody would be speaking to us. He didn't go into details. So who exactly are you, and what's your status?"

"Ah, I hoped that Mr. Crane would have explained a little more. However," the inspector took a deep breath. "Let's start from square one. I'm sure you're aware that one of the gentlemen from your dining table, Mr. Veal, has been found dead ..."

"That much I did know."

" ... and that the circumstances are, to say the least, suspicious. Now as it happens, the Head of Security, Mr. Crane, and I are old friends and colleagues - we trained together for the police. He, obviously, left - I didn't. Which means that I am now a detective inspector in the U.K. police - my name is Constable, and this is my colleague, Detective Sergeant Copper. And as we were on board, and our next port is Southampton in the U.K., Mr. Crane has asked us to make some preliminary enquiries into the circumstances of Mr. Veal's death so as to speed things up. So I hope you'll be willing to help us."

Boyle shrugged, apparently more at ease. "Sure. Why not?"

"So really, there are two things I need, Dr. Boyle, and I hope you don't mind if my sergeant here makes a few notes as we go along." Boyle signified assent. "And do I gather you're travelling alone?"

"Yes."

"You're single?"

"I was married. My wife died." The subject sounded an awkward one, and Constable elected to move on swiftly.

"I'm sorry to hear that. So, did you know Mr. Veal before you came aboard this ship?"

"Know him, no. We'd met."

"Now, Dr. Boyle, that doesn't give me a lot to go on. Could you perhaps expand a little more as to how and when?"

"That would be during the course of my work, Mr. Constable. Although, naturally, a man like Veal would be far more interested in my clients than in me personally."

"Sorry, sir, forgive me for interrupting," said Dave Copper, "but I don't really know what we're talking about."

Boyle smiled condescendingly. "Of course - I was forgetting you're British. You wouldn't know. I'm a surgeon - I have clinics in New York and Los Angeles."

"Clinics, doctor? Not hospitals?" persisted Copper. "So what sort of surgery would that be?"

"We undertake visual and structural enhancements, sergeant."

"Oh. Right." Copper looked slightly baffled for a moment, and then beamed as light dawned. "Right! So, cosmetic surgery, then. The old nip and tuck, is that it?"

"I think my clients would be grossly offended if you were to describe it as that."

"And your clients, sir. I'm guessing that, since you mention Los Angeles and New York, that we're talking about film stars, people on TV, celebrities?"

"That's correct."

"And you're well-known because of this? I'd have thought people who need to have a face-lift or a nose job would want to keep it quiet. I know I would."

Lance smiled again. "That, sergeant, is because you live in a very different world. For the people who come to me, it is very often a badge of honour. If you like, it shows their fans how much they value them that they want to present themselves at their best. And they use the best to get the best."

"And you're the best, doctor?"

"In all modesty, sergeant, yes, I am."

"So when, say, a star who was starting to get a bit rough round the edges does an interview for a magazine, they'll say 'Hey, look at my new face - isn't it fabulous? And I got it from Dr. Lance Boyle.' Is that really what you're telling me?"

"Yes."

"Male as well as female?"

"Of course."

"Crazy!" muttered the sergeant, burying his nose in his notebook.

"So you say," resumed Andy Constable, "that you'd come into contact with Mr. Veal, presumably through the sort of thing Sergeant Copper suggests, but you didn't know him on a personal footing?"

"Exactly. And don't ask me where or when, because I honestly couldn't tell you. Sometime or another - maybe once or twice at award ceremonies. I get invited."

Constable made a strenuous effort to keep the faintest tone of distaste out of his voice. "I'm sure you do, doctor, with the kind of clients you describe. And would you by any chance be engaged in any - shall we say, current projects which might have been of interest to Mr. Veal?"

Lance looked puzzled. "Not that I can think of, inspector. What makes you ask that?"

"Because Mr. Veal had made a slightly unusual request in respect of the dining arrangements aboard this ship, doctor. He had particularly asked that you be seated on his table."

"Me?" Lance sounded incredulous. "Why would he want me?"

"Oh, not just you, sir. All of the people at your table were gathered together at the express request of Mr. Veal. Now what do you make of that?"

For some reason, a note of relief seemed to creep into Lance Boyle's manner. "Everyone? Are you serious? But why would he ...?" He tailed off.

"That, Dr. Boyle, is one of the things we're seeking to establish. So far, without success. So have you had any particular conversations with him since you came on board which might throw any light on the matter?"

Lance pulled a face. "Not that I can think of. We've spoken at the dinner table. I've run across him once or twice around the ship, or ashore, but ... no, I can't think of anything that would help you." He smiled broadly. "I'm really not assisting the police in their enquiries at all, am I - isn't that what you say at Scotland Yard, or wherever you work?"

Andy Constable refused to be ruffled. "Well, no matter, doctor. We'll move on to this evening. Now as I'm sure you know, Mr. Veal's body was discovered at just before half past seven in the library on deck 8. So perhaps you can tell us what you were doing in the hour prior to that."

"The only thing I can tell you about that, Mr. Constable, is that I wasn't doing anything. I'd been out on the trip to Seville today, and we hadn't long gotten back, so I went straight to my cabin. I lay down to read a book, but I must have been tired because I dozed off. I only just woke up in time to get ready for dinner."

"I'm surprised you could sleep with all that music and dancing going on, sir," put in Dave Copper. "I'd have thought they were making enough racket to wake the dead ..." He caught his breath in response to his superior officer's frown. "Or, in this case, not. Sorry, guv - wasn't thinking."

"My cabin is on the other side of the ship," explained Lance. "So I wouldn't have seen or heard a thing."

"Then I won't hold you up any longer, doctor," said Constable. "You're free to go for the moment."

At the door, the doctor turned back. "Just one question from me, inspector. Call it professional curiosity, if you will. Have you figured out how Veal died?"

"We have, sir. It didn't take much doing. When he was discovered, he had been stabbed in the back."

"Really?" Boyle sounded astonished. "But ... that's weird."

"There are some weird people about," agreed Constable. "Which is one of the reasons the world needs people like us."

As Lance Boyle left the room, Copper turned to Constable with a snort of irritation. "So, he wouldn't have seen or heard anybody, and nobody would have seen or heard him. Terrific! I don't know what sort of notes I'm supposed to be making, but it seems to me that the more I get, the less we have."

Andy Constable smiled quietly. "Don't get too frustrated, man - it's early days. Although I have to say, I'm always happier with a cast-iron alibi which I can break down. I grant you, no alibi at all can be a pain, because you've got nowhere to start. But we shall see. And there's one point which occurs to me which you may not have thought of."

"What's that, then, guv?"

"The late Mr. Veal was a reporter - his life's work was winkling out people's guilty secrets. But wouldn't you say that a cosmetic surgeon like Dr. Boyle would also be in possession of the secrets, guilty or otherwise, of a lot of stars and celebrities? Can you imagine what sort of gold that could be to Veal, if he could only find a way to start mining it?"

"And doctor-patient confidentiality? How about that, guv?"

"I'm not sure that I'd fancy my chances against the power of money and the much-vaunted American freedom of speech, sergeant. However, let's not get side-tracked. Onwards and upwards. Who's next?"

*

Marisa Mann sashayed into the room - there was no other word to describe it. "They say you want to talk to me."

"If we may. Do please sit down." Andy Constable gestured to the chair in front of the desk. "It's Mrs. Mann, isn't it?"

"Yes. But please, call me Marisa." Marisa draped her tall form artistically in the chair, and her eyes swept up and down the two Britons in what looked for all the world like a professional assessment.

"Oh." Dave Copper's tone expressed surprise at the accent. "I thought you were American, miss."

"I am," replied Marisa. "But I've spent a lot of time out of the States. Why, does it matter?"

"Not at all, miss," resumed Constable, with a glance of irritation at his junior officer. "It's just that my sergeant here prefers to get all his details correct." And in response to Marisa's slightly startled look, "It's being a policeman, you see. I dare say you've been made aware of what has happened on the ship this evening," he continued. "The death of Mr. Veal. Well, as I am a British police inspector - my name is Constable, by the way - the ship's security officer, who happens to be an old friend of mine, has asked me and Sergeant Copper here to ask some questions on his behalf. I hope you'll help us out - that's if that's not a problem."

"No, not at all. Why should it be?"

Constable chose to ignore the counter-question. "So, just to get a few basic facts, Mrs. Mann. I'm assuming you came on board the ship at Genoa like everyone else?" A nod. "And have you been off the ship since?"

"I did some shopping in Barcelona. And I went on the trip to Seville today."

"But not in Cartagena?"

"No. I stayed on board and spent a day around the pool. But that was boring - there was hardly anyone around - so I took the trip today."

"In common with many others, I gather," remarked Constable. "And when you got back, miss?"

"I went to the spa to get my nails done." Marisa displayed an awesome array of scarlet talons. "Look, what's the point of all these questions? Why do you want to know what I did? Do you think I have something to do with this?"

"We simply don't know, miss," replied Constable. "But as we have nowhere else to start, we're starting with the people who shared a dining table with Mr. Veal. So, did you know Mr. Veal?"

"Before I came on this ship? No. Not at all." Marisa's assertion was firm.

"I see." Constable's tone gave nothing away. "And have you had much contact with him during the voyage?"

"As little as I could manage, inspector," returned Marisa grimly. "He was a journalist, as I'm sure you know, and not my favourite type. I like to be able to choose who I give interviews to and when. I don't appreciate being pursued by some grubby little muck-raking hack whose only interest is in digging up some dirt."

If Andy Constable was taken aback by Marisa's sudden vehemence, he declined to show it. "Muck-raking? No, that can't be very pleasant," he mused. "Although if there's no muck to be raked, then of course there's nothing to worry about, is there? As is the case with you, I assume?"

"No." Marisa laughed, a little shakily. "No, of course not. I was just speaking generally, that's all."

"But that would certainly explain it."

"Explain what? What do you mean?"

"About Mr. Veal's request."

"What request? What are you talking about?"

"Oh, sorry, Mrs. Mann - I assumed you knew," smiled Constable blandly. "It seems that Mr. Veal had put in a request before the cruise that he should be seated at the same dinner table as you."

"Me? What, and they let him do that? But that's ..." Marisa seemed lost for words.

"So you see, Mrs. Mann, we do have a particular reason for wanting to ask you these questions. And for asking about your movements once you came back aboard the ship this afternoon. So if you wouldn't mind ..."

Marisa seemed to gather her thoughts. "So ... I got off the bus when we got back to the ship, and I went straight to my cabin to drop off my bag. And then I went on up to the spa for my manicure, and I thought I'd be late because my appointment was for six o'clock and the bus had been delayed, but the girl was very good and said it didn't matter a bit. You can ask her - she'll tell you. Her name's Leah."

"And you were there how long?"

"Around three-quarters of an hour."

"And after that?"

"I went back to my cabin to do my hair and get ready for dinner."

"Alone?"

"Yes, of course. Who do you think I was with?"

"And did you see anyone on your way to the cabin? Which is where, by the way?"

"On deck 7, in the middle of the ship. 7235, if you really want to know. And I have no idea if anybody saw me - there may have been someone in the corridor, but I wasn't really paying attention. And then I'd just got downstairs in the lift to go in for dinner, and I heard the announcement about the accident. At least, that's what they were calling it. But you're saying it wasn't."

"No, miss," replied Constable shortly. "It wasn't." He paused for a moment in consideration, then stood abruptly. "Well, thank you for your time, Mrs. Mann. I think we'll call that it for now. We'll come and speak to you again if there's anything else. Copper, if you'd like to get the door for the lady."

Marisa got to her feet and, with a somewhat uncertain look at the suddenness of her dismissal, left the room.

"Fabulous!" grunted Dave Copper. "There's another one with no motive and no alibi. Mind you, did you clock those nails? She wouldn't have needed a murder weapon - she could just have stuck the guy with one of those."

"Female of the species deadlier, and all that?"

"Hmmm, maybe. You know, it's funny, guv, she's got this glamorous aura about her, but something's a bit off. Don't ask me what. Anyway, not my type - I don't like tall women." He shrugged. "I'll figure it out. But my notebook's starting to get bored - 'I didn't know him, I didn't see him, I wasn't there'. Am I beginning to detect a pattern in all this, guv?"

"I think what we're beginning to detect, sergeant," responded Constable, "is a very resourceful journalist who has managed to get something, goodness knows what, on a number of very prominent potential head-liner victims, the revelations about which would do his journalistic career a power of good."

"Not, on reflection, the smartest career move the late Mr. Veal ever made, in the light of events, though, guv, if he let on what he knew. What is it they say - dead men tell no tales?"

"Oh, I'm sure Mr. Veal will manage to tell us a few tales before we've finished," said Constable. "We just have to be at least as clever as he was."

"Ah well, no problem, then," grinned Copper. "Is this where I dust off the celebrated power of positive thinking yet again?"

"I was under the impression you never put it back in its box, young David. Right - three down, three to go. Let's bash on."

Chapter 5

Phil Anders took his seat opposite Constable at the inspector's invitation and regarded the man across the desk with what was doubtless intended to be a firm gaze. The slight side-to-side flickering of his eyes betrayed an inner unease.

"We have a dead body on our hands, Mr. Anders," said Constable abruptly, without preamble. "I want you to help me find out why."

Phil appeared taken aback by the inspector's aggression. "But ... why should you think it's got anything to do with me? I didn't know him."

"So, you're aware of what I'm talking about, sir? The death of Mr. Veal."

"Of course I am. What, you don't think it's all over the ship by now? Stabbed, I heard. Is that right?" Constable declined to react. "We knew at dinner - our waiter told us. But that still doesn't explain why you want to talk to me, and hey, who the hell are you anyway?"

"The security officer didn't explain?"

"He did not. They just cooped us up next door, and then they've been bringing us through one after another like some kind of suspects."

Constable smiled gently. "In fact, Mr. Anders, you've put your finger on it. I'm afraid that in a way, that's exactly what you are. I think I'd better explain." With a slight sigh, he introduced himself and laid out how the two Britons had been drawn into the investigation. "So, you see, sir, it's really a question of helping out an old friend. My sergeant here and I haven't actually got any official status above and beyond what the ship's authorities have given us, and of course you're at perfect liberty not to answer any of our questions if you prefer not to. But I'm hoping that won't be the case."

Phil seemed reassured. "No ... no, of course not. I'm glad to help. Only I don't see how I can."

"Well, just a little background, and I hope you don't object if Sergeant Copper makes some notes. Full name is?"

"Philip Anders."

"And you're from ...?"

70

"Australia. Sydney. Why?"

"No particular reason, sir. Idle curiosity - you never know when the smallest fact may be relevant." Constable took in the artfully informal mixture of exquisitely-tailored suit with rolled-back cuffs, combined with a silk open-necked shirt in a subdued pattern of tropical flowers, casual shoes in mirror-finish patent leather, and an enormous and complex wrist-watch bearing the logo of a leading Formula 1 racing team. A substantial signet ring gleamed on one finger - Constable suspected that what looked like silver was probably platinum. "So, can I ask what brings you aboard the *Empress of the Oceans*?"

Phil smiled lazily. "Oh, a bit of business, a bit of pleasure."

"You wouldn't care to elaborate, I suppose."

"It's a free ride, inspector. My dad's company got the invite, and I offered to take it up. It gave me a chance to follow up a few contacts in the Far East and Europe, plus you never know who you're going to meet on a trip like this."

"And these contacts. Business contacts?"

"Inspector, I'm sure my father's work in the public relations industry would bore you silly."

"I dare say you're right, sir," agreed Constable with a laugh. The evasion did not escape him. "So, moving on to this evening. Now, you say you didn't know Mr. Veal, but I'm assuming you knew who he was? A reporter on the 'National Investigator'?"

"Yes, I knew that. He didn't make any secret of it - pretty much the opposite."

"Ah, so you had dealings with him?"

"Dealings? What? I don't know what you mean."

"I mean you must have had some conversations with him at some point, I assume," insisted Constable. "Otherwise you wouldn't have said what you said."

"Oh, that. Well, yes, I suppose." Phil displayed an odd reluctance to elaborate, but the inspector waited patiently in expectant silence until the younger man had no choice but to continue. "I mean, he was at the same dinner table, so we spoke like you do, but that's it."

"And beyond that, around the ship, you didn't socialise?"

"No, not at all. We may have exchanged a few words in passing. Why, has somebody said something?"

"Not that I've heard, Mr. Anders. So, to sum up, you and Mr.

Veal weren't close at all?"

"Far from it," asserted Phil with an almost excessive degree of vehemence. "He wasn't my kind of guy at all. Sort of creepy, I thought. Seems to me that he'd sneak up on people. So I didn't mix with him. So I don't see why you would think that I had anything to do with ... well, anything, really."

Andy Constable decided to change tack. "So, moving on then to today, Mr. Anders, we're asking all the people on your dining table if they can account for their movements this evening. Oh, purely for the purpose of eliminating anyone obviously not involved," he added hastily. "But it helps to rule out certain people if we can."

"Why just our dining table, inspector? There are thousands of people on this ship. It could have been anybody who killed Veal."

"You're absolutely right, Mr. Anders, and don't think we're not aware of the fact. But I have a special reason for concentrating on your dining companions ..." It became obvious in the ensuing pause that Constable was not intending to respond to Phil's interrogative look. "So I'd be glad if you can just tell me what you were doing after, say, six o'clock today."

"Well, at six I'd just got back on board ..."

"Oh? Where had you been, sir?"

"The ... the bus tour. The one to Seville."

"And were you alone on the trip?"

"What, apart from the other forty people on my coach, you mean? Not to mention the other buses."

Constable smiled. "I mean, did you travel alone or with friends."

Phil's answer was elaborately casual. "Well, Marisa Mann was booked on the same bus as me."

"Well, Mr. Anders," said Constable comfortably, "Mrs. Mann is a young lady with considerable attractions, isn't she? And I take it you're single yourself."

"Here, what are you implying?"

"Nothing at all, Mr. Anders," returned Constable smoothly. "Anyway, you spent the day together - nothing in the world wrong with that. And the buses returned to the ship around six, that we know already. What about after that?"

"I went up to one of the bars for a drink."

"And which bar would that be, sir?"

"The one out by the pool on the top deck."

"That's the 'Crowning Glory', isn't it?" put in Dave Copper, looking up from the book where he was briskly scribbling notes. "Yes, sir, I know the one. So did you stay there for long, sir? I mean, can anyone confirm that?" His tone indicated that he had no great hopes of a positive answer. His expectations swiftly came true.

"Probably not," replied Phil. "Everybody was hanging over the side of the ship watching what was going on down below, and there was no way I could get anywhere near. Anyway, all that noise was too much - all I wanted was a quiet drink, so I just went down to my cabin and finished my drink on my balcony."

"Alone?"

"Alone. Sorry if that's inconvenient."

"The truth is never inconvenient, Mr. Anders," resumed Constable. "And after that, you ...?"

"I just had a quick shower, changed, took the stairs to go down to the restaurant, and I'd just got down to the bar when all hell kicked off. Yes, that's right, there was some screaming, and I saw the Security Officer go charging off, and you two went chasing after him. That was you, wasn't it?"

"Yes, it was," agreed Constable.

"So there you are, then." Phil was triumphant. "That's where I was when they discovered the body. So that sounds like an alibi to me."

"Sadly, it's not as simple as that, Mr. Anders. But thank you for your account anyway." Constable glanced across to Copper. "I take it you have all that, sergeant?"

"Oh yes, sir." Copper's tone was gloomy. "In fine detail."

"In which case," said Constable cheerfully, "I don't think we need to keep Mr. Anders a second longer." He turned back to Phil. "For the moment, that is, sir. I expect we shall need to speak to you again if anything crops up. But I dare say you won't mind that, will you?"

"No. No, of course not." With a look of what seemed like relief mixed with apprehension, Phil escaped from the room.

"I'm saying nothing," muttered Copper as the door closed.

"No, I don't really think you need to," said his superior. "Par for the course - no useful information of any kind, except for something lurking beneath the surface which it now becomes our job to winkle out. There seems to be quite a lot of money there, and not too much information about where it comes from. He's jumpy about something, that's certain, despite the smooth exterior. Something of a lounge lizard, I think."

"Do you reckon he's got designs on the fair Marisa, guv? Do you think he's afraid all this business is going to put a spoke in the wheel of his crafty schemes?"

"I can't see why it should, if they've both got nothing to do with Veal's death. And you can't say that the lady's afraid of a bit of notoriety. She seems rather to court it. But as for Mr. Anders - well, that may be a different matter. We shall see."

*

"Yes, I knew him."

"Thank the lord for that!" grunted Dave Copper under his breath.

Andy Constable had explained the situation to Anita Holm, who sat brisk and upright in the chair across the desk, exuding an air of eagerness to help.

"Do you know, Miss Holm, I think you've made my sergeant's day. He's been complaining to me of a lack of information to put in his little book, and you sound as if you may be able to remedy that. So I'm going to place you in his tender hands. Sergeant, over to you."

"You are the Anita Holm we've seen on TV, aren't you, miss?"

"That's right, sergeant," glowed Anita graciously. "But I didn't know that my fame had reached back across the pond since I left England. I'm flattered."

"Yes, we get your shows on the repeats channel on cable. I don't usually watch them," Copper continued, "but I had a girlfriend who loved all that arty stuff with collages and shabby chic and chiffon scarves and whatnot. Not really my taste," he blundered on, "and I could never see how anyone could afford several hundred quid for an old trunk with a few labels on it, but that's just me." And in response to a meaningful throat-clearing from his superior, "Anyway, let's get back to you. You knew Mr. Veal, you say?"

"I did, sergeant. Not particularly well, I have to say, but since we were both journalists of a kind, our paths did tend to cross from time to time. Usually on television talk shows. We were both quite frequent guests on the Friday Late Show."

"Not doing the same thing, of course?"

"Heavens, no!" Anita's tinkling laugh rang out. "No, no, quite different. They would have me in to comment on a developing fashion like ... oh, I don't know, a sudden fad for wildly expensive Madagascan coffee beans among stars attending the Cannes Film Festival, or the fact that this year's must-have piece of art was a sculpture created from llama droppings by some dear little girl from the Peruvian Andes. Now Ira Veal would be on for a totally different reason, as you can imagine. With him, there was always a story which he had uncovered which had some element of sleaze or scandal or fraud, and I'm sure you don't need me to tell you how much the media love that sort of thing. Especially in America, where the laws seem to allow all sorts of speculations and revelations, even before things come to trial."

Dave Copper was intrigued. "What sort of things are we talking about then, miss?"

Anita thought for a moment. "I remember one case - oh, there was quite a lot of fuss about that one. There was a very famous spiritualist who was conducting séances for couples who couldn't have children, and she was claiming that she could get in touch with the spirits of the children who might have been. Emma Nation, her name was. People were paying her thousands of dollars, and she was purporting to produce physical evidence of these imaginary children." Anita shook her head sadly. "I'm afraid there are some very gullible people about, sergeant, especially on that side of the Atlantic, although I suppose I really shouldn't say so. Anyway, Ira got someone to go in under cover, and exposed the whole thing for the fraud it was. Huge fuss, of course, and the woman ended up in prison. Oh, and then there was that author - a woman called Paige Turner. Wrote the sort of books which show up in airport bookshops at bargain prices - not great literature, but they sell by the million. Anyway, it turned out that she was getting everything written for her by teams of ghost writers in the Far East for a pittance, passing it off as her own work, and then posing as a great philanthropist by pretending to donate the majority of the profits to some charitable foundation which was in fact her own offshore company, hidden through a string of holding corporations. And Ira uncovered it all!"

"So Mr. Veal might well be described as a force for good in the world?"

Anita considered for a moment. "I suppose you might say that, yes, sergeant. Of course," she went on, "you couldn't actually like him. He was a grumpy old devil with no social graces at all, and you couldn't really say that he contributed much to the gaiety of the conversation at the dinner table."

"Which makes it a little odd, wouldn't you say, madam, that the guest list on your dinner table was in fact specially put together by Mr. Veal himself."

"Really?" Anita sounded amazed. "Why on earth would he do that?"

"We were rather hoping that you might tell us that, Miss Holm." Andy Constable decided to take over the questioning.

Anita's shrug was expressive. "I can't imagine why you should think that, inspector."

"And, of course, no run-ins with him yourself, I'm assuming?"

"Really, inspector, what do you take me for?" said Anita with a light laugh. "No, my life is an open book - nothing to interest the likes of Ira Veal there. Unlike some others, as I'm sure you can guess."

"Well," responded Constable comfortably, "I'm glad we can put you so easily out of the frame. So perhaps you can help us with the other aspect of our enquiries, which is what the other people on your table were doing today in the run-up to the discovery of Mr. Veal's body."

"Oh dear. I'm afraid you're going to be disappointed there, Mr. Constable, because I don't think I saw anyone from our party, if you want to call it that, between breakfast time and dinner. I saw Baxter - Mr. Wall, that is - early on today, and I thought we might spend the day together. We've known each other for simply ages, and I thought it would be fun, but apparently he'd already arranged to go off on this outing to Seville. I think most of the others had - in fact, the cathedral there is wonderful, but I'd already seen it when I was on holiday in Spain a few years ago. But no, I wanted to go on the tour to Jerez, to visit all the sherry houses."

"Any special reason?"

"Oh, goodness, inspector, you're looking at me as if I'm

some kind of alcoholic! No it's just ... I really shouldn't be telling you this, because it's all highly confidential, but I dare say I can trust you. When I heard I was coming on this trip, I got in touch with one of the major sherry producers and, together with their American advertising agency, they are going to mount the most enormous campaign. In fact, they have more or less sponsored me, and together we are going to make sherry THE fashionable drink of the season in the United States."

"Quite a scheme, Miss Holm." Constable sounded impressed. "And I imagine that, with the size of the American market and what I gather is your considerable influence in it, that would be worth a great deal of money."

"I have the feeling that you suspect something underhand, inspector," said Anita. "You're quite wrong, of course - it's simply the way things work in the world of fashion. So anyway, off I went on this afternoon's tour round the bodegas, made a few notes, and then came back. I did get myself, I have to confess, just the tiniest bit tiddly on the free tastings, so when we got back to the ship I was planning to send some material off to my office, but in fact I went straight to my cabin and took a nap."

"I suppose that there's no point in asking you if you happened to see any of your friends when you returned to the ship, madam," enquired Copper.

Anita smiled helplessly. "Sorry, sergeant. There were so many people milling about in the atrium that I didn't notice anyone in particular. And I'm afraid that when I went to my cabin, I must have gone out like a light. Sleeping the sleep of the just, obviously." The tinkling laugh sounded again. "And then, of course, it was time for dinner. And then - well, I'm sure you are in a much better position to say what happened after that than I am."

"What a nice helpful lady," murmured Dave Copper, one eyebrow raised, the irony plainly audible in his voice, as the door closed behind Anita.

"As you say," agreed Andy Constable in the same vein. "Full of useful information, not a care in the world."

"Shall I go after her and bang the handcuffs on her straight away, guv?" asked Copper, not entirely joking. "If she's that open, sweet and innocent, she's obviously hiding some gigantic guilty secret and, as the least likely suspect, is constitutionally bound to have done it."

Constable laughed. "I think we'd need to base a case on something a little more concrete than that, sergeant. But here's one thought for you to consider while you're compiling your dossier. She said that she was intending to send some stuff off to her office after she got back to the ship. Well, she couldn't exactly pop out to the nearest street corner and pop something in the post box, could she? The only way she's going to be able to file some copy, or whatever it was she planned, would be if she were to email it home."

"And that means," Copper took up the thought, "that she would have to go to the Internet Lounge to do it. So, so far, she's the only person with a sniff of an opportunity of being in the right place at the right time."

*

"I'm really sorry to have kept you waiting for so long." said Andy Constable, as the two detectives entered the room where the other interviewees had been kept, to find Jacqueline Best sitting quietly reading. She closed the small book, placed it in her handbag, and looked up.

"That's not a problem. I've had Sanjay here to keep me company." She nodded towards the uniformed man sitting unobtrusively in the corner of the room. "Would you like me to come through?" She made to rise.

"No, there's no need for that. We may as well stay here." Constable turned to the security officer. "Thank you, Sanjay - I think we can let you go now. But if you could find Mr. Crane and tell him we're nearly finished here, but I'd like a word with him, I'd be grateful."

Sanjay gave a half-salute. "Of course, sir. I'll let him know." The door closed behind him.

"I'm sure you'd like to know what's been going on, madam," said Constable, taking a seat and gesturing Copper to do the same. Introductions and a brief explanation ensued. "And so I need to ask you the same questions which we've already asked everybody else."

"Fortunately, inspector, you've saved the Best until last." Jacqueline permitted herself a small smile. "I'm sorry, inspector, perhaps that wasn't in the best of taste, under the circumstances, but it's a little joke everybody seems to make, so I thought I'd get it out of the way early on. I expect I'm just a little nervous."

"I imagine you would be, Mrs. Best. Or do you prefer the title - it's Pastor, I think, isn't it?"

"I prefer 'Pastor Best', if you don't mind, inspector. Or 'Reverend'. I like to think that, wherever I am, I'm doing the Lord's work, and I like to remind myself of that fact. First name Jacqueline, sergeant, if you need to know."

Dave Copper took in the long black brocade skirt, the black silk blouse enhanced with a discreet but elaborate pattern of black bugle-beads, with leg-of-mutton sleeves showing a hint of white lace at the cuff, and a white lace jabot adorned with a brooch bearing a significant pearl, and mused quietly to himself that the Lord's work appeared to pay well.

"So," continued Constable, "you're a minister with ...?"

"The Community of the Great Shepherd, inspector. It's an evangelical mission my late husband started some years ago. He was the sole founder and Leading Light - everything was his creation." Jacqueline looked upwards. "After the Great Creator, of course."

Constable cleared his throat. "I have to confess, I've never heard of you, but I'm afraid I'm not very well informed about ... that sort of thing." He glanced across at Copper who, he detected, seemed to be straining every nerve to keep a straight face. "American religions, I mean."

"Oh, there are many small religious groups in America," said Jacqueline dismissively, "but many of them are not what you'd call mainstream. We are. We have our own television channel and millions of contributors. And now we have flocks all over. Mostly in the States, but we have many friends in Africa too."

"And - forgive me - you mentioned your 'late' husband."

"Yes." Jacqueline adopted a wistful air. "He was a lot older than me. He passed over a little while back, and left me to carry the Light alone."

"I'm sorry." Constable's sympathy sounded genuine. "Had you been together long?"

"Why no, as it happens, inspector. Just a couple of years, in fact, but as soon as I met him, it was as if a revelation had come over me. I saw all the work he was doing, and I wanted to be part of that. It was like a rushing wind. We married. In fact, my late husband performed the ceremony himself, according to the rite of the Community. It was very romantic. Then he ordained me into the Community as his helpmate, and we devoted ourselves to the work until the day he was gathered. And now I continue to bear the burden."

"And this cruise? Is that part of your work?"

Jacqueline laughed. "Gracious no, inspector, not at all. I'm here at the very generous suggestion of the head of one of the networks which carry our channel. He was a great friend of my dear husband, and he believed that a trip like this might go some way to easing my grief."

"And there is always the possibility, I suppose, Pastor Best, that among a guest list such as we have on board the ship, there may even be some who might wish to know more about your Community and offer it their support."

"Do you know, inspector, I never thought of that. What a very clever suggestion." Jacqueline gazed steadily into Constable's eyes without a flicker of irony.

"Which brings us to the question of Mr. Veal."

"Indeed. Poor dear man. I shall be remembering him in my prayers."

"Tell me, was Mr. Veal known to you beforehand?"

"Before I came on the ship? No, not at all. I believe I'd heard of him, but the 'National Investigator' isn't really the kind of newspaper I like to read. I understand it deals with the more unsavoury things in life, and I prefer something more uplifting."

"So despite the fact that you were sharing a table at dinner, you didn't actually strike up an acquaintance?"

"You're correct, inspector. And somehow, we always seemed to be at opposite ends of the table, so we hardly spoke."

"So, you wouldn't go so far as to say that you sought out his company."

"Why, no, inspector. Why should I?"

"Which makes it a little strange, wouldn't you agree, Pastor Best, that Mr. Veal seems to have made a point of actively seeking out yours."

Jacqueline Best blinked. "I don't understand you, Mr. Constable. What are you saying?"

"Merely that it has been made known to us that, before the ship sailed, Mr. Veal had used some contacts to ensure that he would be sharing a table in the restaurant with certain people. Your name was among them. Would you care to hazard a guess as to why?"

"I simply have no idea." Jacqueline permitted herself a small quiet smile. "But I imagine that it would be rather more your job than mine to find out." There was a hint of a challenge in the words.

Constable declined to pick up the gauntlet. "Moving on then, Reverend, we come to today. Did you leave the ship?"

"Oh, of course, inspector. I wouldn't miss the chance to visit one of the great cathedrals of the world, so of course I was on one of the buses which took the tour to Seville. And do you know, there is what used to be a mosque right in the middle of the cathedral. Such an example of peace and harmony."

Andy Constable was in no mood to discuss the role of peace and harmony in the religious history of Spain. "And we know you would have come back to the ship at about six with the others. What then?"

"Well, I was just passing through the lounge downstairs when I heard the music coming from the dockside, so I went out on to the deck down there by the lifeboats and watched for a while. Then I realised that it was time for my visit to the chapel ..."

"They have a chapel on the ship?" interrupted Dave Copper. "I never knew that."

"Oh, you should go, sergeant. It's very small, but it's exquisite. Such beautiful ceiling paintings. It's just round the corner from the casino - perhaps not the most fortunate placing. I always try to go there for a few quiet moments around six-thirty every day."

"And today was no different, Reverend? Six-thirty, you say?" Copper made another brief note in his book. "And you spent how long there?"

"About fifteen minutes, I guess. And then I went on up to my cabin."

"I don't suppose there's the remotest chance that you saw anyone who can confirm that, madam?" Copper's tone indicated that he did not hold out much hope.

"Well, yes and no, sergeant." Copper looked up quizzically. "Yes, I did see someone. That nice Anita Holm was just going off up the corridor as I came round the corner from the lift. Our cabins are close to each other, you know. But I don't believe she saw me, because she was going in the other direction with her back to me."

"And once you reached your cabin, I'm guessing you stayed there and didn't go out until you went down for dinner?" A calm quiet smile was his answer. Copper closed his notebook with a snap and looked across at his superior officer. "Well, guv, I think I've just about got all the crucial information."

Constable took the cue. "That being the case, Pastor Best, I don't think we need hold you up any longer. I'm sure we shall be able to find you if there's anything else we need to speak to you about."

"That would be my pleasure. Gentlemen." With a gracious nod of the head, Jacqueline left the room as the inspector stood to hold the door open for her.

Dave Copper slumped in his chair with a snort of disbelief. "Guv, is it me, or was that one of the most lunatic pieces of guff I've ever heard? Is she for real?"

"I've learnt by now to be very wary of judging people's authenticity and motivation when it's a question of faith," responded Andy Constable. "And if there's one thing I think we can safely say, that was a lady with no lack of faith in herself."

"Hmmm." Copper sounded dubious. "I've heard a bit about some of these American organisations with their television appeals and their crowds of followers. Haven't there been a few scandals over the years about embezzling funds? Do you think there's a possibility that Ira Veal was on the trail of something of the sort? What's that old saying about serving God and Mammon? I'm no judge, but I'm guessing that the lady isn't short of a bit of Mammon."

"Yes, well, there's another old saying - 'Judge not, that ye be not judged'. Mind you, as far as I know, there's no saying about not gathering evidence. So I'm just thinking about where we go next."

As if in response to his remark, the telephone on the desk rang. After a moment during which the two detectives looked at one another, Constable decided to answer.

"Hello?"

"Andy? It's Derek. I'm glad you're still there. I gather from Sanjay that you'd like a word, which is very convenient, because I wanted a word with you too. I've just had a buzz from the doctor, and he says he's got some information which he reckons is going to interest us, and would we like to go down to his office. It's in the Medical Centre down on Deck Zero. Meet you down there in five?"

Chapter 6

The entrance to the Medical Centre presented a very different face from the rest of the ship. Just one floor above, on the lowest deck of passenger cabins, carpeted corridors stretched into the distance, welcoming with the soft earthy tones of wood-grain and warm with the glow of subtle concealed lighting. Below, all was harsh fluorescent tubes and the uncompromising glare of brutal white-painted steel. Derek Crane waited at the Centre's door.

"How's it going, guys? Got anywhere yet, do you think?"

"Bit early to say," replied Andy Constable, "although you never know what may jump out at second look, if I get the chance to trawl through the copious notes which my young colleague here has been making so assiduously."

"You jest, guv," countered Dave Copper. "I think you'll find it's mostly the same rubbish repeated over and over again, about how nobody knew anybody and everybody wouldn't want to do anybody any harm. If you can find some gold in that, good luck to you."

"Don't go underestimating your boss's talents, sergeant," said Crane. "From what I remember of him, needles in haystacks are his speciality."

"I know, I know," admitted Copper. "I'm just suffering the effects of advanced writer's cramp. Anyway, the guv's got this theory that each of these celebs has got a secret which our Mr. Veal had managed to winkle out, and we don't need to look any further for our perpetrator, and eventually his penetrating interrogation technique will reveal all. As ever."

"You two do realise I'm standing here listening, don't you?" pointed out Constable with a half-smile on his face. "Although, to be honest, Derek, this irreverent whipper-snapper's summary isn't so far from the truth. But I need to talk to some more people. So why are we standing out here instead of finding out whatever your doctor friend has on his mind?"

"Good point," said Crane, pulling open the Medical Centre door. "After you."

A blue-uniformed nurse looked up from behind a desk as the three entered. In her thirties, with a pleasant face and a hearty appearance which suggested that she would be equally at home administering an injection to a nervous five-year-old, assisting with the removal of a recalcitrant bicuspid, or helping to subdue an over-enthusiastic intoxicated rugby-player, she had an air of calm authority which no crisis would ever be allowed to ruffle. "Mr. Crane. Just one moment, and I'll fetch the doctor for you." She started to rise.

"Stay where you are, Jenny - I'm here. Come in, gentlemen, come on in." Doctor Holliday emerged through a door marked 'Dispensary' and greeted his visitors cheerfully. "Nice to see someone healthy for a change. You'll be wanting to visit my latest guest, then? Although, sad to say, he's not really up to receiving callers."

"Why is it," Constable murmured, half to himself, "that medical people have to be so damned jolly around dead bodies?"

"Ah, well, that's the officially approved physician's position," replied the doctor. "Half way between Schadenfreude and Memento Mori. You've got two options - you can either mope about while your patients are dying all around you, or else you can keep cheery and hope that some lucky accident will enable you to help at least some of them to pull through. I belong to the second school - laugh in the face of death, because the bugger's going to get you in the end."

"I've got a police surgeon at home like that," said Constable. "Nothing he enjoys more than a nice grisly corpse. I should put you in touch with one another - you could compare notes."

"Sorry to butt into your fun," said Crane, "but isn't there something rather more serious we should be talking about? Doc, you said you had something to tell us."

"And so I do," rejoined the doctor, in no way repressed. "Follow me, gentlemen, and I will take you to Mr. Veal's new stateroom. Not quite as roomy as one would wish, but he's really in no position to complain." The doctor led the way into a small side room, where the body of Ira Veal lay face-down on a hospital bed, covered by a sheet. The four men crowded round the bed.

"Just a couple of things I wanted to mention. The first one may be nothing to do with anything, but I thought you'd want to know." The doctor drew back the sheet and rolled Veal's body slightly to one side, and pointed to a zone around the midriff, which looked as if it bore a number of small puncture marks.

85

"Injections?" enquired Copper. "Drugs, are you saying?"

"Hold your horses, sergeant," said Holliday good-humouredly. "Drugs, yes. Something naughty, probably not. Far more likely to have been insulin - the pattern's typical, and I'd be rather more inclined to think that the late Mr. Veal was a diabetic than that he was dabbling in illegal substances. There are tests - if you want, I could ..."

"That may not be necessary, doc," observed Crane. "If he's diabetic, there'll surely be stuff in his cabin. We can check."

"Fine."

"You mentioned two things, doctor," said Constable. "What's the other?"

"Ah, now this one's a lot more interesting, inspector." The doctor's eyes lit up. "I'm actually rather proud of myself with this one. Now, take a look at this - you'll remember that when Mr. Veal was found, it was sticking in his back, but I took the liberty of removing it when we removed his clothes - oh don't worry, if you're concerned about fingerprints, they'll still be there. Surgical gloves all the way. We're not fools down here, you know. I made notes and took pictures, and I've got my nurse Jenny as a witness. Here." He picked up a stainless steel dish and removed the cloth covering it, to reveal the green glass shaft which the others had previously seen half-buried in Veal's body.

"I know what that is!" exclaimed Crane suddenly. "It's a glass pen. They sell them in the ship's shop. It's part of the souvenirs range from Italy. They do a gift set with the pen shaft made of Merano glass from Venice, plus some fancy bronze nibs and a bottle of special ink. Supposed to be for calligraphy enthusiasts or some such."

"Strayed a bit from its original purpose, wouldn't you say, guv?" commented Copper, peering more closely. "I mean, I know they say the pen is mightier than the sword, but you don't expect people to go round using them as murder weapons."

"Well, just before you go jumping to too many conclusions, sergeant," interrupted the doctor, "would you like to take a second look at Mr. Veal. I've not cleaned him up, you know, and as you can see, there's not a lot of blood around the wound." The others looked obediently. "And look - here's his shirt, and there's not a lot of blood on that. Now, I'm not an expert in these matters, and you probably know far more about violent death than I do, but I'm prepared to stick my neck out. You've not got enough bleeding there for a fatal stab wound. Whatever this pen may be, it's not your murder weapon. This man was dead before that ever went in."

*

Dave Copper found Andy Constable leaning on the rail at the stern of the ship, a mug of coffee from the nearby drinks station cradled in his hand. The inspector was gazing morosely at the wake of the ship, a white trail of turbulence, arrow-straight, fading gently towards the misty horizon.

"Morning, guv. I was wondering where you'd got to."

"It's a metaphor," responded Constable, continuing to gaze into the distance.

"You what?"

"That." Constable nodded to indicate the wake. "It's a metaphor for our lives. Yours and mine. As professionals. A sea of facts, all churned up together, but actually all pointing in the same direction. And our job is to take a look at where we've been, interpret it, and then turn through a hundred and eighty degrees and work out where it is we're going. And some days - just a few, mind you, but enough - you have to wonder if you're actually going to get there. And in case you've forgotten, we thought we had a murdered man, and all we had to do was find out who killed him. Now we've got a dead man, who we can't be sure has actually been murdered, or if so how, except that we believe that somebody thinks they murdered him. Can you blame me for suffering from fried brain?"

Copper, almost against his will, was moved. His superior did not often let him into his mind so openly. He cleared his throat. "Two things, guv. You're probably right - we all get doubts, but at the risk of getting boring, this is where I have the advantage, because I usually give the deep philosophical introspection a miss in favour of my famous ..."

"Power of positive thinking!" Constable joined in the chorus, and rewarded Copper with a quiet chuckle. "All right, then, David - as my own private and personal Little Orphan Annie, what is your second point, other than that the sun will come out tomorrow?"

As if on cue, at that moment, a shaft of light from the horizon illuminated their faces as the edge of the sun climbed out of the mist. The two men looked at one another for a moment and then burst out into unrestrained laughter. The mood was broken.

"Sergeant, the day I find out how you do that ..."

"The second thing, guv," pressed on Copper, "is that nobody ever gets anything done without a decent breakfast. We might be a small army, but that's not to stop us marching on our stomachs. There's a chef in the breakfast buffet who makes Eggs Benedict with smoked salmon to order. I've seen him do it, and they look really good. Fancy joining me before we bash on with the daily grind?"

The Eggs Benedict were excellent. So were the newly-baked croissants, still warm, and the red berry compote with crème fraiche. After the third cup of tea, Dave Copper leaned back with a satisfied sigh.

"I'm sure that was supposed to set me up for the day, guv," he remarked, "but to be honest, I'm a bit stuffed. Can't we take the morning off?"

"Tough," retorted Andy Constable, his good humour thoroughly restored. "This was your idea. Live with the consequences."

"Well, it was worth a try," sighed Copper. "So, what's first on the list?"

"Good morning again, gentlemen." A familiar voice sounded behind him. "Are you well this morning?"

"Good morning, Timon." Constable looked up to see the waiter standing alongside their table. "Yes, thank you, although we aren't working quite as hard as you always seem to be."

Timon lowered his voice. "But you are working, sir, aren't you? Everybody says that you are police, and you are trying to find out who it is that killed Mr. Veal."

"You were right when you said there were no secrets aboard this ship, Timon," said Copper. A thought struck him. "Hang on - that's not the only thing you said. I remember now - you said there were things you could tell us, and then you got interrupted. Would those things have been about Mr. Veal, by any chance?"

Timon looked over his shoulder. "I finish my shift here at ten-thirty, sir. Can we talk then?"

*

Lydia Carton looked up with her usual welcoming smile as

the two detectives approached the Guest Relations desk in the atrium. "Good morning, sir. I hope you're enjoying your holiday."

"Hardly that, considering the circumstances," replied Constable.

Lydia's face fell. "I'm sorry, sir. You're right, of course. I'm afraid that came out automatically. We've had orders from the management to carry on as normally as possible and not to answer any questions about what happened to Mr. Veal. I think we're supposed to pretend that nothing out of the ordinary has occurred."

"Yes, well, we unfortunately don't have that luxury," commented Dave Copper.

"So, sir, what can I do for you?" Lydia resumed her usual bright and efficient demeanour.

"We were wanting Mr. Crane. Would you have any idea where he is?"

"I believe he's in the Security Office, sir. One moment ..." Lydia picked up a telephone and tapped a number into it. "Hello, Derek. Your English police friends are looking for you ... no, they're here at the desk ... all right, I will tell them." She looked back up at Constable. "He will be out in just one moment, sir." And turning to a blue-rinsed elderly woman wearing a multi-coloured kaftan and far too much jewellery for the hour of the day, "Yes, madam, how can I help you ...?"

Derek Crane emerged from the corridor behind Guest Relations looking every inch the efficient ship's officer in immaculate crisp whites, making the two Britons feel slightly rumpled by comparison.

"How's tricks, Andy? Feeling a bit more like it this morning?"

"Absolutely. I just ran out of steam a bit last night. After our talk with the doctor, I just wanted to unwind and clear my brain. But having consumed a hearty breakfast at the instigation of my supporting cast here ..." A smiling nod in the direction of Dave Copper. "I am raring to go. So I thought we ought to make a start by taking a look at Mr. Veal's cabin."

"Not a problem. Go right ahead. Do you want me with you?"

"No, that's fine. We'll see what there is to find, if anything, and let you know."

"You'll need his ship card to get in, of course," Crane

89

pointed out. "He'll have had it with him, so I assume the doc's got it in amongst the rest of his bits and pieces. Do you want me to go and ...?"

"No, don't worry. We'll pop down and get it from him." Constable led the way in the direction of the stairs.

"Not a thing." The doctor replaced the last of Ira Veal's clothing back in a neat pile. "There, I've been through all his pockets twice, and there's not even a wallet. Most people don't bother to carry one about the ship - no point, because the card does everything. But no sign of his. And I promise you he hasn't got it on him."

Copper looked around. "No offence, but do you mind if I just check?"

"Ah, now, you wouldn't want to be doing that, sergeant," countered Holliday. "Not unless you've come prepared with your arctic gear."

"Sorry?"

"I'm afraid Mr. Veal is nicely packaged up in one of the compartments in the ship's freezer designed for this exact purpose." The doctor chuckled at Copper's expression of incredulity. "We have to be prepared for all eventualities, boy. You'd be amazed at how many passengers come aboard our ships looking as if they're just about ready to fall off their perch. Sometimes I'm surprised at the percentage we actually manage to get back on to dry land alive and kicking."

"That's all very well." Andy Constable brought the conversation back to the matter in hand. "But it doesn't solve the problem of how we are supposed to get into Mr. Veal's cabin."

"No problem at all," said the doctor. "Just ask the cabin steward who deals with that section of cabins. They've all got pass cards so they can get in to do cleaning and whatnot."

"In which case," said Constable with just a touch of irritation, "I'm not sure why we're standing here talking about it. Come on, sergeant - duty calls."

As the steward, smiling helpfully now in contrast to an initial reluctance to admit the detectives which was soon dispelled by a call to Crane's office, stood back to allow them to enter Veal's cabin, a thought occurred to Dave Copper.

"Have you been in here since yesterday evening?"

"Oh no, sir. I had a call from Mr. Crane yesterday evening, I think very soon after Mr. Veal was found. I had strict instructions not to go in, and not to allow anybody else in either."

"Good. Thanks. We'll take it from here, so you can carry on." Copper led the way into the cabin. "Of course," he remarked over his shoulder, "it's all very well getting in here, guv, but without Mr. Veal's own personal card we won't be able to get into his ..." His voice died away.

The safe stood open. The cabin was not exactly in disarray, but it was clear that drawers had been opened and searched. The coverings on the bed had been thrown back at the foot to reveal Veal's suitcase, apparently stored underneath, which had evidently been pulled out and looked through.

"Safe, were you going to say?" enquired Constable mildly. "Well, it looks as if someone's already taken care of that for us, doesn't it?"

After discovering that the safe held nothing more interesting than Ira Veal's passport and a wallet containing several credit cards and a modest amount of U.S. dollars, Copper crouched down. "And it doesn't look as if there's anything useful in the case either. A couple of pairs of shoes ... a shoulder bag - empty ... some bumf from the ship, itineraries and so on ... and there's this!" Copper held up a small case whose contents were evidently medical in nature.

"Don't get too excited, sergeant," said Constable. "I've seen that sort of thing before. Check with the doctor by all means, but I'm pretty sure that'll be Mr. Veal's equipment for his diabetes - injection pen, and so on."

"Righty-ho, guv. I'll take your word for that." Copper closed the suitcase and pushed it back under the bed, reaching to straighten the covers. "Oh please, no, not that old one!"

"What?"

"The old 'stuff hidden under the mattress' trick." Copper pointed to the corner of the bed, where something was protruding. He pulled it out, and found himself holding half a dozen brown manila files.

"And who says the old tricks aren't the best?" remarked Constable. "Whoever it was after whatever-it-was, they don't seem to have got it, do they?"

Copper was examining the pile of files. "Looks as if we were right in our supposition, guv. About Mr. Veal assembling a group of subjects for investigation, I mean. There seems to be a file here for each of the other people on his table. We've got 'BDW' - that'll be Baxter Wall - 'AH' - that's Anita Holm - 'LB', 'PA', 'JB' ... yes, they're all here. Oh, hang on - no, of course 'MF' is Marisa Fellows."

"Ah, but what's in them?"

"Bits and pieces - a couple of emails - a few scribbled notes - either Veal had the most shocking handwriting, or else some of it's shorthand. That's a bit old school, isn't it, guv?"

"Don't burble, sergeant. Spread it out and we'll take a look. Who's first?"

"Marisa if you like, guv, as she's on top. If you'll pardon the expression." Copper spread out the papers. "It's mostly press clippings." He began to leaf through them. "Stuff about 'Big Sister', her at some film première, blah, blah, her wedding with this guy she's just divorced ... and ..."

"And what?"

"A copy of a birth certificate. American."

"Hers?"

"A chap named Morris Fellows."

"Her father?"

"Can't be. This chap would be about the same age as her. Oh!"

"What?"

"The name, guv. Fellows. What if it's a first husband that nobody knows about? Teenage marriage that went wrong, or some such? That would be quite a tasty story for the likes of Mr. Veal, wouldn't it?"

"I'll tell you what would be even tastier, sergeant. Let's let our imaginations run wild for a moment. What if this is a first husband, and in the excitement of all the fame and money, the charming Marisa quietly forgot his existence and ploughed into these other marriages of hers without the formality of disposing of the first husband?"

"Or, what if she did dispose of him? What if he's lying under a patio somewhere?"

Andy Constable chuckled. "I think we may be getting a bit ahead of ourselves. Surely the simplest thing would be to ask the lady. Which we will do. So let's carry on looking at these files. Who have you got next?"

"There's Jacqueline Best, guv - sorry, 'Pastor Best', since she insists." Copper gave a wry grin. "Two or three things in here. Leaflet about this Community of the Great Shepherd with a picture of the founder - doesn't look as if he'll ever see three-score-years-and-ten again."

"Which of course he won't, having conveniently died and left the lot to the grieving widow."

"Here, guv, I can see why she wouldn't be grieving all that much. Take a look at this." Copper handed over a copy of a short article from an American financial paper about the net worth of various fringe religious organisations, among them the Community of the Great Shepherd. The figure quoted was staggering. "And there's a clipping here from some magazine, about the unexpected marriage of herself with the Dear Leader, or whatever he was. Here, what is it about the women on this ship? They all seem to have some compulsion to marry rich old men. You don't suppose this one bumped the husband off to get her hands on the loot, do you?"

Andy Constable shook his head with a smile. "No evidence as yet, sergeant. And Mrs. Mann's latest former husband is still very much alive and kicking ..."

"For a geriatric."

"... while Miss Holm isn't married at all. Your theory crashes to the ground. So, what about Miss Holm herself? What does Mr. Veal's research have to tell us?"

Copper opened the file. "Even less. There's just a printout of an email which he's received on board. From some guy in London. Talks about a meeting they had during Veal's stop-over. Says he's traced the proceedings, but he can't get hold of the results yet. He's going to do some more digging and email the details to the ship. And that's it."

"I smell private detective, David. What do you think?"

"That's just what I was thinking, guv. Whenever I hear the word proceedings, I always think 'court'. So maybe Miss Holm has been involved in some sort of dispute with someone, and Veal was trying to steal a march in revealing ... whatever it was," he finished rather lamely.

"Okay, so that doesn't tell us a great deal. Bash on. Who's our next candidate for Mr. Veal's attentions?"

"That would be Dr. Lancelot Boyle, M.D. and a few other

initials besides. We've got quite a nice dossier here - loads of pictures of celebs before and after they've been under the knife. Photo of him with some woman in a wedding dress - obviously he'd given her the special treatment before her marriage. And … whoa!"

"What?"

"One or two where the results don't look as if they're exactly what the patient ordered." Copper held up a photo for Constable's examination. "Nasty, eh?"

"As you say. And that's why I'm going to be keeping my crow's feet exactly as they are, thank you very much. But the point is, does any of this tie Dr. Boyle specifically to any of these procedures going wrong? Are we looking at a possible malpractice case?"

Copper riffled swiftly through the papers. "Doesn't seem to be, guv, at least not here. Something about a clinic in Casablanca - no, his name's not mentioned in that. Oh, hold on - there's another email at the bottom of the bundle. And this one is definitely from a private detective - some firm in New York." Copper perused the contents. "Tells Veal that he can find absolutely no trace of a certificate, but he's going to keep looking."

"What kind of certificate?"

"Doesn't say. But just a sec, sir - you just floated the idea of malpractice. What if this certificate is the good doctor's certificate to practice medicine, and it can't be found because it doesn't exist? What if the doctor isn't actually a qualified doctor at all?"

"Wilder still, and wilder, sergeant, as the song nearly goes. We could speculate until the cows come home, but with nothing to steer us in a helpful direction, it's all rather pointless. Bear it all in mind and move on, to …?"

"The extremely smooth Mr. Anders, sir. Much easier here - there's just one piece of paper. It's just a list of dates and flights, by the look of it."

"What, by Anders himself?"

"I assume so." Copper scanned down the list. "Sydney to Bangkok and on to London - several times - London to Accra, London to Paris to Casablanca and back to Marseilles, Miami to Mexico City, Jamaica to London, Madrid to Rio and on to Bogotá - our Mr. Anders gets around a bit, doesn't he?"

"The playboy lifestyle, evidently. Our Mr. Anders wasn't

exactly forthcoming on how he earns his living. I'm guessing he does a lot of sponging off daddy, and I shouldn't be surprised if he manages to make the acquaintance of ladies with, let's say, a fair wodge of disposable income. And you know what they say - follow the money."

"So why would he be of interest to Veal, guv? Anders is not the only gigolo on the planet, if that's what he turns out to be."

"Very true. But there's something, so let's see if we can find out what. And finally, I think, that brings us to Mr. Baxter Wall."

"Correct, sir. Not forgetting the inexplicably absent Mrs. Wall. Maybe she's the one who's lying under a patio, courtesy of her rather tetchy husband, and Ira Veal has discovered the unpleasant truth and was about to blow the gaff."

"Sergeant, will you kindly stop talking like a particularly trashy clichéd crime story and concentrate on what we're doing. Your over-active imagination is going to be the death of you."

"Or her, guv?"

"Stop it!"

"Sorry, guv. So ... there's a couple of cuttings about New York trading firms. One of them's got one firm's name highlighted - that must be the company that Mr. Wall works for. There's a sheet with their name at the top and what I assume is a list of some of their clients, including ... wow, including The ... hmmm, she's not going to be too pleased if that gets out. Clipping from last month's copy of a celebrity mag with Wall and his wife at some opera gala ..."

"So still alive at that point, it would seem."

"As you say, sir. Oh, and we appear to have a couple of sheets of phone records."

"What sort of records?"

"It's a list of numbers called from a mobile - doesn't identify any of them. It's a right old mixture. Some of them are quite long, several minutes, and some of them are just a second or two. I'm guessing that the short ones are probably texts. Oh, hold on - I'm wrong. It's not one mobile, it's two. One sheet shows the numbers called from one phone - the other shows the numbers who have been calling a different phone, and they're all quickie calls, so texts."

"Any indication as to the source of all this? Or how come Veal has it?"

"Not as far as I can see, guv. But it won't have escaped your notice that the words 'journalist' and 'phone-hacking' tend to belong together these days. What if Mr. Veal has been doing his surreptitious bit to track down some underhand activity?"

"What indeed? You know, sergeant, I think we have the material for quite a few interesting conversations in amongst this little lot. You'd better put them under protective custody in your cabin for the time being." Constable glanced at his watch. "Time being the operative word. It's just coming up to half past, and we're due for a word with Timon. Let's pack up here and be off. You can dump those on the way."

As the two turned to leave the cabin, Dave Copper's eye was caught by a gleam of white at floor level. "Hold on a sec, guv."

The sergeant bent and picked up an item which seemed to have slipped down into the crack between the desk unit and the end of the couch. Straightening, he turned it over, revealing it to be a black-and-white photograph of the type which is often referred to euphemistically as 'glamour'. The subject of the photo was a woman, probably in her late twenties, although her exact age was not easy to guess because of the black leather eye-mask she wore. In fact, black leather set the entire tone of her costume, if costume was the right word. Shiny black leather high-heeled boots, cross-laced at the sides, rose to above her knees. One foot rested on an old-fashioned bentwood chair. Above the boots, a matching leather g-string, cut high at the sides, was accompanied by a complex metal-studded bra-cum-shoulder-harness which barely covered the evident charms of the wearer. One hand rested on the hip - the other held a cat-o'-nine-tails, seemingly ready for use. The face, what could be seen of it, wore an enigmatically inviting smile. A long plait of black hair hung over one shoulder. Across the top of the photo, the subject's name in a bold script - 'Tanya Hyde'.

"Well, I'll be horn-swoggled." Copper was evidently somewhat taken aback at his discovery.

"I suspect you probably would be, if that lady had anything to do with it," was Constable's mild response. "I think the clue is in the name."

"So you reckon she's some sort of professional horn-swoggler then, guv?" grinned Copper.

"I'm thinking that she's certainly a professional something, sergeant," continued Constable, "and if you weren't far too young, I'd probably suggest what."

Dave Copper's eyes gleamed. "So, guv, do we detect feet of clay in the irreproachable Mr. Veal? Was he a collector of 'feelthy postcards', or maybe he was one of Tanya Hyde's clients? Or ... has this dropped out of one of our victim files? Is one of the other chaps up for a bit of discipline for being a very naughty boy?"

Constable consulted his watch again. "No time for further speculation now, I'm afraid. You can have fun turning over the possibilities in your fevered brain later. We have to talk to Timon before he goes off shift."

Chapter 7

As Constable and Copper entered the Catherine the Great buffet on the stroke of half past ten, they caught the eye of Timon Tides as he finished clearing an empty table next to one of the picture windows looking out over the passing Atlantic.

"Right, Timon," said Andy Constable briskly. "You said you had some things to tell us. So let's hear them."

"I can't, sir."

Constable cast his eyes heavenwards. "Oh, for crying out loud! Look, there's hardly anyone about now. They've pretty much all had their breakfasts and gone to enjoy whatever delights the ship has to offer today, so there's no danger of being overheard, if that's what's worrying you. So we'll sit down in one of the alcoves, away from prying eyes, and nobody will notice."

"No, sir, it is not that. My boss will notice, and I am not allowed to sit down in my uniform in the restaurant with passengers after I have finished working. It is the company rule."

"So what do we do now?"

"Guv, can I make a suggestion?" said Dave Copper. "How about using Derek Crane's office? That's what you might call backstage, in the crew's quarters."

"Timon?"

"Yes, Mr. Andy - that would be no problem."

"Then we will see you in the Security Office in a couple of minutes."

Derek Crane was rising from behind his desk as the two detectives entered his office. "Good timing, Andy. You've just caught me. I was on my way out this second. What can I do for you?"

"Actually, Derek, keep on walking. We've got one of the crew on his way here with apparently some titbits of information. I think he's a bit jumpy about the whole thing, and he might find it easier to talk to us if you aren't there exuding authority. So can we just use your room to talk to him away from everyone else?"

"Go right ahead, chaps. Any time you like. *Mi casa, su casa*. I must say, you're working well if you've managed to cultivate a snout this quickly."

"Hardly that, Derek," smiled Constable. "Just one of the

waiters."

"Good luck. Keep me posted." Crane was gone.

Constable and Copper had hardly had time to take their seats before a timid tap sounded at the door. In response to Copper's barked 'Come in!', Timon, now in plain T-shirt and jeans, entered the office. Seating himself in response to Constable's gesture, the waiter took a breath.

"You know how it is, sir. Everyone ignores waiters. We are always around at the table doing this or that, and people forget we are there. So they talk as if they were alone in private, and very often it is impossible not to hear what they say. And so in my job you have to develop a very bad memory, or else you would know a lot of secrets about a lot of people."

"Ah, for the old days of 'not in front of the servants'," sighed Constable with mock nostalgia. "However, Timon, I'm thinking that we're sat here because your memory is not as bad as some people might wish it to be. And because it concerns Mr. Veal ..."

"Yes, sir, that is it," nodded Timon. "Because he is dead and also in my job you learn to judge people's faces, and I could tell that some of the things Mr. Veal was saying were causing the others on his table some trouble in the mind."

"Right. Enough of the generalities, Timon. Let's move on to specifics. Give. Notebook at the ready, David?"

"Pen poised as always, guv."

"And in case you're worried about telling us something you shouldn't, rest assured that if it turns out not to relate to Mr. Veal's death, it won't go any further than this room. We can all have selective memories if we have to. Okay?"

"Yes, sir." Timon seemed reassured. "So, one time, at the end of dinner, it was. Everybody on the table had finished their meal ..."

"This was the dinner table which Mr. Veal shared with the others?"

"That's right, sir. And people were getting up and leaving, and Mr. Anders was the last to get up, because he was finishing a brandy which he had ordered with his coffee, and Mr. Veal went round to stand behind him and put a hand on his shoulder, almost as if to stop him. I was taking away some things at the other end of the table, and they did not notice me."

"And what happened?"

"Mr. Veal said, 'You look like you're enjoying your trip, Philip. And you certainly look like you're enjoying your time with Marisa. Let's hope it all ends as you expect.' And Mr. Anders said, 'I have no idea what you're talking about, Veal.' And then Mr. Veal said, 'You certainly get around, don't you?', and Mr. Anders asked what Mr. Veal was implying. And then Mr. Veal said, 'I mean your travel plans, son. What else? You seem to lead a very interesting life.' He said something about having made a little study of Mr. Anders' comings and goings, and Mr. Anders asked why on earth Mr. Veal would be interested in something like that, and Mr. Veal said, 'I think you'd be amazed how much I could find out about your history on the internet. Marisa's too. In fact, sometimes it's even more fascinating what you can't find. In my line of work, it's always good to keep track of where all the beautiful people are going. And in your work too, I expect.' And Mr. Anders was starting to get annoyed, and he told Mr. Veal it was all work for his father and to mind his own business, and Mr. Veal just smiled and said, 'Well, you certainly do get to rack up the air miles. Thailand, South America, Europe, North Africa. But that's the thing about travel, don't you find? It's like a drug. And once you get started, you can never stop.' And then he patted Mr. Anders on the shoulder and said, 'Enjoy the rest of the cruise, Philip. Go have another drink.' And then he went out of the restaurant, looking very pleased, and Mr. Anders sat there for a moment, and then he got up and left too."

Dave Copper looked up. "Some of that certainly fits in with what we know from ..."

"I know what you're going to say, sergeant." The inspector interrupted him swiftly. "But I think it's best, if we're going to keep Timon out of it as a source of information, that we ought to be discreet about our other sources. Agreed?"

"Of course, guv," muttered a chastened Copper. "Sorry."

Constable turned back to Timon. "So, was that it, or is there more?"

"Oh, there is more, sir." Timon now seemed eager to share what he knew. "This was at the start of dinner one evening, early on in the cruise. Mr. Veal had been the first one to arrive at the table, and then Miss Holm was the next. I was pouring water into Mr. Veal's glass when she arrived. And Mr. Veal stood up with a big smile and said 'Anita! How nice! You can come and sit next to me

100

and we can have a good long chat about what you have been doing since we last saw each other.' And Miss Holm seemed to hesitate for a moment, and then she smiled too and said, 'Ira. Yes, that would be lovely.', but you remember what I said about people's faces, and I could tell she didn't mean it, but she didn't really have a choice, so she sat next to Mr. Veal."

"And, of course, you couldn't help overhearing what they said?" suggested Copper hopefully, pen hovering expectantly.

"It's just that I had my job to do, sir," replied Timon, a touch defensively. "And besides, nobody from my other tables had come in yet. So I took them some bread while they were waiting, and yes, I heard them talking."

"And it is possibly very helpful that you did, Timon," said Constable with a sideways look at his colleague. "So carry on, please."

"I didn't hear it all," explained Timon, "but Mr. Veal was talking about the programmes which Miss Holm does on the television, and about how she can be very influential in people's lives. I remember him laughing about one time when she was supporting a new fashion for people to try hanging their pictures upside down on the walls of their rooms, because it was supposed to make them consider the world in a different way. He said she should be careful what she did, or she would make herself look ridiculous."

"And how did Miss Holm seem to take his remarks?"

"Oh, she laughed along with him at first. She seemed to agree that sometimes fashion could be absurd, but that she only promoted things she believed in, and then Mr. Veal said, 'Anita, I think that's a wonderful thing. If there's one thing I can't stand, it's hypocrisy. It is so good to meet a woman with the courage of her convictions, and yours are certainly a great source of joy to me.' He said that, in fact, when he stopped over in London, he was in touch with a friend of his, and he expected to have all sorts of extra material on the subject."

"Did he explain what he meant?"

"He did not have the chance, Mr. Andy, because Dr. Boyle and Mrs. Mann both came to the table at that moment. I thought it must be because he was meaning to write an article about Miss Holm in his paper. But I did notice that it was then that she stopped laughing."

101

"Okay." Andy Constable reflected for a moment. "That sounds as if it may give us something to chew over. Anything else?"

"Only one more thing, sir. I was working in the buffet restaurant one morning at one of the clearing stations like I usually do, and Mrs. Best was sitting at a table nearby, all alone ..."

"I hope you remembered to call her 'Pastor Best'," commented Copper. "That's what she prefers, and you don't want to damage your chances of a nice tip from the lady."

"It is not easy to remember that she is a preacher, sir," pointed out Timon. "She does not look like any priest I have ever seen before. And anyway," he continued, "I did not speak to her at all then, because Mr. Veal was passing the table, and he stopped. He said he would like to have the chance to have a good long talk with her at some time, because he was sure that hers was a very interesting story. And Pastor Best said that she would always be glad of the opportunity to spread the news of her work in future. And then Mr. Veal said, 'Actually, Jacqueline ... it is Jacqueline, isn't it? Unless you'd prefer me to use your other name? No, I'm more interested in the past than the future. Your career before you met your husband, the story of how you met, that strange marriage ceremony of yours, things like that.' And the lady said that surely his readers had better things to do than follow petty gossip, and Mr. Veal said, 'On the contrary. That's exactly what they love. They want to know how you became the Shepherd's Crook, or whatever the title is. And of course, the story of your tragic loss.' But I thought that he did not sound very sympathetic when he said it."

"You know, Timon," remarked Constable admiringly, "I could do with more witnesses like you in my work. I don't usually get decent verbatim reports like this. Normally it's a case of 'something like' or 'I thought he said'. For a man with a dodgy memory, yours is remarkably accurate."

"And, if I may say so, guv, remarkably annoying," said Copper, scribbling furiously. "Spare a thought for those of us trying to keep up."

"It is the job training, sir," answered Timon. "They teach us to remember the meal order for a whole table at once, because the management think it looks unprofessional if we write things down. And sometimes it is a table with eight or ten people on it."

"So, coming back to this conversation you overheard, was that it?"

"Almost, sir. After that last remark, Pastor Best just looked up at Mr. Veal without saying anything, and he shrugged and said, 'Well, I dare say you'll want to talk to me at some other time.' And then he started to move away, but then he turned back and said, "Oh, just one thing. I never did hear exactly how your husband died." And then he walked away, and she watched him go and then got up and left. And I cleared away her breakfast - she had hardly eaten anything."

As the Security Office door closed behind Timon, Dave Copper stretched. "Ah, that's better. I was getting a bit scrunched up sat there writing all that lot down. He goes on a bit, our Timon, doesn't he?"

"Maybe," replied Andy Constable, "but potentially valuable as a witness."

"I just wish we'd known we were going to get tangled up in all this business before we came away, guv," remarked Copper wryly. "I would have sneaked one of our useful interview room recorders into my suitcase, and saved myself a nasty dose of writer's cramp." He flexed his fingers with a wince.

"Your noble sacrifice is appreciated, David. And I'm sure there's some food for thought in amongst that lot."

"Please don't mention food, guv," pleaded Copper. "I should have known that last croissant was a bridge too far."

"No self-control, that's the trouble with the young of today. Come on, let's go and grab some elevenses while we chew over - sorry, while we mull over what Timon's told us. Maybe a caffeine boost will perk you up."

"Guv, your jokes are getting as bad as mine."

"Yes," agreed Constable with a grin, "but I outrank you, so you have to put up with it. Move. What's that bar Derek took us to when we first came aboard?"

*

Up on Deck 9, the Hermitage Bar was living up to its name - not a soul was to be seen, apart from the barman who was busying himself polishing an already immaculate mirror etched with an image of the imperial St. Petersburg palace. As the two detectives approached, he abandoned his task and gave a welcoming smile.

103

"Good morning, gentlemen. What would you like?"

"We just want coffees, if that's all right." Constable looked around. "You're not exactly inundated with customers, are you?"

The barman shook his head. "Not at this time of day, sir. Especially when it is sunny. Most people are up on the pool deck, or else in the Neptune Bar at the stern. So yes, just coffees is no problem. What can I get you?"

"One cappuccino and ... David?"

"Espresso, please, guv. That might just about jump-start me."

"Very good, sir. And if I may have your card ... thank you. Please, take a seat, and I will bring them over."

A few moments later, the barman appeared at the booth the detectives had chosen. "If you would just sign here, Mr. Constable ... thank you. Is there anything else I can get you?"

"No, thank you ..." Constable twisted his head to read the name badge. "No, thank you, Ryan - we'll be fine."

"Very good, sir." The barman seemed reluctant to leave the table. "Sir ... Mr. Constable. Am I right - it is you?"

Constable felt sure he knew what was coming. "By which you mean ...?"

"You are the English policeman who is trying to find out about Mr. Veal's death."

"Yes, I am," admitted Constable, "with the assistance of my colleague here." Copper nodded, took a sip of his coffee, and lifted the cup in greeting. "I'm a British detective inspector, and Mr. Copper here works with me. And I suppose you know this because the talk is all over the ship, and every single member of the crew is filled with wild speculation based on no evidence at all. Correct?"

Ryan looked abashed. "You are right, sir. Everybody says you are doing interviews with people who are suspected, and that it must have been somebody Mr. Veal knew - maybe someone on his table. Although we have all been told not to talk about it. But ..."

"But what?"

"But, sir, there were times I heard Mr. Veal speaking to some of those people, and it has been worrying me that it might be important."

"So you'd like the chance to tell us, just in case?"

Ryan's brow cleared. "Yes, sir."

"In that case, as you're not exactly overrun with customers, you'd better sit down and tell us all about it."

"Oh goody," interposed Dave Copper. "Does this mean I get the chance to make copious notes yet again, guv?"

"I'm afraid so, sergeant."

"In which case, Ryan ..." Copper drained his coffee cup. "I'll probably be needing another one of these, and this time, better make it a large one."

As Ryan, a fresh coffee placed in front of Copper, seated himself, Andy Constable leaned forward. "So, Ryan ... Ryan what?"

"Ryan da Rocas, sir. I am from Brazil."

"And do you just work in this bar?"

"Oh no, sir. I move around, like everyone else. I work here sometimes, but also I work in the Crowning Glory upstairs on the pool deck, and sometimes down in the Diadem."

"Which means you get all sorts of chances to overhear conversations. Very useful. And you knew Mr. Veal?"

"Only as a customer, sir. He would come to the bar downstairs for a cocktail before dinner. Always a Manhattan. But he was not like the other passengers."

"In what way?"

"Well, sir, everybody on the ship is here to have a good time. They are all guests of the company, so they are laughing and joking and mixing with the other passengers and making friends. Mr. Veal was not like that."

"I remember saying he didn't look the cheeriest of chappies when we first saw him, guv," commented Copper.

"So you're saying Mr. Veal did not mix with the others?"

"Yes and no, sir. I mean, he would speak to them, but it never looked as if anyone was having much fun."

"Got an example?"

"I remember one evening, down in the Diadem Bar, the famous blonde young lady from his table ..."

"You mean Marisa Mann?"

"Yes sir, that is the lady. She was sitting on one of the bar stools, and I had just given her a champagne cocktail, and she was sitting there and playing with her hair, and I thought it was very funny, because most of the men in the bar were looking at her, but you could see that the ladies with them were getting very annoyed because of this."

"I can imagine that," said Constable. "Mrs. Mann does have a habit of attracting attention."

"But then Mr. Veal came up behind her and sat on the next stool," continued Ryan, "and he asked for his usual, and while I was pouring it he said, 'Marisa, at last we can have that talk I was hoping for.' And she said that she didn't have the time because it was almost the hour to go in to dinner, and he said that he hoped she would make time because he was fascinated by her. He said that he was sure there was a lot of family background that his readers would love to know. 'Everyone knows about you and Yehuda Mann and that famous divorce,' he said, 'but there's a big gap in your past, Marisa, and I'm curious as to why.' And the lady said that there would be no point, because her parents were dead and she had no family, and Mr. Veal said that he knew that wasn't true, and that he happened to have some documents about what he thought must be a family member - someone called Morris Fellows. He said, 'Your name used to be Fellows, didn't it, Marisa? So who's Morris? What relation to you, I wonder. Let's speculate a little. Maybe he was your parents' son. Could Morris be your brother, Marisa? And if you have no family, then what happened to him?' But she did not answer, because just then the bell sounded for the opening of the restaurant doors, and everyone went in to dinner."

"More questions than answers, as usual, guv," remarked Copper. "I suppose we should be used to this by now."

"So, Ryan, any other useful titbits that you may have overheard?" Constable sounded confident of a positive answer. He was not to be disappointed.

"Of course, sir. The barman hears everything," replied Ryan with a smile.

"And thank the lord for it," said Constable in the same vein. "Although I'm not sure that my colleague here would wholeheartedly agree, considering the amount of note-taking he has to do."

"Don't mind me, guv - I'm just here for the donkey work."

"I remember one time I heard him say something to one of the other gentlemen on his table, Mr. Wall. It was in the bar after dinner, sir, but I don't see how it can have been important."

Andy Constable's tone was avuncular and reassuring. "Why

don't you just tell us, Ryan, and then we can decide if it's important or not."

"I have to say, Ryan, I'm impressed with your memory for names," said Dave Copper. "How do you do it?"

"It is just habit, sir. Every time someone orders a drink, we take their card. And the passengers like it when you remember what they are called. It is good for tips," explained Ryan simply.

"So you were going to tell us about this conversation," Constable reminded Ryan.

"Very well, sir. It was in the main bar up in the Maria Theresa Lounge after dinner - you know, where they have the band and the dancing. We are usually very busy at that time because many of the passengers go there for a cocktail after dinner before going to the show in the Theatre Royal. And Mr. Wall was sitting at the bar with the English lady, who I think he knew before coming on to the ship ..."

"Miss Holm?"

"That's right, sir. Mr. Veal went up to them and said, 'Didn't get a chance to talk to you two tonight over dinner. Another opportunity missed,' and he gave a smile which I did not think looked all that friendly. And then Mr. Wall said that sorry, they didn't really have time now because they were just having a quick drink before moving on, and Mr. Veal asked what they were planning. 'Going to the show?' he said. 'Or maybe you should try the casino tonight. After all, everyone enjoys a little gamble. Me, I enjoy roulette. But I wouldn't dare go near the blackjack tables. Those dealers - you could never tell if they were cheating you, could you?' And then I put his drink down for him, and he thanked me, and by the time he turned back, Mr. Wall and Miss Holm had gone."

"Possible gambling habit, guv?" suggested Copper. "Do you think that might be what Veal was driving at? That wouldn't be too good for the public image of either of those two, would it?"

"It's one possibility, sergeant," replied Constable. "We may think of others. So, Ryan, is that it?"

"I think so, sir." Ryan got to his feet. "Oh no, there is one other thing."

"Excellent," remarked Copper with only the merest tinge of irony in his voice. "I've still got a couple of blank pages left in this notebook."

"Ignore him, Ryan," responded Constable. "We'll happily listen to anything you have to tell us."

"It wasn't something that Mr. Veal said, sir - it was something he heard."

"Go on," said Constable, intrigued.

"It was at the start of the week - I can't remember exactly which evening. But I was working down in the Diadem Bar, and it was a quiet moment so I was taking the opportunity to go around to some of the tables to collect empty glasses. It is usually the bar waiters' job, but one of the guys had been transferred upstairs to the Maria Theresa because they were busy, and the girl was taking a break. So I went round a corner to one of the booths, and the American doctor, Dr. Boyle, and Mr. Anders the Australian gentleman were sitting there together, and I was just in time to hear Mr. Anders say to Dr. Boyle, 'The thing is, the people who use your services need my services too, so let's not forget that.' And then, because I was there, he quickly stopped speaking and took a drink from his glass."

"Am I supposed to make a note of this, guv?" enquired Copper. "Only I can't see the relevance. We know Boyle has all sorts of celebrity patients, and we know Anders is involved in the public relations business. And where does Veal come in anyway?"

"Ryan?"

"I don't know if it meant anything, sir," admitted Ryan, "but I believe that Mr. Veal thought it did. I say this, because I went round the other side of the partition to the other booth which backs on to the one where the two gentlemen were sitting, and Mr. Veal was there, and he was writing something down in a little notebook. He must have been able to overhear the conversation between the other two. And the thing was, he looked very happy, and I thought this was unusual, because I had not seen Mr. Veal smile very much at all. Not like that. He seemed really pleased. I did not speak to him and he did not notice me, and then I just came back to the bar."

"And that was all?"

"Yes, sir."

"Okay, then, Ryan." Andy Constable stood. "Thank you for that. We'll let you get back to ..." He looked around the still deserted bar. "To whatever it is you have to do."

"I really have no idea what all that lot boils down to, guv," said Copper in lowered tones, looking in the direction of Ryan's retreating back as Constable resumed his seat. "But there's one thing that strikes me."

"I dare say it's the same thing that strikes me, David," said the inspector. "Mr. Veal had a little notebook."

"Spot on, sir," agreed Copper. "But no sign of it in his cabin. Do you suppose that's what our murderer was looking for in his safe?"

"Reasonable supposition, I grant you. Except, of course, that you say murderer. Which one? The one who thinks they did it, but according to what the doc tells us, didn't, or the one who actually did it, except that at the moment we have no idea how?"

"When you put it like that, guv, it just makes my head hurt. Can I make a suggestion?"

"You may."

"How's about if I go and lock my own little notebook away nice and cosy in my own cabin safe, and then unwind with a bit of a swim in the pool. Then maybe we can grab a cool beer and go and find some lunch in the hope of nourishing my exhausted brain?"

Constable smiled. "You're right. It won't do us any harm to forget about this business for a while - give the batteries a chance to recharge. Pool it is - we might even be able to pretend, for maybe as much as five minutes, that we're on holiday."

*

The insistent tapping on the door eventually roused Dave Copper from a profound sleep, and he forced himself to stagger to the cabin door.

"Your siestas seem to be getting longer and longer," remarked Constable at the sight of the bleary face before him. He entered the cabin as Copper held back the door, and took a seat as the sergeant stepped into the shower room.

"Sorry, guv, but I was totally zonked," called Copper above the sound of running water. He reappeared a few moments later, drying his face and towelling tousled wet hair. "I've just stuck my head under the tap. It's my own fault. Two beers with lunch at a table in the sunshine, and I was good for nothing except to crash out."

"I thought there was something odd when you didn't answer your phone."

109

"Turned the ringer off, guv. I thought I needed my sleep."

"And now you feel all the better for it?"

"On the contrary, guv - I feel absolutely ghastly."

Constable got to his feet. "Medicinal tea, that's what I prescribe." He consulted his watch. "Just gone five. We're too late for tea in the Maria Theresa, plus you're not exactly dressed for an elegant social occasion." He cast an eye over Copper's rumpled shorts. "Bung a shirt on, and we'll toddle in the direction of the buffet and see if we can wake your brain up. By the way, in case you were wondering, I'm feeling absolutely marvellous, but I can't do this all on my own, so I need you to come and make your contribution."

"Thrilled to hear that, guv." Copper's voice came muffled from somewhere inside the polo shirt he was pulling over his head. "Conduct me where you will - I'll follow." And in response to his superior's surprised look, "Shakespeare, I think, but don't ask me which play." He grinned. "I must be waking up after all."

As the two detectives emerged from the scenic lift, they collided with a young woman heading briskly past the open doors. Garlands of paper flowers cascaded to the floor.

"Oh, I'm so sorry, sir."

"That's quite all right - no harm done." Constable bent to help the girl retrieve the fallen items. "It's Portia, isn't it?"

Portia Carr froze for a moment, and then recognition lit up her face. "Yes, it is, Mr. Constable. I hope you're enjoying yourself?"

"More to the point, Portia, how are you?" asked Constable, as Dave Copper gathered up the last of the garlands. "How are you feeling? Have you got over last night's trauma?"

"I think so, sir. To be honest, I've been too busy to have much time to worry about it. There are so many activities for the passengers, that we're always dashing from one to another."

"Well, as long as it hasn't been preying on your mind, that's a good thing."

"No, sir, it hasn't really." A pause. "Although, I have been thinking ... I did hear something, and I wondered whether ..."

"Here we go again," muttered Copper in the background.

"What, something relevant to Mr. Veal?" enquired Constable. "Which you would like to tell me about?"

"Shall I pop down for my notebook, guv - again?" put in

110

Copper.

Portia shook her head. "Oh no, I haven't got the time now. I'm on my way to the salsa class by the pool. It starts in a few minutes. That's what these are for." She indicated the floral garlands.

"Later?"

Portia looked troubled. "I don't know when. After the salsa I've got a dance rehearsal for the show, and then you'll be at dinner, and the show is after that. And my friend Tom was out on one of the trips with me so you might want to talk to him, but he's a croupier in the casino so he'll be working until late ..."

Constable stopped Portia before she ran out of breath completely. "Don't worry, Portia. Shall we leave it until tomorrow morning, and then you won't be in such a rush. How about nine o'clock in the Security Office? Bring your friend Tom, and we'll have a chat then."

"That's fine, sir," said Portia with relief. "I don't start work until ten tomorrow." She glanced at her watch. "I must go, sir. I shall be late."

"Good luck in the show tonight," called Copper after Portia's retreating back. "We might come and watch you."

"I'll give you a wave," smiled Portia over her shoulder.

"Pretty girl," remarked Copper casually, as the Britons entered the buffet restaurant.

"I thought you weren't fond of tall women," countered Constable as the two made for the drinks station.

"I can make exceptions," grinned Copper. "Now, the real question is, will a slice of that chocolate gateau ruin my dinner?"

111

Chapter 8

It didn't.

By common but unspoken consent, the subject of the death of Ira Veal was resolutely avoided for the remainder of the evening. Dave Copper, for all his sometimes irreverent approach to the business of investigation, was occasionally surprisingly intuitive when it came to gauging his superior's state of mind. And as he ploughed through the mountainous slice of cake while his colleague sipped a mug of Earl Grey alongside him, he could tell that this was one of those occasions when the inspector preferred to let his mind quietly turn over, however unconsciously, the facts of a case. Andy Constable, he knew, always needed his quiet moments. And so the atmosphere remained relaxed, the talk kept to inconsequentialities.

"You know, guv," pointed out Copper as the pair headed for their cabins after tea. "We've never taken a proper look right round the ship. Not really our fault, I know," he added hastily, intent on skirting round any unpleasant topics. "But I don't suppose I shall get a chance to take a cruise on one of these mega-ships again any time soon, so I wouldn't mind a chance to check everything out. I'll be able to wind them all up at the station when we get back. What do you think?"

"I think you have a very good point, David." Constable checked his watch. "I'm for a quick shower, and we'll have plenty of time before dinner."

"So where do we start?" asked a freshly-shaved Copper a brisk ten minutes later as the two emerged from their cabins simultaneously. He held up a plan of the vessel. "I've got the ship-nav, so all being well we shan't get too lost."

"Start at the top and work down?" suggested Constable. "This was your idea, so go ahead."

On the open deck, high towards the bow of the ship, the breeze was strong enough to make leaning into it a necessity as the *Empress* forged steadily northwards into a brisk head-wind at a determined 23 knots. Although the sun still shone from a cloud-scattered sky, the temperatures had declined noticeably from the Mediterranean warmth of previous days, and a bank of heavy cloud boiling up on the horizon was a reminder that the ship was heading into northern waters. Dave Copper peered over the railing at the projecting bridge-wings two decks below.

"Hope they're keeping a good watch down there, guv," he remarked. "From the look of those clouds, we could be heading into choppy waters." He gave a small grim smile to himself at the implication of his words.

"Didn't hear any of that," called Constable from the other side of the deck. "Too windy."

"Thank the lord," murmured Copper to himself. "Me and my big mouth. I said," he called back aloud, "let's head off before we topple into the water."

Further aft, the air was altogether calmer. A net-enclosed tennis court and a golf driving station, complete with giant screen to register the trajectory of the player's shot, were part of a small but impressive complex of sporting facilities, while a spiral staircase led down into the interior of the ship, where a large and expensively-equipped gym stood virtually deserted, apart from one middle-aged woman, her leotard stretched further than the manufacturers ever intended, walking on a treadmill with an expression of dogged determination.

"Not tempted to join in?" Constable raised a single eyebrow in facetious enquiry.

"Too late now," returned his colleague. "If it's all the same to you, guv, I'll stay podgy until we get off the ship, and turn over a new leaf next week."

"Can't say I blame you," said Constable. "You'd have to walk from here to Southampton on that thing in order to work off that slab of cake you had. Let's carry on - at the very least you can take the stairs."

"Down? Then I'm in."

Seven decks of cabins later - "Now I know why they call them 'tall ships', guv," quipped Copper - the staircase opened out on to the main public rooms. There were bars ranging in theme from the most formal kind of London gentlemen's club to a neon-lit ice bar whose main attraction was a stupendous and bewildering array of vodkas. Partly-curtained entrances gave tantalising glimpses of intimate speciality restaurants offering cuisine from the extremes of east and west. A show-lounge held a sprinkling of passengers paying very little attention to a pianist playing a selection of songs from the musicals. A parade of shops displayed a range of wares, from shelves of the most mundane, toothpaste or socks, to artfully-lit showcases with a dazzling display of the most glittering of designer watches and jewellery at eye-watering prices. There was an art gallery, displaying prints and etchings on every subject from populist and classical to abstract and bizarre, all available to purchase for a substantial fee, shipping included - "And you'll notice, for all the zeros on the price tag, that there's not an original work among them," murmured Constable out of the side of his mouth. And through a wall of picture windows could be seen the teak-planked promenade deck, lifeboats suspended above, where a handful of hardy individuals, muffled against the brisk breeze, leaned on the rail and gazed at the horizon, wrapped in their own private thoughts.

Another deck down, the stairs gave on to even more bars - "The throughput of alcohol on this ship must be tremendous, guv," observed Copper. "No wonder they have a doctor." - and a casino where, even at this early hour of the evening, the ranks of gaming machines, their flashing lights stretching into the mirrored distance as their electronic theme tunes tinkled in an incessant cacophony, played host to surprisingly large numbers of acolytes, their eyes staring fixedly at the ever-changing displays on the screens and their hands firmly grasping the cardboard tubs containing their playing tokens. At the deserted roulette and blackjack tables, wheels were gently spun and dummy hands were dealt as croupiers stood with expectant half-smiles, waiting in vain at that early hour for a customer. Past the casino, a nightclub with a decorative theme featuring the flight deck of a starship held out the promise of inter-galactic late-night entertainment, and at the forward end of the deck the doors to the Theatre Royal, shining with all the angular Art Deco glamour of a classic 1930s cinema foyer, remained firmly shut, with a 'Closed For Rehearsals' notice to forbid entrance.

"And that's it," said Dave Copper as the two returned to the atrium. "She's not what you'd call a small ship, is she?"

"Have you ever considered a career as a detective, David?" enquired Andy Constable mildly. "Because I think your observational skills may be going to waste."

Copper ignored the remark. "One thing that struck me, guv. For all the goodness-knows-how-many people there are supposed to be aboard, there's not all that many about. So where are they all?"

Constable glanced at the clock above the Guest Relations desk. "Look at the time. Getting on for seven. They're mostly up in their cabins getting ready for dinner, I dare say."

"Which would account for the fact that we don't have any witnesses for ... er, that thing we're not talking about ..."

"And will continue not talking about, David, if you don't mind. We're off duty."

"Sorry, guv."

"Tomorrow will do. So let's track down somewhere for you to have your regulation disgusting pre-dinner cocktail - we'll go and see if we can find a bar where there's nobody we know. I shall have a small dry sherry, and then we'll concentrate on whatever culinary delights the ship is offering tonight."

"You're the boss."

"I know. Satisfying, isn't it?" smiled Constable, and headed back towards the stairs.

*

"Your menu, sir." An unfamiliar face greeted Andy Constable as he took his seat in the Imperial Dining Room.

Dave Copper looked around. "No Timon this evening? What's happened to him?"

"He has been transferred to the Ambassador Restaurant this evening," explained the newcomer. "That's our special Club restaurant. One of the other waiters is not well, so Timon is taking his place just for this evening. So I will be looking after you in his place for tonight. My name is Jonas. But do not worry - Timon will be back here as usual for tomorrow's Gala Night."

"Gala Night?" Constable asked. "What's that?"

"It is the special formal night at the end of every cruise, sir. It is a tradition on all the OceanSea ships. Everyone gets dressed up in their best, and the theme will be 'A Masked Ball', so people will be wearing masks, and there will be a special menu for dinner, and then the Grand Unmasking in the Maria Theresa ballroom at the end of the evening. It is always a big occasion."

Constable looked doubtful. "Well, we'll see about that. In the meantime, I suppose we should concentrate on this evening and decide what we're having to eat tonight."

"I will leave you to look at the menu, sir," said the waiter,

115

and moved smoothly on to an adjacent table.

"In their best?" echoed Copper. "I don't know about you, guv, but I'm not sure that a formal night is exactly my thing."

"Plus," added the inspector, "as I have brought neither my best bib nor my tucker, whatever that may actually be, I think we would be a little under-dressed for the occasion. We may need a Plan B. But the question for the moment is, would the tuna ceviche followed by the grouper be too much fish and fish, or do I prefer the guinea fowl?"

"Guinea fowl would go better with the red Burgundy which I'm planning on drinking with my chateaubriand," observed Copper.

"You, David, are acquiring a worrying taste for the finer things in life," said Constable. "How you propose to maintain this on a sergeant's salary when we get back home is something of a mystery to me."

"Try not to think about it, guv," replied Copper with a grin. "You'll only ruin your appetite. Take a look at the wine list instead." He passed the leather-bound folder across the table. "Why don't you distract yourself by choosing which wine it is we're actually having?"

Dinner completed, the two detectives found themselves strolling casually among the crowds of passengers now thronging the atrium and its surrounding areas. Bars were satisfying a brisk demand for after-dinner liqueurs and speciality coffees. Browsers were idly turning over price labels in the art gallery with expressions ranging from incredulity to contempt. In the perfumery, ladies of a certain age were wielding the tester sprays of exotic fragrances bearing the name and endorsement of glamorous stars forty years their junior. In the gift shop, a variety of souvenirs, from teddy bears in the uniform of a ship's captain to globes the size of bowling balls bearing a map of the world, its countries crafted from every semi-precious stone imaginable, were being pored over, discussed, and discarded.

"Look, guv," said Copper, pointing at the goods on one of the displays. "There's one of those pen sets which Derek told us about - that one's exactly the same as the one sticking in ... you know."

The sales assistant behind the counter pounced in a flash at the slightest prospect of a sale. "Would you like to take a closer look at the pens, sir?"

"No, thanks," said Copper hastily. "I was just wondering. Tell me," he enquired casually, "do you sell many of these?"

"No, sir," replied the assistant. "I don't think we've actually sold any so far."

"Okay. Well, thanks anyway," said Copper, beating a rapid retreat as the assistant's face fell at the loss of a potential customer.

Out on the boat deck, the fresh breeze which swirled around even on the sheltered side of the ship was soon sufficient to drive Constable and Copper back into the comfort of the interior. Copper consulted his watch.

"The show starts in about twenty minutes, guv. Do you want to head for the theatre so's we can get a decent seat?"

In the Theatre Royal, the Art Deco theme of the doors was continued in the interior to dazzling effect. Etched glass panels featuring classical figures in sinuous poses lined the walls. Multi-faceted mirrored columns supported the upper level, and a turquoise-and-gold curtain embroidered in geometric shapes billowed gently at the front of the stage in sympathy with the movement of the ship. Soft-footed waiters circulated along the rows of deeply-upholstered turquoise seats, soliciting drinks orders for the forthcoming entertainment. Mere minutes later, the lights dimmed, and the audience's chatter fell to an expectant murmur. With a sudden crash of cymbals and a brazen fanfare, an announcement echoed over the loudspeakers - "Ladies and Gentlemen, Mesdames et Messieurs, Meine Damen und Herren, Señores y Señoras - *The Empress of the Oceans* is proud to present the highlight of your cruise, truly the finest show afloat, featuring the stars of the Seven Seas - Ladies and Gentlemen, we give you 'Command Performance'!"

The show was a spectacular entertainment worthy of its setting. The rich sound of an invisible orchestra swelled into glorious harmonies. Strobes flashed and coloured lights whirled. Leading singers crooned sultry ballads or moved to pulsating rhythms. Dancers swayed and gyrated with a flash of sequins and a swirl of ostrich plumes. Staircases rose out of the floor and opulently-swagged draperies flew in from above. And in a stupendous finale, with the entire cast on-stage and an enthusiastic audience applauding in thunderous unison, the

117

auditorium was filled with showers of golden and turquoise tinsel accompanied by cascading pyrotechnics.

As the applause faded and the lights came back up, Dave Copper turned to Andy Constable. "I reckon the only word for that is 'Wow!', don't you, guv?"

"Well, you couldn't call it understated by any means," agreed his companion. "But you can't blame them for pushing the boat out, no pun intended, when it's a showcase in front of probably the most influential audience they'll ever have. If they can't sell this ship on the back of that, they're in the wrong business." He gave Copper a sideways look. "And did you enjoy the performance by your friend Portia?"

Copper grinned in reply. "I think you could safely say that, guv. I particularly liked that costume she was almost wearing during the finale."

"Yes, well, try not to drool too much when we're talking to her tomorrow. But for now, tonight is tonight, and I haven't forgotten that you had an ambition to lose some money in the casino."

"I think if you remember rightly, guv, it was you that had the hankering for a turn on the roulette wheel. But I'll happily come and watch you show me how it's done."

*

The following morning, the telephone ringing at Dave Copper's bedside seemed to have a particularly jolly tone.

"I'm assuming that's you, guv, because I can't think of anyone else who would be calling at this hideous hour."

"Of course it's me, David," came the cheerful answer. "I am up, I am showered, I am full of the joys of spring and raring to go. Do you mean to tell me that you're not?"

"The thing is, guv," replied Copper, "that I'm not the one brandishing a fistful of dollars. How on earth you managed to walk away from the tables last night over a hundred quid to the good will be a source of amazement to me for some considerable time."

"Power of positive thinking!" retorted his superior. The delight was still evident in his tone. "You should try it some time!" And, over-riding Copper's splutter of protest, "Come on, get your kit on. It's nearly eight. Breakfast, and then we have work to do. I'm knocking on your door in exactly five minutes."

As the detectives approached the door of Derek Crane's office an hour later, they were greeted by two young faces bearing expressions in varying degrees of apprehension.

"Good morning, Portia." Constable's greeting was affable. "I'd just like to tell you, before we do anything, how much we enjoyed the show last night. And my colleague David here thought you were particularly good. In fact, I remember him remarking that he ..."

"Yes, it was great," interrupted Copper. He favoured his superior with an almost-genuine smile. "I'm sure Portia doesn't want to be embarrassed by a flood of compliments. Especially as I expect she's pushed for time. Sir."

Constable's air sobered. "You're right, of course." He turned to Portia's companion. "And I assume you're Tom. Portia said she'd bring you along." He held out his hand.

"That's right, sir." The young man shook the inspector's hand. He was a tall slim gangling youth who looked barely out of his teens, with dark brown hair and eyes, a prominent Adam's apple, and an accent that hinted at the East End of London. "Tom Bowler. I work in the casino mostly, but I also help out with the animation team when they're escorting excursions or doing activities around the ship."

"Tom calls the bingo every day," added Portia. "He's very good at coaxing people into buying extra tickets."

"I thought I recognised you," remarked Copper. "You were working on the next roulette table to us, the one where that guy was winning huge amounts of money."

Tom smiled quietly. "That must have been quite early on in the evening, sir. After that, the gentleman went away to celebrate at the bar with his friends, but he came back later and, unfortunately for him, he lost it all again. It's the luck of the tables, sir. But he did leave me a good tip from his first session, so I was quite happy."

"Fascinating as all this is, it isn't actually getting us anywhere," broke in Constable. "So, since you suggest that Portia and Tom do not have unlimited time, shall we get on with it?" He tapped at the door of Derek Crane's office and, in response to the call of 'Come in', put his head into the room. "Derek, I've got a couple of staff members here I'd like a chat with. Okay if I use next door as before?" The reply was obviously in the affirmative, and

119

Constable led the way as the small group took seats in the adjacent office.

"So, Portia, where shall we start?" said Constable. "You know who we are, and I suppose you've told Tom about us." Tom alongside her nodded. "And you said you'd heard or seen something which may have a bearing on Mr. Veal's death, or his relationship with the other passengers he had dealings with. Is that fair to say?"

"Yes, sir."

"So, specifics. Would these have been events on or off the ship?"

"Both really, sir. I remember the trip the day before yesterday, when we did the excursion to Jerez."

"And were you both on that one?"

"No, sir," said Portia. "Just me."

"I was on one of the buses that went to Seville that day," explained Tom.

"So who out of our group went on your trip, Portia?"

"Mr. Veal was there, but also Miss Holm. That was why I remember it, because of the trouble."

Copper looked up from his notebook where he had been unconsciously doodling on the cover. "And what trouble was that?"

Portia shifted uneasily. "I don't really know if I ought to say, because it didn't actually come to anything. We'd been to visit the bodegas, which was the main reason for the excursion, and we'd had the guided tours and the tastings and everything, and then there was some free time afterwards when we dropped people off in the centre of Jerez, for shopping and so on. Some people like to go shopping if they ever get the chance. Anyway, we were in a square where there were several souvenir shops, and I was just sitting quietly in the shade waiting for everyone when suddenly I heard raised voices from one of the shops. I went to find out what it was, and it turned out that Miss Holm was being accused by the shop-keeper of having stolen something - a little silver box, I think. I ran to fetch our guide, because I only speak a very little Spanish, and he came and took over, and in fact it was all a mistake anyway. The shop was very small and very cluttered, and it seems that Miss Holm had been looking around, and she must have brushed against this box on one of the shelves and knocked

120

it into her bag without realising. Of course, the guide explained all this, and Miss Holm looked very embarrassed and said of course she would pay for the box, but the shopkeeper said no, that was all right, and in fact he ended up apologising, and he gave Miss Holm a silk scarf as a gift, and then we all got back on the bus and came away. But it was quite unpleasant at the time." Portia's voice held a tremor of tension at the memory.

"So what has this to do with anything about Ira Veal?" enquired a puzzled Dave Copper.

"It was when we got back on the bus," continued Portia. "They were just about to close the door, and I was going up the aisle doing a head count, to make sure we hadn't left anyone behind, and Mr. Veal was sitting in the seat behind Miss Holm, and as I passed them he leaned forward and spoke to her between the seats."

"And you overheard what he said?"

"Yes, sir. He said something about it being lucky that the courier was on hand to straighten things out, and he expected that they were probably used to it because things like that were happening all the time. And he said 'Old habits die hard, eh, Anita?', but I don't think she answered him, and then the bus started off, so I went to sit down."

"And was that it for that trip?" asked Andy Constable.

"For the trip itself, yes, sir," answered Portia. "But there was one other thing when we got back to the ship in Cadiz."

"Oh yes," joined in Tom, "because I was there then, wasn't I? Your bus from Jerez and mine from Seville both got back at the same time, didn't they?"

"That's right," agreed Portia. "And I didn't see Miss Holm go, but Mr. Veal was quite slow to get off the bus, and then he noticed that Australian gentleman ..."

"Philip Anders?"

"Yes, sir. He saw him standing talking to a group of men, and he went over to him, but just as he got there, Mr. Anders shook hands with one of the men and they left."

"And these were what ... other passengers?"

"Oh no, sir, I don't think so."

"So locals, then?"

"Maybe." Portia sounded doubtful. "They didn't look very Spanish."

"They could have been," pointed out Tom. "There's a lot of North African ancestry round here still, even after the Moors left. They told us that in the part of Seville cathedral that used to be a mosque."

"So where does Mr. Veal come in?" persisted Copper.

"He just watched these friends of Mr. Anders walk off," said Portia, "and then Mr. Veal sort of sidled up behind him and said 'Meeting some contacts, Philip?', and Mr. Anders just laughed and said it was nothing, it was just some old friends and it was always good to keep in touch, and Mr. Veal said, 'Yes, but the trouble with some old friends is that they never let go, do they?' Mr. Anders just shrugged and walked back on board the ship."

"Bit of a coincidence, these old friends of Philip Anders being in just the right place as he was getting off the bus from Seville, wasn't it, guv?" commented Copper.

"Oh no, sergeant," contradicted Tom. "Mr. Anders didn't go on the Seville trip. At least, he wasn't on my coach."

"I thought he said he did, guv," said Copper, leafing back through his notebook. "It's here somewhere. I'm sure he said something about spending time with Marisa Mann, because he was on the same bus as her."

"Are you absolutely sure, Tom?" asked Constable. "Might he have been on one of the other buses?"

"All I know is, he wasn't on mine, and Marisa Mann was." Tom sounded positive. "Look, I'll show you." He pulled out a smart-phone from his pocket. "I took quite a few photos while I was on the trip, and Mrs. Mann was usually around somewhere."

"Loves the camera, by all accounts, guv," said Copper. "She's famous for it." Tom was scrolling through the pictures on his screen. "Look, there she is in one group - here's another - here's one my friend Sally took of the two of us together, because she said my mates at home would turn green when they saw it ..."

"And not a sign of Mr. Anders in any one of them," observed Constable. "I think that may need to be looked into a little further. Maybe the gentleman had other fish to fry."

"Must be pretty important fish, if they're dragging him away from the fair Marisa," said Copper. "He does seem to spend a fair amount of time with her."

"Oh!" A thought seemed to have occurred suddenly to Tom. "I do remember one thing that happened in the casino one

122

evening. That involved Mrs. Mann too. I was just coming back from a break, and I came past a group of people crowded around a table, and Mrs. Mann was there alongside Mr. ... I think he's an American doctor ..."

"Dr. Boyle?"

"I think so, inspector. Anyway, Mrs. Mann and the gentleman were standing alongside one another, but they weren't speaking, and Mr. Veal went up behind them ..."

"He seems to have done that a lot, guv," remarked Copper.

"... and I heard him say 'Not having a nice long chat? I am surprised, considering you two have so much to talk about.' It looked as if they were pretending not to hear him, but Mr. Veal carried on and said something about surgery achieving miracles, but you had to be careful and to know when to stop. He said 'Can't do every miracle, though, can you, doc?', but then I went back to my table, so I don't know if anything else was said."

Portia turned to Tom. "Was that the evening I came to watch you after the show was finished?" Tom shrugged. Portia turned back to the inspector. "Because if it was, I think I was there too. I don't mean I saw Mrs. Mann and Dr. Boyle - I think they must have gone by then - but Mr. Veal was still there. He was standing in the crowd watching the players at Tom's table ..."

"I've noticed that there are a lot more people who like to watch the gambling rather than actually participating," observed Constable. "Less of a strain on the finances, I imagine."

"Well, yes, that's the point," said Portia eagerly. "Mr. Veal sort of said the same thing to Mr. Wall."

"You know Mr. Wall?"

"Yes, sir," confirmed Portia. "He was one of the passengers on the tour of Genoa that I was escorting, and I remember him because he left the tour part way through and we had terrible trouble finding him when it was time to come back to the ship. But anyway, he was standing next to me at Tom's table - watching, not playing - and Mr. Veal came up alongside him and said 'Not tempted into a gamble, Baxter? I should have thought this kind of activity would be just up your street - your Wall Street, I should say!' And Mr. Wall gave a sort of sickly grin, and Mr. Veal said something about surely he needed to find ways to justify all those ill-gotten gains of his - 'Or is it those huge losses?' he said. 'I get so confused.' But just then someone had a big win, and there was a round of applause from the crowd, and I didn't hear any more. That was all, really."

Constable took a look at the clock on the wall. "Well, you two, I think that's given us a few things to chew over. And as the time's getting on, I don't want to get you into trouble by keeping you away from your work. If anything else occurs to you, you can easily get in touch with us through Mr. Crane."

"You could talk to Sally if you like," suggested Tom as he made for the door. "Do you know her - Sally Forth, from the Excursions Desk? She was on the Seville trip, and she goes on several of the tours, so she may have heard something."

"It's a thought," said Constable. "We'll check her out." He watched the door close behind the two young people.

"What a busy little bee this Ira Veal was," commented Copper. "He doesn't seem to have been able to keep his nose out of other people's business."

"Which of course was only doing his job," countered Andy Constable, "but it's no sort of smart career move if it ends up getting you killed. And I'm still not terribly happy that we don't know how he died." He uncoiled himself from his chair. "Come on - we'll see if Sally Forth can tell us anything we don't know. If we can track her down."

"Well, at least we know one thing, guv," said Dave Copper. "She won't be off somewhere on a shore excursion."

*

The Excursions Desk was unlit and unmanned as the two detectives returned to the atrium - "Not really surprising, guv, considering there's nowhere left to Excursh to," quipped Copper - but Lydia Carton was at her customary place behind the Guest Services Desk.

"Sorry to bother you, Lydia," said Constable, "but we're wanting to track down Sally Forth from the travel team. We need a private word with her. Is there any way you can help us?"

"Of course, sir," smiled Lydia. She tapped the name into her keyboard, consulted the displayed list, and punched a code into her phone. "Shouldn't be a moment, sir - I've paged her to call me." Moments later, the phone rang. "Hello, Sally ... yes, there's no problem, but I have Mr. Constable here at the desk. He says he wants to speak to you ... no, I think somewhere quiet would be better, by the sound of it ... all right, I'll tell him." She replaced the receiver. "Sally says, can she meet you in five minutes in the Card Room. It's just along there, one deck up, and there probably won't be anyone in there at this time of the day."

"Thank you, Lydia. We'll find it."

The Card Room lay silent, virtually invisible and unnoticed behind heavy glass doors flanked by velvet curtains. Four card tables and their attendant chairs were strategically placed about the room, with only two deep leather armchairs flanking a mock baronial fireplace as additional furniture. A sombre atmosphere reigned.

"The bridge players are obviously expected to take their game extremely seriously," said Constable. "No distractions allowed."

After only a minute or two, the door was pushed open, and Sally Forth entered the room. Her face wore a look of apprehension. "You wanted me, sir? Is there a problem? Have I done something?"

"Not in the least, Sally." Constable smiled to put the evidently nervous girl at her ease. "No, it's just that various people have been able to give us some information about things they've seen or heard relating to Mr. Veal, and we think you may be able to do so as well."

"Well, I'll try, sir." Sally still sounded uncertain, as Constable gestured her to one of the armchairs and seated himself in the other, while Dave Copper unobtrusively took position behind Sally in one of the upright chairs, notebook at the ready.

"It's like putting a jigsaw together," explained Constable. "And it looks as if the large pieces are the people who were sharing a table at dinner with Mr. Veal. But the smaller pieces are the bits which link those people to each other, and most particularly to Mr. Veal. Having had a chat with your friends Tom and Portia, we're pretty sure that escorting your guests on excursions provides plenty of opportunities to catch useful snippets, and that's what we need. So can you cast your mind back, and see if you can remember any conversations or incidents between any of them?"

"We have so many passengers on board, sir, it's not that easy." Sally frowned in thought.

"I'm sure you can think of something," coaxed Constable. "After all, I should think Mr. Veal would tend to stick in the mind somewhat. He wasn't cast in what you might call the mould of the typical passenger."

"That's true, sir," admitted Sally. "I do recall one time, quite early on in the cruise, I think, when I was working at the desk, and Dr. Boyle was standing there looking through some folders about the ports of call, and Mr. Veal came over and saw what he was doing and said 'Isn't it a shame, Lance, that we aren't going to be calling at Casablanca? You could have looked up some old friends.' And Dr. Boyle said that he didn't have any friends in Casablanca, and Mr. Veal said he thought that Dr. Boyle used to practice there, and he was obviously mistaken. 'Not the worst of mistakes, though, is it, Lance?' he said. 'I can think of much bigger ones - can't you?' And then he walked away, and Dr. Boyle carried on leafing through the folders, although it seemed to me that he was looking without seeing, if you know what I mean."

"That's not the first time we've heard Casablanca mentioned, is it, guv," interposed Copper. "Somebody seems to have North Africa on the brain."

"So that was it regarding Dr. Boyle?" Constable ignored the interruption from his colleague.

"Well, yes and no," said Sally. "I mean, it wasn't anything to do with Mr. Veal, but there was a bit of an odd moment between Dr. Boyle and Mrs. Mann. It was on the Seville trip," she continued, "and Mrs. Mann was on my bus, and I suppose Dr. Boyle must have been on one of the other ones, but all the buses arrived together at the drop-off point, and some people were due to go off on a walking tour and one group was going straight to the cathedral. But anyway, because it had been quite a long drive up from Cadiz, we gave everyone fifteen minutes to get a drink or to go to the loo, and I popped in to have a coffee in one of the cafes, and Mrs. Mann came and sat down at a table by me, and then Dr. Boyle came and joined her. I didn't mean to eavesdrop, but their table was just the other side of a pillar from me, and I couldn't get away without them seeing me. Anyway, they were talking in quite low voices, so I didn't hear too much, but it did sound like quite an argument."

"To what effect?"

"Mrs. Mann was saying that as far as she was concerned she didn't know Dr. Boyle, and she would carry on not knowing him. And Dr. Boyle said that that sort of silence came at a price,

126

and he thought that, with all her money, it was a small enough price to pay. 'And of course, Marisa,' he said, 'we both know it's not truly your money at all, is it?' And she said she had friends too, and Dr. Boyle should be careful about what he said, and Dr. Boyle said 'Let's see how many of those friends stick around when they hear what I have to say.' He said he wanted his share of what she'd got, all on account of what he'd done, or else the story would get out. But then the guide came round calling for everyone to get ready for their tours, so they got up and left separately, and I carried on with the trip."

"Sounds like the potential for an interesting case of blackmail, sir," said Copper. "Wonder what the lady's been up to. It's just a pity that Ira Veal wasn't involved. We might have had a sniff of a motive."

"Patience, sergeant - there may be more to come. Now, Sally," resumed Constable, "how about any trips Mr. Veal went on?"

Sally considered. "I can only think of one that I escorted, sir, and that was in Barcelona."

"Tell us about it."

"It was the tour that visited the Segrada Familia church."

"That's the one with all the knobby towers, right?" said Copper.

"Yes, sergeant, it is," replied Constable patiently. "We've all seen the pictures. But I'm assuming that the architecture was not the relevant point, Sally?"

"No, sir, although I suppose that's why most people go. But I think that it was because it's a very famous church that Pastor Best joined the tour."

"Along with Mr. Veal."

"Yes, sir. Not together, obviously. Our guide took us into the church and conducted us round explaining things as normal, and then at the end there were a few minutes of free time for people to look around on their own, so everyone went off in different directions. I was just going to look in one of the side chapels that we'd missed, and I saw Pastor Best in there on her own with her head in her hands. I thought she must be praying, so I stopped to one side just inside the entrance, but then Mr. Veal came in and went right up to her and interrupted her, and said 'Ah, Jacqueline, we meet again. I assume you're praying for the forgiveness of sins?' and she said something about everybody having something they needed forgiveness for, even him, and he said what about the Eleventh Commandment, 'Thou Shalt Not Get Found Out', and I thought he said something about why should a pastor hide anything. But then I realised that I really shouldn't be listening to a private conversation, so I slipped out and went and found the guide just as the group was getting back together. And Pastor Best and Mr. Veal joined us a few moments after that."

"Strikes me, guv," said Copper, as Sally left the room a minute or two later, having exhausted her fund of revelations, "that Mr. Veal would have been rather keen on sin. I should think it provided him with quite a tasty living."

"His problem being," responded Constable, "that it seems to be other people's sins which have found him out. Not quite the result he was hoping for."

Chapter 9

"Any progress, guys?" asked Derek Crane.

The approach of lunchtime had fostered an agreement to abandon the investigation for the time being in favour of a refuelling break, and the mechanics of negotiating a way through generous portions of enormous Mediterranean prawns in the Catherine the Great buffet restaurant while remaining relatively un-messy had rendered a coherent discussion of the case totally impossible. But now, with the meal behind them, and relaxing in the Neptune Bar on the after-deck with a brace of coffees to hand, Andy Constable was drawing breath to open the subject of Ira Veal when Derek's arrival at his shoulder gave a rather unnecessary kick-start to the proceedings.

"Not so bad, Derek," he replied. "We've had a number of conversations with a number of people, so I think the next step is probably to trawl through David's notes and see what we can analyse from them. I'm sure we'll still have questions to ask, and with a bit of luck we may find out what those actually are."

"Good," said Crane. "Not wanting to rush you at all, and don't think I don't appreciate the favour you're doing me in taking this on in the first place, but it is Friday already, and we'll be docking tomorrow before we know it. And the thing is, once we get into port, the ship is going to be crawling with police and security anyway."

"That's a bit of overkill, isn't it?" said Dave Copper. "Sorry, no joke intended, but surely you're not bringing in the entire Hampshire Constabulary just to investigate the murder of one American journalist, however notorious he may be."

"Oh, didn't you know?" Crane looked surprised. "Of course, I forget you've been out of the U.K. for a couple of weeks, and you probably haven't caught up with the media. No, it's nothing to do with Ira Veal. It's for Sunday."

"What happens on Sunday?" asked Constable.

"It's the royal christening of the ship," explained Crane. "We've got the Duchess of Middlesex coming down to do a big public ceremony on the quayside - champagne, balloons, fireworks, the lot. And the last thing the company would want is an unsolved murder hanging over us to put a dampener on the proceedings. We really can't have H.R.H. embarrassed in any way, so I really was hoping ..."

"Point taken, Derek. We'll shut ourselves away with David's little book and see what we can do."

The gratitude on Crane's face was plain. "Look, if there's anything else you need ..."

"We'll ask," Constable forestalled him. "Leave us to it. Come along, sergeant - back on duty. Sink the remains of that coffee, and we'll go and ensconce ourselves in my suite and decide what's next."

*

Back in the comfort of Constable's cabin, the two detectives cast a brief glance out of the windows at the ocean beyond. The Bay of Biscay seemed to be living up to its traditional reputation. A strong north-westerly wind was finding a way through the merest crack around the door to the balcony to produce a tiny, barely-audible but unsettling whistle, while a rolling procession of seas from the north-east, each one seemingly fractionally higher than the one before, was causing the *Empress* to begin to bury her bow ever-deeper into the waves as she shouldered her way through them with an increasing pitching motion. A tumble of purplish-grey clouds filled the horizon.

"Looks as if we may be in for a stormy night," remarked Dave Copper.

"Many a true word," retorted Andy Constable grimly. "Especially so for at least one of the people on that list of ours. Come hell or high water ..." He took another look out of the window at the deteriorating weather beyond, "... or even a combination of both, I'm absolutely determined to get to the bottom of this business, if not for our own satisfaction, then as a favour to Derek, and to the ship as well. She's been good enough to bring us home - the least we can do is return the kindness and not send her off on her career with some unsolved mystery hanging over her like an evil omen."

"You're really a bit of an old romantic, aren't you, guv?" said Copper with a smile. And in response to a half-serious warning look from his superior, "But I promise not to spread it around the station when we get back."

"You'd better not!" said Constable, and then relaxed. "Not that a soul would believe you, anyway. Okay, plonk yourself down,

130

get the notebook out, and we'll try to make sense of what we have so far."

"First things first, guv. Are we absolutely certain that the people on my little list are the only ones we should be considering? There's a ship-full of people out there."

"True, but we have to take into account that Veal seems to have deliberately assembled that table of people and nobody else, so we assume that they were all his specific targets."

"Until somebody made him theirs," agreed Copper.

"Therefore, as nobody's mentioned any contacts between Veal and anyone else, your little list is the only show in town. And all, according to Derek Crane, members of the great and the good. Not a nice routine Saturday night domestic bash on the head with a blunt instrument such as we are used to at home." Constable sighed. "No, we're more into Iago's territory."

"Now you've lost me completely, guv," said a baffled Copper. "I don't remember anyone on board called Iago."

"In Shakespeare, sergeant. 'Othello, The Moor of Venice'. Don't tell me your education skipped that one?"

"Oh, *that* Iago," said Copper. "No, our year did 'A Midsummer Night's Dream'. So where does Iago fit in?"

"Something he says. 'Who steals my purse steals trash'."

"So? I still don't get it."

"Meaning you can rob somebody, and that's just material possessions. But he goes on to say 'But he that filches from me my good name, Robs me of that which not enriches him, And makes me poor indeed'."

Copper caught on. "And that was Veal's game. He went through life having a great time destroying people's reputations. People like the ones on his table. And someone decided that, for them, this was a spectacularly bad idea. Which brings us back to our little list."

"So, who do we start with ...?"

"Mr. Baxter D. Wall was the first one we spoke to, guv."

"As good as any. So what have we got on him?"

Copper began to leaf through the pages of his pad. "American. Works for some sort of big financial firm in New York, so he's obviously up to his ears in money. Bit aggressive when he first came in, but that needn't tell us anything. Wife should have been on the trip with him, but didn't come for some unknown reason. Don't know if there's anything in that. Says he'd never met Veal before coming on this trip, although he'd heard of his paper, and says he doesn't have any idea why Veal would be interested in him. And as for the time of the murder, says he was in the gym but can't quote anyone to verify it. In fact, he seemed almost proud of the fact that he couldn't give us an alibi."

"And cocky people make great murder suspects," observed Constable. "But not quite enough to convict him on its own. So much for what he had to say about himself. What about what we've learnt from our various informants?"

Copper started turning pages. "That's going to take a bit more finding, guv. I've got stuff dotted about all over the place. Hang on - here's something. The barman guy ..."

"Ryan?"

"Yes, sir. He heard Veal say something to Wall in the bar about gambling in the casino, about making sure the dealers weren't cheating, or something of the kind."

"You mean he suspected Wall of having some sort of arrangement with one of the croupiers? I can't see how that could be. Those tables are really closely monitored, what with all the CCTV, and a pit-boss casting a beady eye over everything. There's no way Wall could get away with anything underhand in that department."

"No, and how could Veal know about it anyway? But if you remember, guv, I wondered whether he might have got a whiff of a gambling habit which could hurt Wall in his business dealings. In fact, that ties up with something ... hold on while I find it." The sound of riffling paper. "Yes, here it is. It was when Wall was actually in the casino. Portia told us this morning. Again, it was something about gambling, and he made a really lame joke about his name - you know, Wall, and Wall Street - and some remark about ill-gotten gains." Copper let out a derisive snort. "Difficult to imagine somebody like Veal having a puritanical streak, but journalists can always pile it on when they want to, I suppose."

"Any other comments?"

"Not that I can think of, guv."

"What about in the file in Veal's cabin?"

"I've got it next door if you want to check, guv, but as far as I recall it was some articles about the firm he worked for, and a couple of sheets of phone records, but we couldn't tell what they related to."

"We'll have another look at those but, if that's it for the moment, we'll move on. And the next contestant who wants to play 'Spot The Murderer' is ...?"

"Dr. Lancelot Boyle, guv, but call him Lance."

"How very chummy."

"As you say, guv. Another American - plastic surgeon to the stars. Well, he'll be used to having blood on his hands, won't he?" The quip was rewarded with a stony look from the inspector. "Sorry, guv. Anyway, very high-powered, by the look of it. Thinks a lot of himself. Says he'd met Veal but didn't know him well, and can't think of any reason why Veal would be interested in him particularly, other than in the way of the celebrities he's done work for. Very surprised that Veal wanted him on the same table as him."

"And his whereabouts when Veal was killed?"

"Even less helpful, guv. Said he was tired when he got back from that day's trip, so he went to his cabin and just crashed out. No witnesses, of course."

"It's a bit of a pain that all these people seem to be single, with the exception of Mr. Wall, whose absent wife is no help at all. No useful spouses to confirm people's locations. And before you start resurrecting your theory about half of them being buried under patios, we shall consider what we've actually been told rather than indulging in flights of wild speculation. So who said what to whom?"

Copper puffed out his cheeks as he began to trawl back through his notes.

"I can wait," drawled Constable helpfully as he leaned back on the sofa.

"No need," replied Copper with a grin. "Ask and you shall receive. There's this. It's something that Sally heard. Veal made some remarks to Boyle about having old friends in Casablanca, because he had practised there, and it seems Boyle flatly denied anything of the kind. And here's another thing she told us, which doesn't involve Veal, but it's rather odd, if you think about it. There was that conversation where Marisa Mann denied knowing Boyle, but it sounds as if he had some kind of hold over her." Copper glanced at Constable, and was intrigued by the quiet smile which was developing on his features. "Any thoughts as to what that might be, guv?"

"Very, very tiny ones, sergeant," said Constable. "And I don't want to frighten them away. Leave them alone for the moment, and they may grow of their own accord."

Copper continued to flip back and forth between the pages in his notebook. "The only other thing that I can find about Boyle at the moment is something said between him and Phil Anders in the bar, when Anders was going on about having customers in common who both needed their services. But both were connected with doing work for celebs - so what? I can't see that it has any particular significance."

"But," countered Constable, "if I remember rightly, Ryan seemed to think that Ira Veal thought it did, if his reaction to what he was hearing was anything to go by. So what, I wonder, did Ira Veal hear that so far doesn't click with us? Maybe there was something in his file that connects."

"The file ... the file ..." More sounds of turning pages. "Here you go, guv. Mug shots of Boyle's clients - quite a lot of pretty ladies, and one or two pretty men. Something about a clinic in Casablanca - *that's* where I remember it from! - but no specific mention of the doctor in that." Copper looked up from his perusal of his notes. "Am I getting fixated on Casablanca, guv? It just seems to keep cropping up. After all, it's a place with something of a reputation these days, isn't it?"

"Time was, sergeant, when Casablanca had a reputation for quite a number of things," said Constable. "Which I am going to put aside in my box of tiny, tiny thoughts for the moment. Anything else in the file?"

"Only that email from the New York private detective about a certificate, but we don't know what sort - do you suppose there's any chance of contacting these people and finding out more?"

"It's worth a try."

"And I've just had a thought, guv - maybe we can get access to Veal's emails on board to find out if there's been anything more since he died."

"Hmmm. That might take some doing, but it could be helpful if it's possible. For now, let's just work our way through what we've got. Who's next?"

"That would be Marisa Fellows, guv - sorry, Marisa Mann."

"The blessing of not being a follower of the tabloids, sergeant," intoned Constable, "is that I don't get confused by trying to keep track of the various entanglements which these celebrities seem to get themselves involved with on a daily basis."

"You're probably wise," confessed Copper.

"But fortunately," continued Constable, "you seem to have got over your initial tongue-hanging-out-in-admiration phase, so I can look forward to a professional analysis of the facts about the lady. So please proceed."

"Just the facts, ma'am, eh? I'm sure I've heard that line before, sir." The inspector's single raised eyebrow discouraged Copper from any further attempt at levity. For the moment. "Well, really only what I told you when we first clapped eyes on her. Glamour by the bucket-load, and she trades on it for all she's worth. I didn't know anything about her before she turned up on the 'Big Sister' reality show, and she didn't offer any other information, but now that she's got all that cash from her divorce, I doubt if she feels the need to. American, she says, and never knew Veal before coming on this ship, although she did have a pretty strong aversion to a ... hang on ... yes, here it is ... 'muck-raking hack' when the subject came up. Don't know if that's a general thing, or whether there's some history there that she's not telling us. But as for the murder, it sounds as if she's got a sort of alibi for at least some of the time in question, because she was having her nails done." Copper laughed. "I feel quite sorry for the poor girl, guv. It must take an awful lot of effort to maintain that look all the time."

"I'm sure you have no idea," returned Constable, with a quirky smile which Copper could not quite fathom. "So, if that's the sum of your knowledge, what does Veal's secret file add to it?"

"Not a great deal. More press clippings than you can shake a stick at, and ... oh, yes. There was that birth certificate for the mysterious Morris Fellows, about whose identity we know no more. Except that ..."

"Except that what?"

"Hold on a sec, guv, while I find it. Here. According to something Ryan heard. Veal seems to have had a particular interest in Morris. He sounds as if he had some theory that maybe he was Marisa's brother, and he asked Marisa whatever had happened to him."

"And your counter-theory, I believe, was that he's under a patio somewhere."

"Well, you have to admit, guv, murders do tend to come in twos. Look at last week in San Pablo."

"Let's not fret too much about Morris's alleged untimely end," said Constable. "I'm rather more interested in what Sally heard between Marisa and Boyle on the Seville trip. That little row about money, and it sounded as if he was putting pressure on her."

"But Veal wasn't around then, guv," Copper pointed out. "He was in Jerez."

"No," countered the inspector, "but Tom Bowler was around when Marisa and Boyle were together in the casino one night. And he heard Veal say something about the two of them having a lot to talk about. Well, maybe the row in Seville was that talk."

"D'you know, guv, I'm beginning to feel quite glad I'm not an investigative journalist," remarked Copper. "All this malarkey is far more confusing than the stuff a simple detective sergeant has to make sense of on a daily basis."

"You should get used to it," said Constable. "That's if you ever want to go for promotion and make inspector."

"What, and miss the pleasure of working for you, sir?" grinned Copper. "Not likely. I know when I'm having a good time."

"In that case, you'd better get your nose back to the grindstone. Your next one under the spotlight is ...?"

"We're back to Phil Anders and his globe-trotting activities, which everyone seems to have been going on about. Can't necessarily see why they should - Australian, works for his father's company which is a big international P.R. firm, so I suppose it's only logical that he should get about a bit. Speaking of getting around, there's the Marisa factor to consider. But obviously the jet-setting was what interested Veal - in fact, the only thing in his file on Anders was that list of travel arrangements."

"Which I seem to recall got brought up in a conversation which took place in the restaurant, according to Timon."

"Yes, guv ... here we are. Veal made some sort of waspish remark to Anders about his relationship with Marisa Mann, and then seemed to be trying to goad him by going on about researching his travels and listing all the places he'd been to.

Surely it can't have been something as simple as jealousy? Anders getting a lot of what Veal would have liked to have?"

"I think there's more to it than that. And again, don't forget that snippet which Portia told us about, when people were getting off buses in Cadiz."

"Oh yes, I remember. I've got that here somewhere." A pause. "Portia ... Cadiz ... right, got it. She saw Anders talking to some people on the dockside there, and Veal saw them too and made some comment about looking up old contacts."

"These were the people she described as 'not looking very Spanish'? Yes, well, thank goodness for politically correct terminology. I think we can make a guess as to what she meant. I believe Tom had it right when he mentioned the Moorish ancestry, but maybe not that distant in terms of time. Right, so there we are, on the quayside, and Anders has just got off the bus from Seville ..."

"Hang on, guv. That's not right."

"But I distinctly remember from when we first talked to him, he said he got off the Seville bus, went for a drink, and then went down to his cabin because he couldn't put up with all the racket that was going on with the sail-away party. Check it in your notes."

"I don't need to, guv. I remember that as well. But I also remember that Tom Bowler, who actually did go to Seville, said that he wasn't on their bus, and he doesn't appear in any of the photos which have got Marisa Mann in them."

"You're absolutely right, David - I missed that," admitted Constable. "Well spotted. So our Mr. Anders, as well as having no alibi for the time of the murder - yet another one! - has been spinning tales about where he was and what he was doing all day. That's worth revisiting. But not just at this second."

"Want to move on then, guv?" asked Copper. A nod from the inspector. "In which case, the next one we spoke to was Anita Holm."

"Of course," said Constable. "Nice helpful English lady. Actually knew Ira Veal beforehand, which came as a great surprise, although as I recall she didn't especially like him, which I suspect doesn't surprise anyone at all. What do your notes say?"

"Only pretty much what I knew about her before from having seen her on TV. Pops up offering all sorts of totally useless

137

helpful advice about what colour you should be painting your great-granny's Georgian writing desk in order to make it fashionable, or which undiscovered Caribbean island you should go for your holiday if you want to spend a fortune being bitten to death by mosquitoes and being unable to get a decent cold beer. She knew Veal because she'd shared the couch with him on any number of talk shows, but not what you'd call matey with him. Told us a couple of tales about how he'd gone after people with reputation-breaking stories, but of course she'd never had any sort of problem with him herself. And as for the day of the murder, she said she spent it on her own, went to Jerez, downed one or two too many sherries, and toddled off to her cabin to snooze it off."

"Just a second, there, David. Can you find the notes you made from when we were talking to Portia earlier about that Jerez trip?"

"I can, guv. In fact, they're just ... here! So, what do you want to know?"

"I think Portia said," said Constable slowly, thinking it through, "that far from being on her own on that Jerez trip, Veal was on it too, and in fact, he was around when that incident, whatever it was, occurred in the souvenir shop. Correct me if I'm wrong."

"No, you're absolutely right, guv. That was when he made this remark that Portia heard about old habits dying hard. Why, do you suppose he knew that the fact that she was a bit squiffy was in fact a pointer to a historic drinking problem which the lady was trying to keep quiet?"

"I do know she was quite eager to tell us that she wasn't an alcoholic. So perhaps the lady did protest too much."

Copper was turning more pages as the inspector spoke. "And there's another thing here - a conversation which Timon heard at the dinner table when Veal and Anita Holm were there alone, before the others turned up. Apparently going on about her house-doctoring guru-ing activities and saying something about the courage of her convictions. Do you reckon this ties in? He'd got wind that she'd been up before the beak for Drunk and Disorderly or Driving Under the Influence? That's not the kind of thing a respectable English lady wants to see all over the papers, is it?"

"It is not," agreed Constable. "So, what's in Veal's dossier on her?"

"Precious little, guv, but what there is links in a treat. That email from London, from the guy we think is a private detective, talking about researching records and promising to send further information as soon as he had it." Copper looked up. "You know, sir, I'm thinking we do need to get into Veal's in-box somehow."

"I'll speak to Derek. A ship this size, with computer terminals in every nook and cranny, there's bound to be some kind of I.T. geek on board who can find a way into the system. Which I think now brings us to the last of our six candidates."

"And so it does, guv," confirmed Copper. A smile crept across his features. "Ah, now I'm not sure I get this one at all."

"And you are of course referring to ...?"

"The saintly Pastor Best, sir. Jacqueline Best. I may not know much about religion, but I know fish when I smell it."

"And Jacqueline Best smells fishy to you, does she, sergeant?" said Constable. "Well, I wouldn't go so far as to contradict you, but I'd be interested in your reasons for saying so."

"Too good to be true? Holier than thou? I don't know, guv - maybe I've just become a cynic because of all the nonsense that gets talked to us every day on the job. You know, somebody standing there blatantly saying 'It wasn't me' when there's no-one else for miles. But my toes just start to curl when I hear all the talk about the good works, when the lady's obviously rolling in it because of all the dosh all the poor suckers are sending in."

"So not entirely convinced by the pitch, would it be fair to say?"

"Fair assessment, guv," admitted Copper with a rueful grin. "So I assume you'd like some plain facts, untempered with personal comments?"

"It might be better."

"Righty-ho, sir. So, here goes." The notebook was consulted once more. "Yet another one who says she didn't know Veal beforehand, although she might have heard of him or his paper, and another one who sounded surprised at Veal's inclusion of her on the dinner table. As for her movements on the day of his death, says she spent the whole day on the trip to Seville ..."

"Which we know Veal was not on."

"Correct, guv. And when she got back, she watched the

band and the dancers, went to the chapel, and then up to her cabin. Not offering anybody to verify the story - she didn't see anyone except Anita Holm, who didn't see her, so she won't be able to corroborate."

"And how about items in the file?" asked Constable. "No matter what she may say about Veal, there obviously must have been some reason for his interest in her."

"Looks as if he and I may have something in common, which is rather a scary thought. Loads of stuff about the Community of the Great Shepherd, largely focussing on the financial side of things - money coming out of their ears, and so on." Copper broke off. "See, it's not just me, guv." He perused further. "Mention of her old man - ah, now that reminds me. I'm sure there was something Timon mentioned, which I shall track down for you in just ... a ... sec." Further riffling of pages. "And here we have it. One breakfast time, Timon heard Veal making what seemed to be insinuations about Mrs. Best's past and her marriage to her husband, and Veal asked how her husband died. Sounds as if his remarks were pretty pointed."

"He probably subscribes to your theory that the late Mr. Best is lying in a shallow grave somewhere next to Morris Fellows," laughed Constable. "Anything else from Timon?"

"Sorry, no, that seems to have been it. But ... you know, I'm going to get repetitive stress injury from all this page to-ing and fro-ing ... right, it's here. From this morning. And the blessed pastor is betrayed by her fondness for cathedrals, only this time it's the Segrada Familia in Barcelona rather than in Seville."

"Although," commented Constable, "I've got an idea that the Segrada Familia is a basilica rather than a cathedral, but we won't split hairs. And who is our informant on this occasion?"

"That would be Sally Forth," replied Copper. "Escorting one of her trips. And while they were in the church, Sally overheard Veal when he caught Pastor Best praying and talked about the forgiveness of sins."

"Oh yes, I remember. Mention was made of the Commandments, I believe, except that it wasn't 'Thou Shalt Not Kill' which he fastened on to, but the much more fun 'Thou Shalt Not Get Found Out'."

"Correct in every syllable, sir. So what, we wonders, yes we wonders, has the good lady been up to."

140

"Precious little." Copper winced. "That will teach you not to do extremely bad Gollum impressions, sergeant. At least, precious little that we know about as yet. So is that it?"

Copper snapped his notebook shut with a sigh of relief. "That's all we know."

"All ye know on earth, and all ye need to know, eh?" quoted Constable. And in response to his colleague's look of enquiry, "Keats, sergeant. One of the odes. Yes, I know, I really must get out of the habit of quoting dead authors at you. But in fact, all this which we've been going through is definitely not all we need to know. There's more, and I think we're going to need the input of Derek Crane to lay hold of whatever it may be." He picked up the telephone on his desk and dialled a number. "Hello, Guest Relations? ... Could you please put out a call for Mr. Derek Crane and ask him if he would get in touch with Cabin 6218 ... Thank you." He replaced the receiver. "Now we wait."

*

"Sorry to have kept you hanging about, Andy."

"Not a problem, Derek. Come in and sit down." Andy Constable looked his friend up and down. "You're looking a bit frazzled. What's up?"

Crane threw himself into an armchair. "I've just spent over an hour pouring oil on troubled waters. The wife of the Argentinian cultural attaché in Madrid, of all people, was throwing a major wobbly because she was missing a pair of diamond earrings which she wanted to wear at tonight's do, and she swore she'd locked them away in her safe, and the cabin stewardess must have stolen them. Great kerfuffle, accusations flying in all directions, floods of tears and protestations of innocence from the stewardess, threats to sue the line from the husband - I get the impression that the lady is extremely high-maintenance - some serious schmoozing on my part with a view to avoiding a major diplomatic incident, and then what happens? After I quietly and calmly suggest that we search the suite, just in case the earrings happen to have been accidentally misplaced, and the lady instantly climbs back on her high horse because she's offended that I'm doubting her word, damn me, what happens? We find the earrings tucked away in the toe of one of her evening shoes where she had put them for safe-keeping because she didn't trust the safe to be secure enough! Madam

141

Attaché doesn't know whether to laugh or cry, so she compromises by having a fit of the vapours while her husband tries to calm her down, I'm left to salve the wounded pride of an unjustly-accused crew member, and I finally manage to escape to the relative sanity of your cabin." He assayed a smile. "You don't suppose I could hide out here for the rest of the voyage, do you?"

"You have my considerable sympathies, old mate," replied Constable with a laugh, "but not a chance. Although I have to say, compared with your trials and tribulations, the question of solving a nice cosy murder on your little ship seems almost trivial."

"Sergeant," Crane addressed Dave Copper, "your inspector has a cruel way with words. How to make a man feel guilty."

"Oh, you don't know the half of it," murmured Copper under his breath.

Crane sat up. "Okay, Andy, so what do you want from me?"

Constable considered for a moment. "Three things, Derek. Firstly, do you have some sort of computer techie on board?"

"Of course we do. Two or three of them. The system is still bedding itself in, and we've got odd terminals going off-line all over the place all the time, so they're kept pretty busy. Why?"

"Because I think there's some unfinished business with emails to and from Ira Veal. After all, he was working at the terminal in the Internet Lounge when he died, and I'd like to know if there are any that have come to the ship since then. I want to take a look at his in-box. Can that be done?"

"I don't see why not. I'm sure I can get one of our lot to be a gamekeeper-turned-poacher and hack into the system. And it's not as if Veal's going to complain about an intrusion into his privacy. I'll put the word out when I get back to my office. Next?"

Constable ran his fingers through his hair in a characteristic gesture. "I really need to see the doctor."

Crane smiled sympathetically. "Is it the weather? Because the ship's moving about quite a lot more than she was in the Med, and some people are starting to find it a bit uncomfortable. But they're handing out tablets at Guest Relations if you need them."

"No, no, it's nothing like that." There was irritation in the inspector's tone. "Sorry, Derek, I don't mean to be ratty. It's just that I'm starting to feel a bit frustrated. We've got a barrow-load of odd bits of information pointing in all sorts of directions, but the thing that is stymieing me is that we still don't know how Veal died. So if I can have a word with the doctor, and maybe another look at the body, perhaps we'll get some pointers."

"Let me call him." Crane picked up the phone and dialled. "Hello, Jenny, it's Derek Crane. Can I have a word with the doc, please? ... Are you, indeed? ... That wasn't very clever of him, was it? So how long do you think you'll be? ... Okay, can you ask Eamonn to page me when he's free? Thanks." Crane laughed. "Doc's a bit tied up at the moment. One of the fitness instructors in the gym was doing a run on a treadmill up there, turned to speak to a passenger who was asking him something, missed his footing, and fell off and broke his arm. Not too serious by the sound of it, but at the moment, the Medical Centre is acting as an A & E Department while they straighten out some bones and put a cast on the arm. They're going to let me know when it's sorted. So that's two out of your three. What's the third?"

"This one might be a bit tricky. I'd like a chance to go over the cabins of the people on Veal's dinner table."

"Ah. That's an interesting one. I'm not sure how we stand on jurisdiction on that. People might get a bit funny, especially if there isn't any specific evidence - the sort that we could take before a magistrate if you were at home. Plus, the Americans particularly are likely to kick up a fuss, I should think. You know how they are with rights and liberties."

"On the other hand," argued Constable, "you could say that, as we're on the high seas, national jurisdictions don't apply. Treat the captain as the magistrate, if you like - ask him."

"Or ..." said Dave Copper tentatively.

"Or what?"

"Or you could operate under the 'what the eye doesn't see' rule, guv," suggested Copper. "There's this gala bash on this evening, which I think we've decided we're not bothered about, but I expect everybody else will be there for all the special jollification. Why not wait until everyone is conveniently out of the way in the restaurant, and then craftily sneak in with one of Derek's useful pass-cards. We can take a look and see if there's anything to find, and if we do it carefully, nobody need know we've ever been there. Unless it's the clincher as to who we're looking for, of course, and then it won't matter whether they know or not. How's that for a plan?"

"David," said Constable, "you are sly, crafty, sneaky, and underhand, and I love it! Your upward progress through the police force is assured if this is the way you plan to go on." He looked at Crane. "Well, Derek? What do you think?"

"You know, Andy," replied the ship's officer, "there's been this funny buzzing in my ears. I never heard a word of that. Let me get back down to my office - I'd better file a report on this blasted earrings business for the record - and I'll contact you when I've got a few ducks lined up." He sighed as he stood. "There's a theory that this job is glamorous, guys. Maybe I should have done what my school teachers suggested, and trained as a plumber." The cabin door closed behind him.

Chapter 10

Andy Constable sat alone in his cabin, lights turned off, letting the ideas turn slowly over in his head in the gathering gloom as the fading light of a cloud-covered Atlantic afternoon gave way to an unusually early twilight. Threads of thought drifted lazily, formed into hazy patterns, and then just as quickly dissolved before they could become properly coherent. Odd words of conversation would surface, swirl about on the edge of sight, and then vanish from view once more before the eye could focus on them properly.

"I'm gagging for a cup of tea," Dave Copper had said. "Shall we pop up to the buffet and get one while we're waiting for Derek to get back to us?"

"No, you go if you want to, David," Constable had replied. "I'm just going to stay here quietly and unwind for a while."

"I get it, guv." Copper gave a smile of understanding. "You want to do your thinking bit without me cluttering up the landscape, don't you?" A quiet nod came in reply. "In which case, I reckon I'll pop next door, chuck some shorts on, and see if I can grab a last swim of the trip up on deck. Thank goodness they heat that pool - I wouldn't fancy it much otherwise. But then I can tell the guys at the station when we get back that I've swum the Atlantic, and no word of a lie! That'll get them scratching their heads. And then I'll have a cuppa, and come back in about an hour. How does that sound?"

"Very good. Off you go, and I will see you later."

As if by arrangement, the tap on the cabin door coincided precisely with the ringing of the telephone, jolting Constable from his musings. He seized the receiver. "Yes? ... Yes, hold on one second, Derek, just let me get the door before the junior ranks beat it down altogether ..." He stepped to the door and opened it, then returned and picked up the phone once more as a still-tousle-haired Copper stepped into the room. "I'm back ... that's good. And you've got him there now? ... Excellent. Give us two minutes, and we'll be down." He hung up. "That couldn't have been better timed," he said in response to Copper's quizzical look. "Derek's spoken to his tame geek about the emails, and he doesn't seem to think there's a problem. They're down in his office at the

145

moment, and we are cordially invited to join them. And as I assume you are refreshed and reinvigorated by your bracing dip ...?" He was rewarded by a happy smile. "Shall we go?"

In Derek Crane's office, his chair was occupied by an owlish individual with spiky ginger hair, a t-shirt with an aggressive death's head motif, and an apparent age of about fifteen.

"This is Scott Freeman," said Crane in introduction. "He's our main I.T. man on board, so if there's anything he can't do with a computer, it's because it can't be done."

"I am so old," murmured Constable to Copper out of the side of his mouth. "And I thought it was just policemen who were getting younger."

"I'm with you, guv," responded Copper in like vein. "Shall we both just put in for retirement now and have done?"

"So, Derek says you want in to the emails of one of the passengers?" said Scott. "No sweat. Have you got his ship-card?"

"Unfortunately not," answered Crane. "It seems to have disappeared. Overboard, probably."

"No worries. What's his cabin number?" Crane told him, and Scott began to type into the computer keyboard. "Okay, here he is - Mr. Ira Tobias Veal, American citizen, age 57, address blah blah blah, credit card number 4216 ..."

"I don't think we need to go into all the personal data," interrupted the inspector. "At least, not for now. It's just his email traffic that we need to see."

"No probs." More clicking of the computer keys.

"But I'm sure all these passenger email accounts are password-protected," objected Crane. "And we haven't got his password. How are you going to get around that?"

Scott rewarded him with a look, eyes cast skywards, and a snort of derision. "Amateurs," he muttered under his breath. "Ins or outs?" he asked.

"Both, preferably."

A few more clicks, and Scott turned the screen round to face the detectives. "So, which of those emails do you want printed?"

"Andy?"

Constable surveyed the list. "There's only about a dozen. Can we have the lot?"

"Course you can," replied Scott, and administered one final

click with a flourish. In the corner of the office, a printer obediently sprang to life, and a subdued whirring hum told of pages being generated. "Is that it, Derek?"

"Thanks a lot, Scott. Yes, you can get back to whatever it is you were doing."

"The System, of course," grinned Scott. "What else?" A few more clicks, and the computer screen reverted to the OceanSea logo. "See you." With a nod to the other three, he slid from the chair and was gone.

"System? What system?" wondered Copper.

"That," wryly explained Crane, "is his dream system of a mathematical formula to beat the odds at roulette. Which is why I try to stay on the right side of Scott. If this system of his ever comes to anything, I want to know about it before anyone starts trying it out on our ships."

The printer had finished churning out sheets, and Crane gathered them up. "You'd better have these, Andy. You know what you're looking for."

"I wouldn't go so far as to say that," said Constable, "but we live in hopes." He began to leaf through the pages. "Stuff between him and his editor - deadline for a story about some Russian oligarch buying up American sports teams - he wants him to follow up rumours about the love life of one of the Scandinavian princesses and a Portuguese tennis player, photo included - hmmm, good-looking woman - and so on, and so on - ah, here we are. One about Anita Holm." He browsed the contents. "What's that saying about old sins and long shadows? Here's a pretty old sin - that's, what, about twenty years ago. This chap in London says he's tracked her down in the lists of the West London Magistrates Court. Found guilty, sentenced to three months, suspended for two years. Basically, whatever it was, go away and don't do it again."

"Drunken youthful prank, guv?" suggested Copper. "Is that from the days when they used to go around knocking off policemen's helmets?"

"I think you've been reading a little too much Bertie Wooster," said Constable. "But whatever it was, it doesn't sound too alarming. Three months suspended is what you'd probably get for going through a red light on your bike. Doesn't sound like the stuff of great journalism to me. Let's take a look at the others."

147

Copper peered over his shoulder. "That's one from the detective in New York, guv. Mentions Morris Fellows - says he can't find a sniff of him after the age of eighteen. And another one about Lance Boyle."

"Yes, thank you, sergeant, I can read. The man who was trying to trace a certificate of some kind. And he says he's not got one but two, and he hopes they're what Veal was looking for."

Constable riffled through the sheaf of paper. "So where are they? They're certainly not here."

"Attached, guv. Look." Copper pointed to the sheet in the inspector's hand. "He's sent copies of whatever-it-was as an attachment."

"Which we don't have. Great!" said Constable in frustration. "Can we not get back in and get them?"

"Not without Scott," said Crane. "This system is a mystery to me. I just do the monkey-see-monkey-do stuff on it. But don't worry. I'll track him down, get him back, and have him print off whatever's missing."

"Thanks. Now about the doctor ..."

As if possessed with psychic powers, the telephone on Derek Crane's desk rang. "Hello ... yes, thanks for getting back to me, doc. It's my friend Andy Constable ... no, he's fine, but he's more concerned with that patient of yours who isn't. He wants to have another chat with you about Mr. Veal, and maybe cast an eye over him again. Can that be done? ... So how long is that going to take? ... Okay, well, I think he may be busy around then, but how about half past eight or thereabouts? ... Great. We'll see you down there then."

"So what's happening?"

"Eamonn says he's finished with the broken arm, but he's going to be tied up for the next hour with his evening surgery. He's free after that, but by then it'll be coming up to seven thirty, and I thought that you'd want to be carrying out your surreptitious examination of your suspects' cabins as soon as you can, so I suggest we go down to the Medical Centre while everybody is still in the restaurant firing off party poppers and giving the rest of the crew their stage-managed round of applause for doing the job they're paid for."

"That sounds fine, Derek. And I don't know if you'll want to tag along, especially as we can't really get into these cabins without you."

"On balance," said Crane, "I think the less I know about any unauthorised searches, the better. But I may be able to mislay my master pass-card or accidentally let it fall into your pocket, if that will suit you."

"Guv," interrupted Dave Copper, "if we're going to be doing all this, and missing our special dinner into the bargain, is there any chance we could get something to eat first? I'm starving, and you know I can never detect on an empty stomach."

"This man is always hungry," remarked Copper to Crane. "Okay, David, since I don't want you fainting on the job, we will go and feed your worm."

"There'll be food up in the Catherine the Great," pointed out Crane. "And I'd be very surprised if there are many people up there at the moment with dinner coming up. You should have the place to yourselves."

"Back soon," said Copper cheerily, and led the way out the door.

*

"Happy now?" Constable asked Copper, as the latter wiped away the last lingering traces of pasta sauce from his lips.

Copper was in no way discomfited. "Can't think straight if you're rumbling inside, guv. Dave Copper's First Rule of Policing." He looked around the buffet restaurant, deserted now except for a small group of waiting staff folding napkins in a corner, and a solitary soul seated as far away from the food serving area as possible, attempting to read a book with a slightly queasy expression on their face, a chequered rug over their knees, and taking occasional sips from a glass of water. "Looks as if Derek was right - everyone's pushed off elsewhere, apart from the lone stranger over there."

"Yes, well, not everyone's such a robust sailor as you are," said Constable. "Packing it away while the ship's bouncing up and down."

"Hardly moving at all, guv." Copper dismissed any thoughts of seasickness. "No, I'm fully fit and ready to go, if you are. And, as it's coming up to half past seven, I suppose we'd better get on." He rose to his feet.

"It might be a wise precaution," observed Constable, "to check that the people in question are all actually down in the

149

restaurant. It might be somewhat embarrassing to walk into one of the cabins to find the occupant still in possession and naked. There would be awkward questions to answer."

"I reckon if we can find something significant, sir, you're more likely to be asking the awkward questions. But this," grinned Copper, "is because I have an overwhelming level of confidence in my superior."

"You are, of course, completely justified." Constable returned the smile. "But some of my fellow-inspectors would take a dim view of remarks like that. I think you should send up a small prayer of thanks that you're working for me."

"I do, guv, on a daily basis. So, shall we go and take a sly nosey through the door of the restaurant to check on our pigeons?"

"I do occasionally feel it would be helpful to restrict your intake of cliché-ridden detective fiction, sergeant," said Constable as he led the way towards the lifts. "But in essence, yes, and then we shall go and get the pass-card which Derek will have so kindly left lying about unattended, and be about our work."

As the two detectives emerged from the lifts at the atrium level, the last straggles of passengers were finishing their drinks in the Diadem Bar and making their way towards the dining room. Sedate American women in long satin gowns, their hair coiffed in up-swept styles in homage to the 1960s, and men in white dinner-jackets set off with jaunty red bow ties, mingled with Italian twenty-somethings in vertiginous heels and clinging lace dresses, cut to cover the most strategic areas with a minimum amount of leeway for decency, and their sleekly-brilliantined escorts in shiny two-toned suits from Milan. The majority were wearing eye-masks, ranging from small discreet dominoes for the men to flamboyant creations of sequins and peacock plumes for the women. As the chattering crowd drifted towards the restaurant, Constable and Copper followed in their wake.

"Excuse me, sirs." The maître d' stepped in front of them at the doors. "Tonight is Gala Night, and the dress code for the restaurant is formal." He looked the two Britons up and down, taking in the inspector's casual wear and Copper's jeans and t-shirt. "May I suggest that you have just enough time to return to your staterooms and change?"

"That's all right," Constable assured him. "We're not coming in. We just wanted to check that some friends of ours are there." A quick glance towards the centre of the restaurant was sufficient to satisfy him. "It's fine, David. They're all there." He turned and headed in the direction of Derek Crane's office.

"Mr. Crane is not here at the moment, sir," explained the security officer manning the office. "But he left this envelope for you, and he said he would be back here in about an hour."

Constable opened the envelope, to reveal the expected pass-card, together with a slip of paper bearing the names of the persons in question and their cabin numbers. As he up-ended the package, a further smaller envelope dropped out. Curious, he tore it open. An unusually-shaped small metallic key was inside, accompanied by a note in Crane's exuberant scrawl - 'This is the over-ride key for all the cabin safes. You may need it. You did NOT get this from me'. Constable pocketed the key without comment. "Thank you, Sanjay," he said. "This is all we need for the moment. We'll come back later. Off we go, David - work to do."

As he pushed open the door of Phil Anders' cabin, Andy Constable felt a faint flutter of unease. Failing to do things by the book, or at least the spirit of the book, was not his customary way of proceeding. Well, not always. He shrugged off the feeling. If criminals did things by the book, there would be no need for him to do his job. "You take the bathroom, and I'll start looking round in here."

"Righty-ho, guv."

A swift search through the wardrobe and cupboards revealed nothing more than the fact that Philip Anders was a man who gave a great deal of thought to his appearance. Well-pressed shirts from formal to Hawaiian hung in neat rows, and jackets, trousers and suits, mostly with designer labels, each had their own dedicated plastic carrying case. Shoes were neatly lined up. A jumble of socks and underwear filled one deep drawer. Under the bed, an extremely sturdy suitcase from an internationally-renowned manufacturer was accompanied by a matching briefcase which held nothing more interesting than a men's lifestyle magazine, brochures from a chain of hotels and a car rental company, and a sealed envelope, hand-addressed to the head of one of London's most celebrated advertising agencies, with a note paper-clipped to it saying 'Phil, make sure you give this to Charles personally'. In the safe, which clicked open without resistance, somewhat to Constable's surprise and relief, there were only a wallet with a selection of credit cards and a modest quantity of banknotes in Euros, sterling, and both Australian and American dollars, and a tiny notebook containing lists of telephone numbers, each only identified by initials. A smart-phone lay there dark and mute.

"Not much in the bathroom, guv," reported Dave Copper as he emerged, "other than the usual wash-kit, an electric razor you could probably use as a remote control to fly a stealth bomber, and a gang of aftershaves, each of which would probably cost me a month's salary for a bottle." He looked around the cabin at the furnishings still standing open from Constable's inspection. "He's a bit of a neatness freak, isn't he, guv? I haven't seen anything this tidy since the Chief Constable came to call at the station."

Constable smiled. "Thank you, David. You're right - it is all obsessively neat. Except for one thing." He gave his attention again to the incongruously-untidy sock drawer. "And here we have ..." His eyebrows rose. "Well, well, well."

"Good grief, guv. He must have been hoping to get exceptionally lucky." In the drawer, beneath a shallow layer of clothing items, lay four cartons. In each, packet after packet of condoms, their cellophane wrappings pristine. "Doesn't seem to have paid off - nothing's opened."

"I think you may find," replied Constable, "that Mr. Anders probably still has hopes of profiting from his little stash of supplies. We'll have a quiet discussion with him on the subject."

"Sooner you than me, guv."

"All right, let's move on."

"What, that's it?" Copper sounded incredulous.

"I think we've learnt all there is to learn here for now, sergeant. So while the little cogs in my brain are quietly going round and round in the background, we shall go and take a look at the next one on the list. Which is ..."

Anita Holm's cabin bore the subtle imprint of a person whose living consisted of pursuing and disseminating thoughts and ideas for a chic lifestyle. Several flower arrangements in contrasting colours were dotted about. A fringed silken pashmina, draped with artful casualness and accompanied by a cleverly arranged pile of cushions, lent an oriental opulence to an

152

otherwise ordinary couch. Two or three magazines, one of them open at an article on Indonesian batik, lay on the coffee table. Anita was evidently a skilled artist - a tooled leather folder contained a sketch-book with a mixture of pencil and pen-and-ink drawings of all manner of items, from fretted Moorish stone screens to a group of urchin children playing in a gutter, their features animated with a few deft strokes. The safe yielded nothing unexpected. Constable briskly scanned through the contents of the wardrobe while Copper, returning from the bathroom with a mute shake of the head, started on the drawers.

"Do we actually know what we're looking for, guv?" he enquired as he burrowed delicately, seeking to leave as little trace of his passage as possible.

"Not precisely," replied his colleague. "Anything incongruous, I suppose. Anything that jars. Anything you're not expecting - a bit odd."

"In that case, how about this?" Copper turned from the desk and held up a small bottle decorated with gold filigree. "Looks like green ink. Isn't that traditionally what nutters use to write letters of complaint to the newspapers? Here, maybe Miss Holm is running a dirty tricks campaign, writing nasty anonymous letters to the press and television about her competitors in the business. I should think it's all pretty cut-throat, so if she can get one over on her rivals, maybe she figures that'll do her career some good."

"Ingenious and inventive as ever, sergeant," responded Constable. "Let me take a look." He took the bottle, glanced at it, weighed it in his hand, musing for a moment, and then handed it back. "Okay. Leave it where you found it. Anything else in there?"

"Not that I can see. It's pretty much all paperwork from the ship - deals on spa treatments, flyers from the shop with special offers on souvenirs, that kind of thing. Nothing personal."

"Then we're on our way again."

In contrast to the previous two cabins, Marisa Mann's presented a picture of total chaos. Cupboards stood open, clothes were scattered across the bed and chairs, lingerie spilled untidily from a half-closed drawer, and discarded single shoes lay forlornly in odd corners. A pile of handbags lurked in the bottom of the wardrobe. Through the open door of the bathroom could be seen an open nail-varnish bottle lying on its side, slowly dripping

153

its glutinous scarlet contents on to the glass shelf beneath.

"Whatever you do," instructed Constable, almost succeeding in keeping a straight face, "make sure you leave everything as you found it. We wouldn't want the slightest clue to betray the fact that we'd been here."

"It's a tough ask, guv," acknowledged Copper with no attempt whatsoever to hide a grin, "but I'll give it my best shot."

Constable picked gingerly through the disarray, with a general feeling of slight irritation that so many obviously expensive items had been treated with such disregard. "You know when you go into the perfume section of a department store and the atmosphere almost knocks you off your feet?" he heard Copper call from the bathroom. "I shouldn't come in here if I were you, guv. I don't reckon there's enough oxygen for the two of us, plus there's enough lotions and potions to float this ship."

One item, neatly encased in a see-through protective cover, caught the inspector's eye - a commemorate issue of 'Hi There!' magazine whose cover's main feature, dominating smaller items concerning errant footballers' wives and the doings of minor European royalty, was a large photograph of the celebrated nuptials of Marisa Fellows and Yehuda Mann, promising a full twenty-seven pages of further coverage inside.

As Copper returned, slightly red in the face - "I've been trying to hold my breath, guv" - Constable handed him the safe key. "Take a look in there."

"Oh my god!"

"What?"

"Well, guv, there's bling, and there's bling. And I have to tell you that I think we've struck the mother-lode."

Lying on a crumpled black velvet cloth was a tumble of jewellery - bracelets, necklaces, earrings, watches. Amongst them, two or three boxes for what were evidently the most precious rings. The glow of rubies, the dark gleam of sapphires, the green glint of emeralds and above all, the dazzle of diamonds threw an ever-changing pattern of reflections all around the cabin. The effect was almost that of opening a box of fireworks.

"Isn't it a jolly good job that you and I are both honest?" remarked Constable mildly. "For lesser mortals, the chance to do a grab and scarper might be irresistible."

"I'll tell you one thing, guv," said Copper. "If that

Argentinian whatnot's wife got a look at these, she'd have a fit of the habdabs for sure. Here, that's a thought - you don't suppose Marisa is a bit of a collector, as you might say, on the side, and that she was responsible for ... no, dammit, the earrings turned up, didn't they? Another fine theory down the pan."

Constable was busily ignoring him and examining the remaining contents of the safe. There was not much to find - aside from a folder of travel papers, the only other item was a passport.

Dave Copper craned his neck as the inspector looked at the identity page. "Why is it passport photos always make you look like Frankenstein's monster?" he wondered. "And she hasn't hung about, getting a passport in the new name, has she? She and this Mann guy only got married five minutes ago. And now that she's divorced, she's going to have to get a new one, isn't she?"

Andy Constable was running his fingers over the page, gazing unfocussed into the distance. "You know, David," he replied ruminatively, "I rather think she is." He came back to himself with a start, and handed the passport back to Copper. "Put it back, lock the safe, and we'll press on. I'm getting very conscious of the time, and in case you've forgotten, we've got a date with a dead man."

When the detectives opened the door to Lance Boyle's cabin, they found a welcome return to order. Clothes were at least hung or folded away in wardrobes or on shelves, but in a faintly haphazard way which indicated a relaxed air to organisation. A small pile of books alongside the bed, all on loan from the ship's library, showed an eclectic taste in reading matter - a biography of Alexander the Great, a slim volume on reiki techniques, and a paperback whodunnit entitled 'Fêted To Die'. In a briefcase tucked under the desk, a magazine with a glowing profile article on Boyle featuring interviews with several satisfied celebrity clients, together with a clutch of leaflets on his clinics in both New York and California and a case containing a quantity of his business cards, hinted that the doctor would be ready at all times to expand his list of patients. And as if to prove the point, at the bottom of the wardrobe, slightly to Constable's surprise, was a doctor's medical bag, small but comprehensive, with stethoscope, dressings, a hypodermic with several phials, and a range of other instruments. In the safe, the by-now-customary wallet and passport.

"At least you can breathe in there," stated Copper as he

emerged from the bathroom after a swift examination. "Just the one aftershave, even if it's the one you have to be able to afford a string of polo ponies to buy. Mind you, I've never seen so many cleansing lotions and moisturisers in one place. He must spend hours gunking up his face. In fact, you could say that our Dr. Boyle is the definition of a slippery customer." He guffawed.

"Most diverting, sergeant," said Constable. "But as Dolly Parton once said, it costs a lot of money to look cheap, so you have to assume that it costs even more to look good. And if Boyle doesn't keep himself looking tip-top, how is he going to convince the stars to spend goodness-knows-how-much on his treatments?"

"You too can have a face like mine, is that it, guv?" Copper grimaced. "Well, you won't find me volunteering to go under the knife any time soon."

Constable did not really pay attention, standing in the centre of the room, hands on hips, looking about him with a faintly abstracted air. "David, my instincts are failing me. I can't find anything that catches my eye, and yet Veal was surely on the trail of something. So what's odd?"

Copper pointed to an item lying in an ashtray, tucked away and almost invisible behind a bottle of sparkling mineral water on the desk. "Aha! Got him!" He pulled the ashtray out and gestured to the cigarette lying within it. "We have discovered the doctor's guilty secret, guv. He's a smoker. How is that going to go down with all the self-righteous bike-riding health freaks in the media? They would probably string him up for betraying the medical profession."

"Easy does it," replied the inspector. "Before you get totally caught up in your flight of fancy, I feel I should draw to your attention the fact that this is an electronic cigarette. As fake as one of Boyle's patients' smiles. The only thing it gives off is a little steam, and not the air of corruption you are so desperately seeking. Bad luck."

Copper's face fell. "Sorry, guv. That's the best I can do. If that's all we've got, I suppose it's on to the next."

Jacqueline Best's cabin showed a taste for calm and reserve which echoed what the detectives had gleaned regarding the pastor's personality. Desk and table surfaces lay clear of clutter, free of paperwork and ornaments other than the customary vase

156

of flowers. A brief glance revealed the bathroom to be spartan in the extreme, only towels and toothbrush in evidence, along with a modest make-up bag containing a small but exquisite selection of cosmetics from extremely expensive Parisian houses. The contents of the wardrobes presented an almost aggressively monochrome appearance - black and white reigned supreme, leavened occasionally with a touch of purple or pastel.

"She doesn't exactly dress to impress, does she, guv?" commented Copper. "You'd think, with the sort of money she's got access to, she'd take the chance to splash out just a bit."

"Two things, David. I think this just shows what a very clever woman she is. Firstly, it's probably good public relations to dress in the character of a sober clerical figure, because if you're asking people to donate their money for good causes, you don't want to give them a chance to think that all the cash isn't going where they think it is. Although I suspect if you looked through the labels and knew what you were about, you would find that none of these clothes exactly came off the bargain rail."

"And secondly?"

"Simple logistics. Black and white. She can mix and match, and only have to carry half the clothes around with her. Clever wardrobe planning."

"Never had you down as a fashion guru, guv, but I'll take your word for it. So what else is to find?"

The suitcase beneath the bed contained a large manila envelope which disgorged a selection of brightly-coloured leaflets detailing projects for the digging of village wells in central Africa, plans for the establishment of schools in remote parts of the Amazonian rain forest, and schemes for the rehabilitation of affected children in some of the war-scarred parts of Asia.

"This lot all seems very worthy, guv," said Copper. "I may be beginning to regret some of the things I said about the lady. There's a lot of good being done here."

"And so there is," agreed Constable. He emptied the last item out of the envelope, a bound folder bearing the title and logo of the Community of the Great Shepherd, and marked 'Highly Confidential' in large red lettering. "Now, what have we here?" He browsed the contents - columns of figures under various geographical headings, lists of incomes and expenditure. "Hmmm. You may not have been so wrong in your judgement after all.

157

True, there's a great deal of money going out, but there's an awful lot more coming in. This needs an accountant, but I know how it looks to me."

Copper had meanwhile been browsing through the drawers of the desk. "One thought, guv - you'd think she'd have a bible, but I can't find one. Oh no, I'm wrong - there's one here. Hold on, though - it's the Gideon Bible supplied by the ship. I reckon everyone must have one - there's one in my cabin, I know. But I'm still surprised that she hasn't got one of her own."

Constable was at the safe, and he swung open the door. "Ah, well that's where you're wrong, sergeant." He held aloft a small well-thumbed thick black book, then looked more closely at it. "No, I take it back. That's where *I'm* wrong. A bible it isn't." The book's black leather cover was embossed with the letters 'JH', while the interior proved to be an address book with innumerable names, addresses and telephone numbers of U.S. senators, members of Congress, ambassadors, prominent figures in the world of entertainment, and many others whose identities Constable could only guess at.

"Perhaps it's her bible of target big donors for this community of hers, guv. Although it looks a bit knocked about. I mean, if she's only been involved with this religion thing for a short while, it probably wouldn't get this towsed. Maybe it used to belong to her husband."

"I'm thinking not," said Constable. "I have a hunch that it has a more professional use than that. Well, we'll stick it back, lock up, and carry on. Time's a-wasting."

"Last one, then, guv," said Copper, as the detectives headed along the corridor towards Baxter Wall's cabin.

"And the biggest last," responded his superior as they arrived at the door. "I'd forgotten he said he had a suite." He checked his watch. "We shall have to get our skates on if we don't want to be late."

"What, for the late Mr. Veal? I don't suppose he'll complain much!"

Constable sighed and pushed open the cabin door. "Shut up and get in."

The suite was identical in size and layout to the inspector's. While Dave Copper started on a search of the dressing-room and by-now-customary bathroom, Andy Constable cast his eyes

158

around the main room. Valuable items lay about, seemingly casually discarded where they fell or had last been used. A laptop from a high-end manufacturer sat open but inactive on the desk. A gold Geneva-made watch lay on its side on a shelf next to a dish containing a selection of gold cuff-links, several studded with precious stones. A half-consumed bottle of vintage champagne sat abandoned in an ice-bucket. A pair of shoes, whose label Constable recognised as being that of one of London's top makers, had evidently been kicked off and left in a jumble under a chair. A recent copy of a leading American financial newspaper, presumably purchased in the last port of call, lay crumpled on a sofa. A clip of banknotes, holding what looked at first glance to be several thousand dollars, lay disregarded on top of a passport on the bedside cabinet, alongside an e-reader in a leather case.

Copper returned from his task in the other rooms. "Nothing untoward that I can find, guv. The usual fiendishly-expensive pongs in the bathroom - what is it about cruises that makes people want to scent themselves up like a Babylonian harlot on the pull? - and I've patted all his suits and whatnot down, but there doesn't seem to be anything to find, unless you count his dodgy taste for pink socks." He took in the contents of the cabin. "Now here, you would say, guv, is a man who doesn't have a particularly secure habit of mind. Obviously far more money than sense. If somebody light-fingered happened on this lot, they could have a field day and be away with the goodies in five seconds flat."

"Evidently money would seem not to be a major source of worry for our Mr. Wall," agreed Constable. A thought struck. "Either that, of course, or else he's in so deep that he can't be bothered with trivialities like a several-thousand-quid watch."

"I'll tell you one thing, guv," said Copper. "I bet we could find out all sorts of stuff if we could take a look at that laptop. And I should think, if the rest of the room's anything to go by, that the security is not exactly top-notch. You wouldn't even need Derek's tame geek to get into it."

"Sadly," retorted the inspector, "we do not have time for you to exercise your computer-burgling skills. Useful as they were in Dammett Worthy. I'm not going to take the chance of you crashing the thing while trawling through innumerable files on a hunt whose quarry you do not even know. Stick to practicalities and open that safe for me. Not, judging by the rest of the cabin, that he'll have bothered to put anything in it."

Constable was wrong. In the safe, notable in their solitude, lay a pair of smart-phones, a set of identical twins. "Interesting," commented Constable. "Why would he want two phones, I ask myself?"

"One for business, one for pleasure?" speculated Copper. "One on and one in the wash? One good, one bad?"

"Ah, now there you may have hit on something. And that would tie in with something we already know, or think we know." Constable consulted his watch once more. "And we'll have to speculate of the hoof, because it's perfect timing for our trip back to the Medical Centre." One final glance around the cabin confirmed that nothing had been disarranged. "Let's close up and be on our way."

Chapter 11

As the Britons trotted down the several flights of stairs to the Medical Centre, Dave Copper couldn't help noticing the curious absence of visible crew members around the various corridors and landings. "Not a soul to be seen, guv. It's a bit odd, isn't it?"

"Not particularly," replied Andy Constable over his shoulder, "if you think about it. This is probably one of the few times, when all the passengers have been getting ready for dinner or are down in the restaurant eating, when the crew get a chance for a break in the middle of their shift. I dare say they jump at it. Which might have turned out as a lucky chance for whoever did for Mr. Veal - nobody about to observe their comings and goings."

It was a few minutes past the half hour when Constable pushed the Medical Centre door open. "Doctor? We're here. Hope we haven't kept you waiting."

Eamonn Holliday poked his head out from the small room where the detectives had first examined Ira Veal's body. "Ah, don't fret about that. You're not the only ones. Derek just called down to say he'd been held up, but he'll be with us in a few minutes. But it's no problem anyway, because I've made a start on my own. Come on in and join the party."

Ira Veal lay on the same bed as before, except that this time he was resting on a large black plastic bag, unzipped to reveal the dead man lying on his back.

"Do you mean to tell me that you actually have a stock of body-bags on this ship, doc?" enquired an amazed Copper.

"You would be astonished at the things there are squirrelled away in the bowels of this ship, laddie," returned the doctor. "There's a Chinese laundry and an entire costume-making department down there. We could put on our own production of 'Aladdin' if we'd a mind to."

"Entertaining as that would be," said Constable, "it's not exactly relevant to the matter in hand. Now, what I needed to ask you, doc ...

"I can guess." The doctor forestalled him. "You're still wanting to know how your man died, right?" Constable nodded. "Thought so. Because, you see, the same question had been

161

bothering me. We've already decided how he didn't die, but that's not going to be a lot of help to you in working out who killed him. So even before you asked, I'd already planned to haul him out of cold storage and take another look at him. I wasn't at all sure that it would do any good, because I've no sort of facilities here on board and I'm not trained in that line of business anyway - that's more one for your forensics and pathology guys when you get the late lamented on shore. But there's no harm in trying, is there? And there is one thing I've noticed which wasn't apparent when he was nice and fresh, so to speak, but which has popped out since."

"And that is?"

"Take a look here." The doctor beckoned, and the detectives drew closer to Veal's head. "See, around the mouth. There looks to be the beginnings of some faint discolouration, almost like the start of a bruise. Do you see that?"

Constable screwed up his eyes. The condition which Holliday was describing was barely visible. "How sure are you, doc?"

"Pretty sure. I know it won't look much to you, but in this business you develop an eye for the incongruous. I dare say you do the same in your job. Trust me, it's there."

"So what does this mean, doc?" enquired Copper with an edge of excitement in his voice. "Are you telling us that he was smothered or stifled or whatever?"

"Oh no, nothing like that at all." The doctor couldn't help smiling as Copper's face fell in an almost comic fashion. "Sorry to pop your balloon, sergeant, but there's nowhere near enough damage done to point towards that. It seems to me that if, say, someone had crept up behind Veal and tried to smother him like that, they'd have needed a lot more pressure over a period of time, and that would have made the bruising much more distinct. And he might well have flailed about, which might have caused other marks in other places, and there's nothing like that to be seen. No," he concluded, "sorry to disappoint, but I can only show you what's there. I can't tell you what it means."

Constable's eye was drawn to a scattering of tiny blood spots among the stubble underneath Veal's chin. "I take it that is blood, doctor. Could that have something to do with it?"

The doctor glanced at Constable's own immaculately-shaved chin. "Bless you, inspector, but you're the lucky man. You look as if you've got the type of beard which succumbs quietly to a normal razor. Unlike our special guest for the evening here, who has the sort of beard growth which my old granddad used to describe as looking like a badger's backside. Coarse as you like, and however careful you are when you shave, you're going to get little spots of blood just like that. It's a great argument for the collarless shirt, but I don't know how far it gets you in a murder investigation."

The sound of the outer door opening was heard, and a slightly breathless Derek Crane in full dress uniform appeared in the doorway. "Hi, chaps. Sorry to have held you up, but I forgot I had to change into the full rig for Gala Night, and what with one thing and another ... anyway, I'm here now. Have I missed all the fun?"

"Absolutely," said the doctor. "We were just about to zip Mr. Veal back up and file him away under pending."

Andy Constable turned his eyes heavenwards. "Am I the only one taking this seriously?" he pleaded. "I'm used to it from Copper here, but if two you start joining together in some sort of joke-fest ..."

Copper came to the rescue. "Just lightening the atmosphere, guv. No disrespect intended. Anyway, I think we'd finished, hadn't we?"

Constable subsided. "Yes. And in answer to your question, Derek, a couple of snippets of information, but how much they tell us I know not."

"Well, perhaps I've got better news for you," said Crane. "I tracked Scott down eventually to the crew mess, and he was going to get access to those email attachments and send them up to the printer in my office. They should be waiting for us upstairs."

In Crane's office, the two sheets in question lay in the printer's out-tray. Constable took them, scanned them wordlessly for a few moments, then stood immobile, frowning slightly, for a good thirty seconds, while Copper and Crane exchanged speculative glances.

"David," said Constable very quietly, "have you got that notebook of yours handy?"

"Here, guv, as always," responded Copper, retrieving it from a trouser pocket. "My complete Ira Veal dossier."

Constable took it and surveyed the cover. On it, Copper had occupied some of the quieter moments during his superior's interviews with suspects and witnesses by indulging in his customary doodling, and the words he had written on the front cover - 'I.V. MURDER' - had come to resemble the illuminated letters of a medieval manuscript. Constable gazed at the cover for several long moments, and a slow smile began to creep across his face, finally reaching his eyes, which blazed in sudden triumph.

"David," he repeated in the same subdued voice. "I believe I may have mentioned before that you are a bloody genius."

"I think you did say something of the sort, guv," replied Copper uncertainly.

"I was right. Come along. Let's go and solve a murder."

*

In the Imperial Dining Room, the cruise director was concluding his farewell speech to a room full of enthusiastically applauding passengers.

"... and so may I say once again, on behalf of OceanSea Cruises, how glad we are that you could all join us on this memorable cruise, and another big thank-you to all my colleagues in the crew who have looked after you so well." Renewed applause and cheering. "Don't forget that the evening's fun is not yet over - the ship's orchestra is waiting for you up in the Maria Theresa Lounge, where there will be dancing and entertainment from our full animation team until the Grand Unmasking at eleven o'clock. So please, go and have a good time. And may I say, finally, if you have enjoyed yourselves with us, please go out and tell all your friends that the *Empress of the Oceans* is the finest ship in all the world." Cries of agreement in several languages. "And if you haven't enjoyed yourselves, ..." A dramatic pause, and then the cruise director put his finger to his lips. "Shhhh!" Laughter and a fresh burst of clapping as the sound system burst forth into a rousing orchestral version of 'Auld Lang Syne', and there was a general stir as people began to rise from their tables and move towards the exit in chattering groups.

"Derek," hissed Andy Constable, "can I suggest you make a beeline for our friends and keep them at their table while everybody else clears the place. If we let them go off, we might have trouble getting them all in one place again. And maybe you could rustle up a couple of your security team to loom meaningfully by the doors, just in case."

"Got you," said Crane. He murmured briefly into his walkie-talkie, and then made for the dinner table where a slightly strained jollity was being replaced by a trace of relief as the group showed signs of breaking up. "Excuse me, ladies and gentlemen, but could I ask you to remain where you are for the time being. My colleague Inspector Constable would like a few words with you before you leave the restaurant."

"I hope he won't take long," objected Marisa Mann. "There's a party going on upstairs, and I don't plan on missing it."

"And I have my packing to do," added Anita Holm. "They say we have to have our suitcases outside our cabins in the corridor by one o'clock in the morning, of all things."

"I'm afraid I must insist," said Constable. "And I'm sorry if this spoils your plans for the evening." There was a hint in his tone that probably more than one evening would be spoilt by what he had to say.

The restaurant's maître d' had in the meantime come up behind Derek Crane and murmured in his ear.

"Of course - we'll do that," he responded. "Ladies and gentlemen, if we could just move to the section in the corner of the restaurant where the tables have already been cleared, it will give the staff a chance to get on with their work. We don't want to spoil their evening as well. And we'll be a little more private."

The request was greeted by a selection of frowns and a grumbling assent on the part of the group as they relocated to a secluded corner of the room. Masks were discarded on the table as all eyes turned to the inspector.

"So, what's this all about, Mr. Constable?" enquired Baxter Wall in a somewhat aggressive voice. "We've told you all we know, at least, I have. I assume everyone here has done the same. So what do you hope to achieve by this?"

"I hope, Mr. Wall, to identify who was responsible for the death of Mr. Ira Veal," replied Constable mildly. "Which I would think everyone here would have an interest in. But, and forgive the mangling of the language, what is most interesting to me is that everyone here would seem to have a reason, to a greater or lesser degree, for wanting Ira Veal dead."

"That's ridiculous," objected Phil Anders. "I'd never met the man, our paths had never crossed before, I knew nothing about him. Why would I want to kill him?"

"But it's not what you knew about Mr. Veal, but rather what he knew about you, Mr. Anders. And about everyone else here, for that matter. To be fair, knew or suspected. And also to be fair, some of the things which I have in mind, I can't prove. Not at the moment, not here and now. And if any of you can tell me I'm wrong, then so much the better for you. But Mr. Veal's position was very different from mine. He had access to the pages of a newspaper with an enormous circulation, and very few restrictions on the material that paper could publish. He didn't necessarily have to prove anything, not to the standards of a court of law. Allegations, suspicions, hints of scandal - these would all be quite enough to destroy in a flash careers and reputations which had been constructed over years."

"Inspector, you're being very vague and mysterious," said Jacqueline Best. "If you have something to say, wouldn't it be better if you just came out and said it?"

"Yeah, right," echoed Baxter Wall. "We don't have all night."

"Of course. Very well then, Mr. Wall. We may as well start with you, as you're so insistent. Now, you're in a very enviable position, Mr. Wall. I know in some circles it is considered vulgar to talk about money, but by all accounts, you're a very wealthy man, and I believe you're the heir to a very considerable fortune and business empire. But I think there's an old saying that 'Much wants more', and while that of itself isn't a bad thing, it can tempt some people into taking the path into less moral activities. One or two of the things which Ira Veal was overheard to say to you could be interpreted as having something to do with a gambling habit. There was a remark about being tempted into a gamble and playing the tables in the casino in order to justify some unspecified ill-gotten gains, and another comment about the possibility of the dealers cheating. But I think that mention of the casino was just a coincidence. I think the sort of money that might be in jeopardy with even a serious gambling habit would probably be regarded as chicken-feed in the lofty financial circles in which you move. Nobody would concern themselves about your reputation if it were as simple as that.

"But I have in mind another sort of gambling, and that is one far more directly connected with those same lofty financial circles of yours. You are involved in some very serious money

166

movements, from what I gather. A very different kind of dealing, and one with potentially massive rewards for the dealers. Or penalties, of course, if things go wrong. We all remember Bulling's Bank in London that went down and took half the financial world with it. Now, what if Ira Veal had an idea that you were involved in something of the sort? What if he had contrived to get someone to hack into phone messages and emails on, say, two phones in the possession of one individual? Goodness knows, phone-hacking and journalism seem to be inextricably linked these days, as my sergeant here pointed out. I wonder what the contents of those calls and emails would reveal. And what if, just to continue the speculation, two phones, whose numbers just happened to coincide with the numbers of the phones Ira Veal was investigating, were found in the possession of one of the people at this table? What conclusion might we draw from that, Mr. Wall?"

Baxter leapt to his feet. "Hey, have you been searching my ...?" he challenged, suddenly breaking off at the implication of his words and subsiding back into his chair.

Constable continued as if there had been no interruption. "I'm not knowledgeable enough to judge whether we might be looking at a question of insider dealing, or this new business of stock-swapping that I've heard about, or whether it's large-scale currency-speculation which has gone spectacularly wrong. It may be none of these things. But the point is, Mr. Wall, that Ira Veal believed he had got hold of something, and it didn't look as if he was going to let it go. And I dare say, as in the City of London where a man's word is his bond, a dealer on Wall Street whose reputation is publicly questioned has no future, and a lot of questions to answer. And that, Mr. Wall, is a perfectly plausible motive for murder."

Baxter D. Wall sat mute in his seat, staring back at the inspector with lips firmly closed.

Constable took a breath and turned to the man seated next to Wall. "And so, Doctor, we come to you."

"And what did Ira Veal's poison pen plan on writing about me?" enquired Lance Boyle. "Something tenuous and damaging to my reputation, no doubt?"

"Now you come to mention it, Dr. Boyle, yes, there have been several theories floated as to why Mr. Veal might have been interested in you as subject matter for his writings. Some of them

167

more fanciful than others. For example, he had compiled a sort of dossier on a number of your celebrity clients, with before and after shots, detailing some of the procedures you might have carried out on them."

"That's hardly a guilty secret, inspector," answered Boyle. "In fact, you could say that the more people in the public eye know what I can do for them, the better it is for my business."

"On the face of it - sorry, that was not meant to be flippant - I'm inclined to agree with you, sir. I imagine good results make for good publicity. But there were also some pictures in that file showing outcomes that were perhaps not so satisfactory. Pictures that might have made prospective clients think again, and as I said before, once the bad word starts getting around, who knows what effect it could have on what I'm assuming is a very lucrative living indeed. And then there was a mysterious reference in an email which spoke of some sort of missing certificate. Again, we wondered what that might mean, and Sergeant Copper here, ever ready with a good idea ..."

Dave Copper, seated discreetly in the background of the proceedings, looked up at his superior with a cross between disbelief and embarrassment.

"... floated the theory that it might be a certificate of qualifications. A certificate to practice. What if, he asked, you had no such document, and your whole career was constructed on a fraudulent foundation?"

"That's ridiculous!" exploded Boyle. "You want qualifications, I can show you qualifications. Get me access to the records from my medical school, and you're gonna have to eat those words!"

"Calm down, doctor," responded Constable. "I said it was a theory, not an accusation. But here's another theory, and it's one based on a conversation overheard between yourself and one of the others here - Mrs. Mann."

Marisa looked up in surprise. "What conversation? And who is saying that they heard ...? I mean, we never ..." Her voice petered out.

"Let's not bother too much about who is our informant," continued Constable. "Suffice to say it's someone whose word we do not doubt. And the burden of this friendly little chat, doctor, was that you were in possession of some information which was not exactly to Mrs. Mann's advantage, and that you were pressuring her to ensure that this information did not reach the public. And although we know that Ira Veal was not present at that time, what if it had come to his attention that you were engaged in such activity? Would the great society surgeon's career survive a revelation that he might be a blackmailer?

"Which very neatly brings us to the case of Marisa Mann. Now, Mrs. Mann, considering the amount of column inches which have been devoted to you in the press, we could almost say your life is an open book. But not quite open, I think - there are a few chapters which have remained firmly closed. I just mentioned the words exchanged between you and Dr. Boyle, which hinted at some knowledge which you might have preferred to keep secret. You were heard to say that you didn't know him, and would never admit that you did. Why so, when one of the crew heard Ira Veal say that, in his opinion, you two would have so much to talk about? Surely it couldn't be something as simple as your having had what my sergeant has so delicately described as 'the old nip and tuck'? As we've come to learn, in the celebrity world, that's almost obligatory. So what if it were something a little more ..." Constable searched for the right word. "Radical. Now we know Ira Veal had in his possession the birth certificate of a certain Morris Fellows. Which was, of course, your surname when you first became famous. Sergeant Copper, with his ever-vivid imagination, raised the possibility that he might be an early husband who had been somehow disposed of in the past. I think the answer lies far closer to the present. So let's turn back to your relationship with Dr. Boyle. The doctor who has famous clinics in America, but who denies vehemently any such activities in Morocco. Specifically, in Casablanca, a place long celebrated for discreet surgery of the ... I think I said 'radical' sort. Let's follow our flight of fancy just a little further. Ira Veal was heard to ask pointedly if Morris Fellows was your brother, and what happened to him. Sergeant Copper speculated that he might be dead. But I don't think Morris Fellows is dead, is he, Marisa? Morris Fellows is very much alive, although maybe his old friends wouldn't recognise him so easily these days. Morris Fellows is sitting here at this table ... isn't he, Marisa?"

The shocked silence, during which all present turned towards Marisa with expressions ranging from shock to incredulity, was broken by an outburst of sobs. "All right! Yes,

169

you're right. I was born male - and every moment of my life was hell! Even from when I was very small, I knew everything was wrong. I was trapped inside someone who wasn't really me. I hated my body, I hated what it made me do, and every time I looked in the mirror I hated myself. You have no idea what it was like ..." Marisa paused, wiped tears away roughly with the back of her hand, and seemed to pull herself together with a shuddering intake of breath. "And so I swore that one day, I would make it right. I took every job I could to get enough money together for surgery. I would do anything - you don't want to know what. I humiliated myself with doctor after doctor in the States, before I found out about places like the hospital in Morocco. That's where I met Dr. Boyle. And after the whole business was over, and don't you dare think that it was quick and easy, because it was nothing like that ... how can I tell you? It was like coming home. It was as if I'd found the real me. And nobody can tell me that that's a crime!"

"Of course it isn't," said Constable gently into the hush that followed. "Nobody would doubt your right to make yourself who you really are." His voice grew stronger. "But what is a crime is to perpetrate a fraud on an elderly man by going through a sham marriage with him in the hope of gaining a vast amount of money, either through inheritance or, as in your case, divorce. You couldn't legally marry Yehuda Mann because, in law, you are still a male, which no doubt is why I'm sure your passport is, although a very good one, a forgery. That famous divorce settlement of yours isn't worth the paper it's written on. So that's the story which you would be desperate for Ira Veal not to tell - the fact that you had criminally defrauded a rich man out of millions, and that your entire public persona is a complete fake. Now that, Marisa Mann, is as good a motive for murder as I have ever heard!"

Chapter 12

"Mr. Anders, you look as if you've had something of a shock," observed Constable mildly.

"I ... I ..." Phil Anders seemed completely lost for words.

"But then," carried on Andy Constable smoothly, "it's turning into something of an evening of revelations. Somebody mentioned to us that they had heard Ira Veal tell you that he hoped your relationship with Marisa turned out as you hoped. I'm guessing that you are only now beginning to understand what he was driving at in his oblique way. But of course, that wasn't the revelation which fostered his interest in you, was it?"

"Forgive me, inspector. I have absolutely no idea what you're driving at," replied Phil.

"Oh really?" enquired Constable comfortably. "Well then, I shall just have to refresh your memory, shan't I? And I think it may well have been part of that same conversation, if that helps you to remember. Mr. Veal, we are informed, was displaying a particular interest in the amount of travelling you do, and most specifically some of the exotic destinations. I believe you called in to Bangkok on your way to join this cruise, didn't you? And I think Mr. Veal mentioned some of the other places you'd been."

"So what?" challenged Phil. "You know I do work for my father. I've told you he does a lot of P.R. business internationally - it's a very connected world."

"Oh, I understand that very well," said Constable. "I realise that, say, an Australian racing driver doesn't stay in Australia. One week he'll be in the Far East, the next he's in Brazil, or Dubai - we know all this. But I believe that Ira Veal was far more interested in the journeys which you may well have taken on your own behalf rather than someone else's. He'd taken the trouble to lay hold of a fairly detailed dossier on your travels. We've seen that - it tots up to quite an impressive total of air miles, as my colleague here put it. And I think Mr. Veal joked that you seemed to have acquired some sort of addiction to travel - he said it was like a drug, didn't he?

"And he said something else which might have been rather worrying for you on another occasion. It was in Cadiz, on the day you told us you took the trip to Seville. But in fact you didn't go to

Seville, did you, and that story was an attempt to divert attention from what you were actually doing on that day. You were seen with a group of men on the quayside in Cadiz, men whose North African appearance caused Mr. Veal to enquire if you were in fact meeting some old contacts. Mr. Veal seems to have been going out of his way to drop hint after hint to you that he had a very good idea how you earn your living - a living for which travelling in support of an international P.R. company might well provide a perfect cover. And I have a confession to make, Mr. Anders - we have searched your cabin." Constable swiftly forestalled Phil's evident intention of voicing a protest. "Oh, I agree - completely unauthorised, probably illegal, a totally unwarranted invasion of your privacy. So let me apologise for that. But just before I do so, Mr. Anders, can you answer me one question? Why would a man who spends time in Bangkok, and Casablanca, and Bogotá, and Lima, need quite such a large consignment of condoms in his luggage? Sergeant Copper's first thought was that you might be hoping to get very lucky, but then, he's a much younger man than I am."

Dave Copper failed to conceal the blush which swept across his features.

"But my first thought, being a far more cynical individual, was that you were hoping to get very, very rich. I think these condoms were not for use but for, how shall I put it, distribution among a whole lot of free-lance employees, who similarly enjoy international travel. Tell me, Mr. Anders, just off the top of your head, what's the current price for pure high-grade cocaine?"

"One word of this," said Phil breathlessly, "one word, and you will find yourself being sued until your eyes pop out. You have nothing but hearsay and speculation, and whatever it was that Ira Veal and his poison pen was hoping to splash about, there isn't a scrap of actual evidence." He laughed grimly. "And now that he's dead, there's not likely to be, is there? That ship's left port, hasn't it?"

"I couldn't have put it better myself," responded Constable. "I'm very well aware that there are some very unpleasant characters in the world we're speaking of. People who would stop at very little to prevent their activities receiving the full scrutiny of a publication like Ira Veal's. So when that ship sailed, as you so graphically put it, might you have been the one who untied her and helped her on her way?"

As it became evident that Phil was not intending to offer any further reply, Constable turned his attention to Anita Holm. "Now, since we have once again broached the subject of journalism with Mr. Anders' rather colourful reference to Mr. Veal and his poison pen, why don't I have a little chat with you, Miss Holm?"

"If you wish, inspector," said Anita. He hands twisted in her lap, and she swallowed nervously. "Although if you're looking for Ira Veal's enemies, I should remind you that I was probably the closest thing he had to a friend aboard this whole ship."

"Yes, I haven't forgotten that, Miss Holm. You certainly seem to have had by far the greatest number of personal contacts with him before this cruise, but I remember you were astonished that he had requested that you be among the numbers sharing a table with him at dinner. And it doesn't seem as if this vague friendship, if that was indeed what it was, was enough to stop his journalistic instincts from following up on what he thought might make very entertaining copy for his readers."

"You've lost me, inspector. I really have no idea what you're referring to."

"Then I'd better be a little more specific. Miss Holm. And I'm afraid his interest in you was fairly transparent. There was an email in his file on you - oh yes, he had a file on everyone - following up on a meeting he'd had with an investigator he'd met in the U.K. on his way here, which made reference to a court appearance you had made in London some years ago. He didn't have the details at the time, but it was enough for Mr. Veal to start making smart remarks about you being a woman with the courage of her convictions. No doubt that set alarm bells ringing with you. And subsequently, a further email came through with more details, but even then no specifics of what this 'conviction' might have involved. But by then, Miss Holm, it seems as if you'd yourself given Ira Veal all the information he needed to confirm the burden of his story. I dare say you won't need me to remind you of that unfortunate incident in Jerez."

Anita flushed. "I'm sure we needn't go into that here, inspector." The words tumbled out in an embarrassed rush. "That was all a complete misunderstanding, as I explained at the time. It was an unfortunate accident, and the gentleman quite

173

understood, once our guide had made it clear to him what had actually happened."

"Yes, of course, Miss Holm. I know there were no repercussions, and the owner of the shop decided not to take the matter further. But afterwards, on the bus, Ira Veal wasn't so easily satisfied. He thought he knew very well what had happened, and it simply confirmed to him what he believed he had already deduced. 'Old habits die hard' - isn't that what he said to you? So here was a delicious story for his pages - the English rose, queen of the talk-show sofas, the pattern of model social behaviour for a generation, revealed to be little more than a common shop-lifter. That would set the laughter rolling round the media world in America, wouldn't it? And might you not resolve to do anything to prevent that happening? Up to and including murder?"

"This is so silly," said Anita with a valiant attempt at nonchalance. "Why would I have stolen a silly little - I can't even remember what it was?"

"A silver box, madam," interjected Dave Copper helpfully, "since you ask."

"Well then." Anita turned to the others in appeal. "I'm not exactly on my uppers, am I? I mean, I could have afforded to buy anything I wanted in that grubby little shop. Why would I bother to steal a cheap little box?"

"I agree, Miss Holm," said Constable. "Why would you bother to steal anything, anywhere? Be it in a souvenir shop in Jerez, or even on board this ship?"

The colour drained from Anita's face as she looked up at Constable. He gazed at her for several long moments, and then seemed to make a decision. "Let's put that to one side for just one moment, and turn our attention to Pastor Best."

"The Best last - is that it again, Mr. Constable?" Jacqueline's voice sounded strong and confident.

"If you say so, Reverend."

"And what supposed misdeeds of the Community of the Great Shepherd do you suppose Mr. Veal was investigating, inspector?" There was a distinct tone of defiance in the words.

"Oh, I don't know that we can identify any such thing," was Constable's candid reply. "Certainly we know, from papers that we've seen, that Veal had a considerable interest in the substantial wealth of your Community."

"People can be very generous," replied Jacqueline simply.

"They can," agreed the inspector. "Quite how generous is evident both from the copies of public information by way of press articles in a file he had about you, and from a brief perusal of some rather more confidential accounting information. Information which showed that the Community's level of expenditure on its no doubt very laudable projects didn't quite match the stratospheric level of income from donors."

"Are you telling me that Ira Veal had gotten hold of copies of our accounts? How the hell did he manage to do that?" Jacqueline's choice of words indicated the beginnings of a crack in the calm facade. "Or are you saying that you have been...?" She bit back her words, and glared accusingly at Constable, whose bland smile provided all the confirmation needed.

"So there might well be many people, readers of the 'National Investigator', who would have been shocked and surprised to learn of the discrepancies in the finances of your Community. There might well have been calls for an investigation into the use of funds. Who knows, people might even have used the word 'embezzlement'. But it doesn't seem to have been only the money side of your life that Mr. Veal was interested in," continued Constable. "He was intrigued by the personal side as well. He was heard, during a visit to a church early on in the cruise, to ask if you were praying for the forgiveness of your sins, and speaking about those sins being found out. On another occasion, he was asking pointed questions about the status of your marriage to your late husband, and even speculating as to the circumstances of his death."

"My late husband's death was perfectly natural, inspector," said Jacqueline hotly, "and I deeply resent any suggestions that it was otherwise. How dare you?"

"I'm making no such suggestions," was the inspector's calm reply. "I'm quite aware that the Reverend Best was a gentleman considerably older than yourself, and nature will take its course. And I do not necessarily subscribe to one of Sergeant Copper's pet theories, which states that very often one death is explained by another. Not always, anyway." He glanced around the company. "So in this instance, Mr. Veal might very well have been barking up the wrong tree.

175

"But his interest, I think, went further back than your involvement with this Community of yours. And now I think it's time for a small confession on my part. Yes, Reverend, we did search your cabin. That's where we found those accounts. But my sergeant here was surprised that we didn't find a bible. Then we found a book which at first glance seemed to fit the bill, except that it wasn't a bible at all, or at least not the conventional sort. It was an extremely well-used address book, full of the names of men of status and wealth, and evidently going back some years. But of course, that couldn't possibly be yours, because the initials embossed on the cover weren't yours. They were 'J.H'. But during a conversation with you, Ira Veal had been heard to refer to your 'other name'. And there was something about 'why should a pastor hide anything'. But of course, that was just a mis-hearing, wasn't it? The actual words he used were 'Pastor Hyde', weren't they? I think it's a reasonable guess that your name before your marriage was Jacqueline Hyde. So, two identities. And I think my guess is confirmed by a photograph which must have dropped out of the file we found in Ira Veal's cabin, and which would have led us to this truth much sooner. I think, Reverend, that this evening is not the first time we've seen you in a mask. Jacqueline Hyde's other persona was Tanya Hyde, a professional lady who provided some extremely explicit disciplinary services to the very high-powered gentlemen whose names were listed in your book. And the disclosure of a secret such as this would have destroyed forever your Community and your source of wealth. A desperate woman might very well resort to murder in an attempt to preserve her secret."

Jacqueline Best drew herself up with dignity. "You may say what you like about money, inspector. I can't deny that temptation can be very great, and we are not all strong enough to resist it. But please remember, before you condemn me utterly, just remember that Mary Magdalene was a woman with a past, and her reputation was saved."

"Nice try, Reverend," was Constable's unsympathetic response, "but still not a justification for murder."

He addressed the entire group once more. "You may all be wondering why I have gone into all this detail. That's because there are always several factors to be taken into account in a murder investigation, and the primary one is usually motive. I think it's fair to say that each of you had a plausible motive for killing Ira Veal."

"Are you trying to say," asked Baxter D. Wall, "that we all did it together in some kind of gigantic conspiracy? A sort of 'Murder On The Occidental Express' at sea? Come on, inspector. If you are, I think you've lost the plot completely."

"Nothing of the kind, Mr. Wall," replied Constable. "Because now we come on to the other two essentials - means, and opportunity. And of course, frustratingly for everyone, the murder took place at a time when each of you was alone and cannot call on anyone else to account for their movements. Almost everyone, that is. Because you, Miss Holm, were seen to leave your cabin during the crucial period. Pastor Best saw you in the corridor outside your cabin, although you did not see her. But you had told us that when you returned to the ship that day, your plan was to send some copy to your office, but in fact you went to your cabin for a nap. Except that you left your cabin - we know that. And it's reasonable to deduce that you were sticking to your original plan to send off this copy by email, and so you went to the Internet Lounge. And that is where you found Ira Veal. And he had some very unpleasant news for you, didn't he? He had received confirmation that your personal history included a court conviction. You knew very well what it was for, and you knew that, being the man he was, he wasn't intending to keep the information quiet. It was too good to waste."

Anita Holm, tense until that moment, suddenly slumped in defeat. "When I arrived, I asked him if he would be finished soon. He said no, but I would. He taunted me, inspector," she admitted. "He asked what I was planning to do with the pieces of my reputation when he'd finished with it. I appealed to him for the sake of friendship, but he said that, in his business, he couldn't afford to have any friends. So I turned and left."

"I'm sure you did, Miss Holm. But let's not leave the story half-told. You came back later, didn't you?"

"Yes," whispered Anita.

"I'm guessing that you went to your cabin in something of a distracted state. I think you agonised, not knowing what to do. Then I think you noticed something you had, perhaps in the drawer of your desk." Constable's voice suddenly changed, and took on an unexpectedly friendlier tone. "Miss Holm, may I offer a

177

word of advice? The next time you are tempted to acquire a little something, perhaps a souvenir, do not keep evidence of it. Throw it overboard. Because in your cabin we found a small fancy bottle containing green ink. The sort of bottle which is contained in the souvenir presentation sets of glass pens which are sold in the ship's shop. Except that the shop has not sold any such items during this voyage. But I think that one of these sets had, let's say, come into your possession, and in your distraught condition you saw the green glass pen, thought how you might use it, returned to the Internet Lounge with it in your hand, and stabbed Ira Veal in the back with it. And then I suspect that you returned to your cabin and tried somehow to pretend the whole thing had never happened."

A murmur of incredulity ran around the group seated at the table.

"I must have been mad," faltered Anita. "If I'd been in my right mind, I would never have wanted to kill anybody."

"Which is fortunate," said Constable, "because however unlikely it may seem, you didn't."

Anita gaped in disbelief. "But ... but ... I don't understand." The baffled faces looking at the inspector showed that Anita was not alone.

"Oh, you stabbed Mr. Veal, we agree on that. But there is something you don't know, which is that when you did so, he was already dead. Now as a medical man, this will interest you, Dr. Boyle. Because the ship's doctor pointed out to us the fact that the stab wound had caused remarkably little blood flow. Certainly nowhere near enough for a fatal wound to the heart. And that baffled us for a while. I remember when we first spoke to you, Dr. Boyle, and told you that Mr. Veal had been stabbed, you were surprised at the information. And until a very short while ago, we still had no idea how Mr. Veal had met his end. But then two missing pieces of the jigsaw fell into place when I was handed two emails which had been sent to Mr. Veal. Certificates, in fact. One was a marriage certificate between you and your wife, doctor. This tied in with a photograph which Mr. Veal had of the two of you, presumably at your wedding."

"But you knew I'd been married - I told you that."

"Indeed you did, doctor. And you also told us that your wife had died. Oh, you were completely candid with us. Well, perhaps

178

not completely. Because what you failed to tell us was that the place of death was your cosmetic surgery clinic in New York, and that the attending physician was yourself. These were clearly stated on the death certificate, which was the other document we received. A document signed by yourself and one other doctor, showing the death as having been through natural causes. I'm guessing that Ira Veal found that cause of death somewhat hard to believe in the context of a cosmetic procedure. And I'm also guessing, although I have absolutely no reason to do so, other than an increasing awareness of the sort of cynical view Ira Veal took of the world, that he may have had an intuition that you might have put pressure on a junior colleague to cover up a cause of death which was, in fact, your fault. As Veal said, you could perform every miracle except that one – raising the dead. So tell me, doctor, how near the mark do he and I hit?"

A long silence followed. "She was beautiful," said Lance Boyle eventually. "Far more beautiful than she ever knew. And we were the happiest couple you could wish to meet. But for some reason, that wasn't enough. She had a fear of growing old - no, of looking old. Maybe she thought I would love her less if her looks started to fade. She was wrong. But I loved her, so I did what she wanted. One or two tiny things at first - we didn't even need to use an anaesthetic. But then she wanted a more major procedure, which I told her over and over again that she didn't need, but in the end I gave in." He gave a huge sigh. "She wouldn't stop bleeding. My assistant and I did everything we could, but by the time a full crash team got to us, it was too late. She'd gone. And yes, you're right. I thought maybe if I could pick up the pieces of my life and somehow carry on, it wouldn't all have gone to waste. So that's what I did. Yes, I pressured the other doctor to sign the certificate. Yes, I lied as to the cause. And yes, that vicious little rat Ira Veal somehow got hold of the facts, and he was going to have a really great time watching me twist in the wind. That's the kind of man who doesn't deserve to go on living."

"Not your decision to make, doctor," responded Constable sternly.

"Well, I will have to live with the consequences of that, won't I, inspector?" said Boyle defiantly. "So if you have worked all that out, I expect you have also worked out how I did it, which you are longing to explain to everyone."

"It gives me no pleasure to do this, doctor, but yes, I believe I have. When you returned to the ship on the day of the murder, you told us you went up to your cabin to read. So why should your path cross with Mr. Veal's? My surmise is that you wanted a fresh book, and went to the ship's library to choose one. And the library also serves as the internet lounge, where Ira Veal was sitting receiving emails. In fact, the very certificates we've just been discussing. So I think he told you what he knew, and the threat to you was obvious. You returned to your cabin where you have your medical bag, and decided on your course of action."

"And you have also figured out what that was, inspector." It was a statement, not a question.

"Yes, I believe I have, but I haven't done it alone. I need to acknowledge the input from Dr. Holliday and from Sergeant Copper who set me on the right path. Dr. Holliday pointed out some markings around the dead man's mouth - not severe enough to signify smothering or strangling, but perhaps the sort of marks which might be left if a cloth impregnated with chloroform or something similar was held over the airways to induce unconsciousness. I don't know if you would have such a chemical in your possession, but it's not impossible. How am I doing so far?"

"Please continue, inspector. I'm sure the others are enjoying seeing a professional at work."

"But then what? My sergeant gave me the answer without even realising it. It was an answer which had been staring us both in the face. He has a notebook, in which he has been recording every detail of all the conversations we have had with each of you, all the information we have picked up from members of the ship's crew who have witnessed certain incidents, and all the various items we have discovered in our searches. I asked him for that notebook earlier this evening, and he handed it over to me. And what had he written on the cover? Both the title of the case, and the solution, in just a couple of words - 'I.V. MURDER'.

"In your medical bag you certainly have a syringe - I've seen it. Now under Ira Veal's chin, there were several small blood spots which were initially dismissed as a shaving rash. But I believe that when the body is put under specialist examination by the pathologist, one of those blood spots will turn out to be the site of an injection. Mr. Veal was unconscious and couldn't struggle while you injected him with … what? Some chemical or other. Again, I have no idea what you would have. Please tell us."

Lance Boyle gave a small rueful smile. "Air, inspector. Nothing more toxic than air. We're not veterinarians - we don't carry a range of chemicals around with us to put animals out of their misery. Or in this case, my misery. But if you know just where and how much to inject, it doesn't take long for the bubble to get to the brain or the lungs and do its work." He gave a deep sigh. "And so, you see, my degradation was complete. I have gone from the idealist who wanted to help people feel better about themselves, to an accidental killer who was too cowardly to face the results of his actions, to an out-and-out murderer." He stood. "So, inspector, I assume this is where you arrest me, read me my rights, and then lock me up."

"I have no powers to do anything of the kind, Dr. Boyle," replied Constable. "But as soon as we reach port tomorrow, I shall be delivering a report to the local police authorities, and you will be handed over to them for further investigation. That is as far as my writ runs." He turned to Derek Crane. "I dare say you'll want to take it from here, Derek."

"Dr. Boyle," said Crane formally, "you will be confined to your cabin for the remainder of the voyage with one of my officers guarding the door. If you wish to contact a legal adviser, you may of course do so, and I will take you to my office to allow you to make that call. I shall arrange for the telephone to your cabin to be disconnected, and I must ask you not to make any attempt to communicate with any other person before we reach port. If you would follow me, please." He led the way towards the door of the restaurant, as his two officers fell in behind Lance Boyle.

Andy Constable turned to Dave Copper. "David," he said softly, ignoring those seated around him, "after all that talking, I'm a little thirsty. I need something to drink."

"Don't blame you, guv. You must be knocked out. But we'll never get anywhere near one of the main bars, what with the Grand Unmasking coming up any minute."

"Enough unmasking for one evening, I think, David. For goodness sake, find me somewhere quiet. You choose."

As the two detectives walked from the dining room, they left behind them a stunned silence.

Epilogue

Andy Constable was drawn into wakefulness by the long low mournful moan of the *Empress's* siren. Heavy still with sleep, his eyes opened reluctantly, and he swung his feet to the floor and padded over to the window, drawing back the curtains as the siren sounded once more. Fog. Fine droplets of condensation covered the furniture of the balcony, but beyond the rail, nothing was to be seen but a featureless white blanket of vapour, occasionally swirling lazily in response to the ship's slowed progress.

Constable returned to his bedside, where his watch had begun an insistent bleeping. Seven-thirty. We're late, he thought - the ship should have docked two hours ago. He stretched, and then ambled in the direction of the bathroom. Restored to a more customary alertness by a quick shave and shower, he dressed swiftly, gathered together the few remaining belongings into his hand luggage holdall, picked up the phone, and dialled.

"Good morning, David. Glad you're actually up and about. Have you looked out of the window? ... No, I've no idea, but I expect somebody will tell us. In the meantime, I assume we still have to do as instructed in the Ocean Times and be clear of our cabins by eight o'clock, so if you're ready, I'm heading for breakfast up in the buffet."

"Morning, guv," was Dave Copper's cheery greeting as the two emerged simultaneously into the corridor. It appeared that even the events of the previous evening could not dampen his irrepressible spirits. The sergeant looked up and down the empty corridor. "Well, they've taken the cases on schedule, anyway. Although I have to say, packing was the last thing I wanted to do when we finished last night."

The evening had concluded for the two detectives with a few drinks in a virtually deserted bar at the stern of the ship, followed by a slightly hunched stroll around the open top deck in the cool dampness of the night. The threatened storm seemed to have been left behind - the air was calmer. There had been little conversation, and a complete avoidance of the subject of murder.

"You must be knackered this morning, guv," suggested Copper tentatively.

"Maybe," agreed the inspector. "Quietly satisfied is probably a better description. But I will tell you one thing - I have an absolutely ravening appetite. So why don't we go and find that egg chef of yours, and he can knock me up a final dish of those Eggs Benedict you always rave about."

As the Britons were sitting back with a final cup of tea at the end of an extremely satisfying breakfast, the uniformed figure of Derek Crane appeared in the doorway of the restaurant. He waved and made a beeline for their table.

"Hello, guys. I thought I might find you up here. Raring to go?"

"In all senses," answered Copper. "We've just been enjoying the customary last hearty meal, courtesy of your fine ship, before being condemned to return to the daily grind."

"Not exactly in the best possible taste, David, considering the circumstances," reproved Constable.

"Which is actually why I came to find you," said Crane. "I've been in contact with your opposite numbers ashore, and they'll be waiting for us when the ship docks ..." He consulted his watch. "... which shouldn't be too long now, fortunately. Fog in the Channel - what can you do? It's all a conspiracy to make my life more complicated. Oh, by the way, I've arranged for you to have special priority disembarkation so you don't have to hang around, and they're going to find your cases for you and bring them to the gangway. Anyway, the point is, Housekeeping need to get on with their work to get the ship cleaned and ready, so I'm just going down to Dr. Boyle's cabin to take him to my office to wait, and I didn't know whether you would want to tag along, just to tie up the last loose end."

"Yes, we'll do that," said Constable, standing. "Difficult to think of a murderer as a victim, but there is a very small part of me that feels just a little sorry for the doctor. After you."

In the corridor outside Boyle's cabin, the three were greeted by a familiar face standing guard.

"Sanjay!" said Constable. "You seem to be everywhere. Can Derek not run this ship without you?"

"It would appear not, sir," replied the smiling Indian. "But I always try to let him think he is in charge."

"Heard anything from him this morning?" enquired Crane, gesturing to the closed door.

"Not a peep, sir. It has been as quiet as the grave all night."

"Well, we'd better rouse him. Got his ship-card?" Sanjay handed over the piece of plastic, which Crane inserted. In response to the bleep, he pushed open the cabin door. "We locked his balcony door last night, just in case anyone tried to get in or out," he explained over his shoulder.

The curtains remained closed. On the bed, by the subdued light of a solitary bedside lamp, Dr. Lance Boyle lay looking almost relaxed and comfortable, his eyes closed. Alongside his hand lay a hypodermic syringe.

"Oh no." Crane emitted an agonised groan. He moved immediately to the bedside, picked up a limp arm in an attempt to feel for a pulse, placed his hand on the doctor's brow, and then gave a deep sigh. "Stone cold," he reported. "Sanjay."

"Sir?"

"Would you please call Dr. Holliday and ask him to come up here as soon as convenient."

"Shall I tell him what has happened, sir?"

"Yes, do. And tell him there's no hurry."

Andy Constable stepped to the window and pulled back the curtains. Outside, through the thinning mist, the ghostly dome of a building could be seen slowly passing.

"That's the chapel at the old Netley Royal Victoria Hospital," said Crane. "We're almost home."

Constable, gazing out, his back to him, did not seem to hear. "Qualis artifex pereo," he murmured.

"What's that, guv?" asked Dave Copper, coming to his side.

"It's what the Emperor Nero said, just before he killed himself," answered Constable. "It means 'What an artist dies in me'. Nero had killed his beautiful young wife too. It just goes to show, there are no new stories." He shook himself slightly. "Come on, David. Get me off this ship."

*

At the head of the gangway, Andy Constable turned to Derek Crane for the last time. "Well, Derek, I won't say it's exactly been a pleasure, but please thank the company for bringing us home."

"I think it's rather more like thanks to you and David for

sorting things out for me," replied Crane. "Without you, I'd have been all at sea."

"That, Derek," said Constable, "is even more atrocious than the worst of Sergeant Copper's puns. I think it's definitely time we were on our way."

As the three shook hands, the inspector noticed the police vehicles drawing up on the quayside. "*Two* cars, Derek?"

"Well, one was going to be for Dr. Boyle. I dare say the news hasn't yet got to them that he's going to need some other form of transport."

"And the other?"

"That's for you. I took the liberty of calling your station, and they said that they've been missing you so much, they'd send a car and driver to bring you home in style."

At the foot of the gangway, as the smiling police constable hefted the luggage into the boot of the patrol car, Constable took one last look up at the *Empress of the Oceans* towering above him.

"Ready to resume normal duties, sergeant?"

"You bet, guv. Let's go back to being ordinary policemen."

"That, sergeant, I very much doubt. Get in. I want to go home."

*   *   *

MORE INSPECTOR CONSTABLE MYSTERIES, AVAILABLE FROM AMAZON

FÊTED TO DIE

Who killed celebrity clairvoyant Horace Cope at the annual fête at Dammett Hall? Did rival Seymour Cummings spot trouble ahead? Did magistrate Lady Lawdown take justice into her own hands? Or has her daughter Laura Biding got a guilty secret?

Detective Inspector Andy Constable and his irreverent colleague Sergeant Dave Copper must try to make sense of the whirl of gossip, rumour and secrets circling the peaceful English village of Dammett Worthy. Throw into the mix a celebrated author, a dodgy solicitor, and a sponging relative, and Constable and Copper really have their work cut out!

(Published on Kindle as MURDERER'S FETE)

JUAN FOOT IN THE GRAVE

What could spoil the fun of a free holiday on the Spanish Costa? For Detective Inspector Andy Constable and his colleague Sergeant Dave Copper, only one thing - the murder of Spanish builder Juan Manuel Laborero.

But why should the death of one manual labourer on a building site make Constable and Copper's free holiday far from carefree? Demolishing the local British community's wall of silence, our detectives soon unearth a whole structure of deceit and corruption. Whose story is without foundation? Who has constructed a false alibi? Has somebody gone plumb loco, or did one of the suspects put the final nail in the coffin? Sparks fly as the truth emerges!

(Published on Kindle as MURDER UNEARTHED)

Printed in Great Britain
by Amazon.co.uk, Ltd.,
Marston Gate.